PRAISE FOR RHINO IN THE ROOM

If you have never been on an African safari, this is as vicariously close as you will get to doing so. If you have, you will recognise the vividly-described sights, smells, sounds and elemental rush of an intense wilderness experience. Rhino in the Room *is far more profound than a fast-paced thriller. It's the story of vanishing wildlife that's happening on our watch.*
—Graham Spence, co-author of *The Elephant Whisperer*

Jill Hedgecock writes with passion about the near extinction of the black rhino and the human predators who stalk it, and she tells an exciting story for YA readers in the process.
—Alan Brennert, Emmy winner, L.A. Law; author of *Molokai*

Hedgecock has a mastery of evocative language and seamlessly guides the reader through the details of both an African safari adventure, as well as the poaching that takes place. The reader experiences everything in such detail that the experience becomes real. The plight of the rhinos is made quite clear and it is difficult not to feel helpless as the novel develops. Rhino eases you slowly into the action, but then holds you tight until the highly charged finish, leaving the reader exhausted and satisfied.
—William Gensburger, *Books 'N Pieces Magazine*

Rhino infuses the sights, sounds and smells of Africa at its most intense and captivating in a coming-of-age story full of adventure on a safari in South Africa. Sit tight. It is a wild ride!
—Wendy Blakeley, Founder, Africa Matters africamattersusa.org and Facebook Africa Mattersusa, Arts Coordinator, Painted Dog Conservation Zimbabwe

Rhino in the Room *is a beautifully written and an intellectually stimulating debut novel from Jill Hedgecock. Its power is in advocating for a worthy cause—that of the rhino, using the storyteller's eye. This is a novel for anyone with an interest in the natural world and the rhino. This is a novel for everyone!*
—Tendai Mwanaka, Mwanaka Media and Publishing Pvt, Ltd.

RHINO
IN THE ROOM

JILL HEDGECOCK

GOSHAWK
PRESS

Published by Goshawk Press

Printed in the United States of America
First Edition: September 2018

10 9 8 7 6 5 4 3 2 1

Hedgecock, Jill
Rhino in the Room

ISBN: 978-1-7322415-0-3

Cover art from original oil painting by Anne Pentland
www.apentland.com

Cover and book design by Andrew Benzie
www.andrewbenziebooks.com

For the wildlife rangers who face death and injury from both poachers and the rhinos they strive to protect. You are the unsung heroes of Africa.

CHAPTER ONE

Why do shortened school days seem to take the longest? Not that I'm anxious to get home after what went down last night. Still, it seems like Mr. Garcia has been droning on forever about some philosophical topic unrelated to U.S. history. I guess that's better than memorizing Civil War dates. I swallow a yawn. This whole class is a waste of time. Learning about the past isn't going to help me become a better fashion designer.

"Okay, now that I've laid the groundwork, let's have a debate," Mr. Garcia says then smooths his thick, black moustache with his thumb and forefinger. "There's no going back. Do you agree or disagree with this statement?"

I shrink down in my seat, hoping he won't call on me. My parents' fight has left my emotions jumbled. Trying to sift through feelings that seem to change moment by moment has left me exhausted. I gaze around the orderly lines of desks. A few of my fellow high school seniors text on phones held under their tan, plastic desktops to shield what they're doing from the teacher. Others smirk. Danny seems to have nodded off. My classmates' expressions suggest they are as bored as I am.

Then I look toward the back of the classroom. My heart sinks a little deeper in my chest when I see my best friend's blanched face. She knows better than anyone that you can't turn back the clock. Her eyes are closed. Her hunched shoulders cause her body to curl in upon itself. Is she having a relapse? Mr. Garcia's words must have reminded Sylvia of her new reality. She'll have to suffer through the flu-like symptoms of malaria on and off for the rest of her life.

"Claire," Mr. Garcia says. "What do you think?"

I startle and turn to face the teacher. My cheeks flame as my mind goes blank. I have no idea what the question is. Lots of students take notes on their computers, but I still use a pencil and paper. That way I can doodle fashion designs if inspiration hits. But I haven't written anything down.

Then I think of Sylvia and remember. Can you go back? Once something happens, is history set in stone? I'm not sure. Certainly, I can erase parts of my fashion design when I'm sketching. But what about Sylvia? She can't go back to a healthy life.

Mr. Garcia frowns at me as if he's getting impatient.

"Maybe?" I say, raising my eyebrows and offering a half-smile.

"Continue," he says.

My mind latches onto the hurtful words I overheard Dad shout last night. My father couldn't have meant what he said.

"Well," I say, "people say things they don't mean all the time, especially when they're angry. Isn't an apology a way of going back?"

"Can you give me an example illustrating the opposing viewpoint?" His smile of encouragement helps my thoughts kick into gear.

I remember what happened in the Parkland and Sandy Hook shootings. The kids who saw their classmates gunned down must be permanently affected by the tragedy.

"Well, I don't think there's any going back for the high school kids at Parkland," I say. "Some of those students started the #NeverAgain movement and others became public advocates for gun control."

"That's a very interesting example," Mr. Garcia says. "What about—"

I'm saved from further discussion by the sound of the bell. A flurry of activity erupts. No one waits for our teacher to dismiss us. Some kids have already bolted out the door. I walk three desks back to where Sylvia sits. She's stuffing her history book into her backpack with more force than necessary.

"Hey," I say, bending over to put my arms around her, "Let's get out of here."

When I let go, she unfolds her tall frame from the seat, slinging her brown bookbag over her shoulder. She's wearing the blue-gray turtleneck sweater and distressed jeans that we ordered online last week when she'd been too ill to go to the mall. Sylvia used to be so energetic that I couldn't keep up with her. Now, she shuffles around like she needs a walker. Kids impatient to get out of the classroom jostle us as we make our way outside. The crisp air is a welcome relief after the stuffy classroom.

"That was cool what you said," Sylvia says. "Danny even woke up."

"Stop it," I say, staring at a hairline fracture in the concrete walkway.

"It's true," she insists. "You're smart and people respect you."

"Seriously," I say, bumping my shoulder against hers. "Stop it."

As we reach the school parking lot, I scan the area for my mother's car. She always parks across the street so she doesn't have to slog through the line of cars in the pick-up lane. But our white Volvo isn't in the usual spot.

Now I'm worried. Mom's never failed to show, never been late. Even after one of hers and Dad's many arguments. But their midnight fight had been worse than normal. My mind replays my parents' words. Usually they kept their voices down, but last night I heard more than I should have. After my mother called my father a bastard, he yelled how he never would have married her if she hadn't been pregnant. I chew on my lower lip, hoping that what I'd said to Mr. Garcia was true that people say things they don't mean when they are angry.

"What would you do differently if you could go back in time?" Sylvia says, unlocking her car with the press of a button. One of Sylvia's thin hands tugs on the door handle until it opens.

"I know what you'd do," I say, deflecting her question.

I punch in my mom's cell number. I had intended to remind Mom about early dismissal this morning, but she hadn't come down to breakfast. The phone rings and rings. It's a hollow sound that feels like an affirmation she's not coming.

Had her fight with Dad sent her over the edge? Had she left him? And in doing so, had she left me too?

"Yeah, mine's a no brainer," Sylvia says, "If I could go back in time, I'd take those stupid malaria pills the way I was supposed to. I'd probably even take extra just to be sure. Hell, if I could do it over again, I wouldn't go to Peru at all."

I nod. Sylvia eases herself into the driver's seat. I try my mom's cell again. No answer.

I probably shouldn't ask. Sylvia's not supposed to drive other teens yet. But what am I supposed to do?

"Hey, can you take me home? My mom's not here, and I can't reach her."

Sylvia glances around. I know she's thinking about getting caught, but if we take the back streets, the chances of being pulled over are slim.

"Get in," she says.

I clamber into the passenger side. Sylvia's frail fingers grip the steering wheel. Stress isn't good for her. Having her drive me home really isn't a good idea.

A couple of kids honk and squeal their tires in celebration of their extra hours of freedom, but Sylvia is careful to avoid any scrutiny and turns slowly out into the main road.

I try Mom's cell once more. But there's no answer. Until now I've managed to brush off my father's outburst as something he said out of anger. But Mom's disappearance has rocked my world once again. Had Mom gotten pregnant to trap my father?

"Crap," Sylvia grumbles, as the traffic light turns red.

What if I'd been a mistake? The air in the car compresses, and I can't take a breath. I suddenly feel as if I'm about to break into a million pieces. I sense Sylvia turn to study me, so I examine my fingernail polish, hoping she thinks that I'm upset about a chipped nail. But my eyes won't focus and keep darting around as if the answer to this horrific question lies within the car's interior.

"Claire?" she says. "What's wrong?"

I shake my head. Afraid that if I say anything, I'll burst into tears.

"Come on. What is it?"

"Nothing," my voice quivers and gives me away.

"You're scaring me," she says.

I take a deep breath. There's no way around it now.

"My mom and dad got in a big fight last night," I whisper then choke out the words that threaten to tear me apart. "And my dad said… he said… he only married my mom because she was pregnant with me. I wasn't… wanted."

"Oh, Claire," Sylvia says. "I'm so sorry."

I can't do this. I can't dump on Sylvia. I need to pull it together. I sit up straight then shrug like it doesn't matter.

"He didn't mean it," I say with a surprising strength of conviction in my voice.

Sylvia reaches out her hand and squeezes mine. I smile and nod. I'm overreacting. Mom forgot about early release day, and I'm blowing things all out of proportion.

The light changes, and the car accelerates through the intersection. Sylvia shifts in her seat and puts her hands back in perfect four and eight position. I can tell she doesn't know what else to say, just like I often can't find the right words when she's suffering another bout of sickness.

I shift in my seat. I want out of this car. I don't want to fall apart in front of Sylvia.

I spot the radio and punch the on button. An old Beatles song is playing. One that Sylvia loves, so I turn up the volume. Ugh. I'll probably be falling asleep with "Yellow Submarine" lyrics stuck in my head. But she smiles, and a bit of pink colors her cheeks. I swallow hard then start to sing. My voice cracks at first, but soon I'm singing the hurt and anger from my soul. Sylvia chimes in too, and we both laugh. Ten minutes later, she pulls into my driveway, and I'm feeling more like myself.

"Thanks again for the ride," I say to Sylvia as I get out of the car.

"It's going to be okay, Claire," Sylvia says.

"Yeah," I say, but my voice rattles. "See you tomorrow."

I pull my sweater close against the chill in the air. The garage door is down so I can't tell if Mom's car is there.

Our two-story house casts a shadow over me as I make my way to the porch, shuffling through the autumn leaves that clutter the front lawn. Behind me, the scrape of metal against concrete announces that Sylvia's rear bumper hit the curb as she backed out into the street. I turn and wave before stepping inside and closing the door behind me.

As I toss my house key on the small table in the entry, I notice my father's briefcase on the floor next to it. A sense of unease flickers through me.

"Dad?" I call out in the direction of the kitchen. "Mom?"

The only response is the tick, tick, tick of Grandma's old cuckoo clock from down the hallway. The noise that usually comforts me now seems more like a warning. Mom was a realtor before she married and she swears every house has an energy fueled by the people who have lived there. I understand what she means. These days my home feels feral, as if it's been neglected for far too long.

I kick off my sandals. As I shove my shoes under the waist-high table, dust poofs into the air. The stairs in front of me are covered in golden dog fur. Mom used to be so meticulous about house cleaning. Now I rarely see the stripes on the living room carpet that prove she's bothered to vacuum. Dishes in the sink are the norm.

Buster woofs to come inside. Proof that Mom definitely isn't home. She always puts our dog out when she leaves the house. I chew on my lower lip as my eyes return to the briefcase. Something feels wrong.

It occurs to me that maybe Dad came home because of the fight. Mom's been depressed about something, but she won't say what's going on. Once, after she'd drunk too much wine, she confessed that she tried to take her own life before she got pregnant with me. Maybe Mom put Buster out for a whole different reason. What if she's taken too many pills? What if she called Dad threatening suicide, and he rushed home, but it was too late? Panic hits. I rush upstairs.

I hear a groan. I imagine Dad sitting on the bed grieving over Mom's dead body. My hand rests on the cold, metal doorknob. My mind screams at me to walk downstairs and go outside, but I twist the handle and push on the door anyway.

The blinds are at half-mast. The afternoon sun streams through the bottom portion of the window and illuminates the lagoon-blue glass vase on the dresser that Mom bought in Italy during their honeymoon. My head turns in slow motion toward the center of the room. I'm confused. The bed is moving.

I blink as I take in thick calves and feet with bulbous toes pointing skyward as if they are trees sprouting from the mattress. My father's dark head of hair, his swimmer's shoulders, the mole on his back about the size of a quarter. His hips pump away. Oh god. I've walked in on my parents having make-up sex.

I take a step back and grip the knob to make a quick exit when it dawns on me that those stubby legs aren't my mother's long and slender legs.

Air rushes from my lungs. The walls compress as reality slams into me: Dad's screwing another woman. She's. In. The. Bed. That. He. Shares. With. My. Mother. In. My. House. The vile taste of rotten eggs fills my mouth. I want to flee, but I can't move.

The woman moans, which breaks my paralysis. I try to sneak backward out of the room, but my heel bangs against the doorframe. I suppress a yelp, but the woman hears the thud. Her eyes widen when she spots me. I don't recognize this blotchy-faced woman. It looks like she's been crying. Her pudgy nose and thin lips make me think of Elmer Fudd. She's not even pretty.

"Jackson," she screeches as she pushes my father off.

Dad's head swivels.

"Oh, crap," he says.

He tries to pull the sheet over himself as he rolls off of her, but my eyes don't flick away quickly enough. I've seen a part of my Dad that no daughter should.

I stumble backward as the walls close in on me like a coffin. The air feels as if it has been sucked from the room. My chest constricts. I clutch my throat. I can't breathe. I have to get out. Somehow my legs do my bidding and I manage to turn and run.

"Claire. Sweetheart. Please. I'm sorry," Dad yells after me.

I plunge down the stairs, two at a time. My head feels as if it's submerged underwater, but I can still hear Dad's pleas for forgiveness. Buster barks and claws at the back door, desperate to get inside, but all I want to do is get out.

I kick Dad's briefcase over when I reach the foyer, jerk open the front door, and slam it behind me. I can't catch my breath. I close my eyes. But it's too late. The image has been seared into my mind.

In this case, Mr. Garcia got it right. There is no going back.

CHAPTER TWO

The Botswana airport terminal waiting area is about the size of two full basketball courts—mega small compared to Los Angeles International. The walls here are covered with advertisements from some company called RMB. The logo has a lion holding a key. One poster announces "RMB at Work" with an image of one of those old railway carts that miners used to haul rocks. I'd rather do that kind of hard physical labor than spend this week on vacation with my father.

Dad shifts in the plastic seat beside me. A safari in South Africa isn't going to undo all the pain his affair has caused Mom and me these last few months. The only reason I agreed to come on this trip was because Aunt Sally begged me to go. She says the divorce proceedings have turned so nasty she fears for Mom's sanity. She's right. Mom has been self-medicating with too much vodka and sleeping until noon. She needs a week-long break from Dad's jerk of a lawyer and divorce papers. Still, I hate that I have to fly across the world and spend time with a cheater. Dad's motivation for arranging this father-daughter trip was guilt, not love.

I clench my hands into fists, remembering the way he came into my room all cheerful and announced how he'd booked our trip. He did it knowing full well I didn't want to go anywhere with him. I had been scribbling in my sketchpad too upset over my parents' separation to even try to work on my portfolio for design school applications. He babbled on about how sorry he was that direct flights to South Africa were sold out but how lucky we were to get last minute reservations. All his false cheer had only served to mire my already turbulent feelings toward him in a cesspool of confusion.

This trip feels like a betrayal of Mom. It infuriates me that he didn't give me a choice. At some level, I want to spend time with him. But it feels like he's trying to buy my forgiveness, so the trip is already pushing us further apart.

"You hungry?" Dad says, glancing away from his African bird-identification book to scan the terminal. "The flight to Johannesburg is only an hour but then we have a long drive to the safari camp."

I shake my head no. A part of me wants to let go of my anger toward him, but I can't find my way to forgiveness. I don't know how I'm going to survive seven days of sharing a tent in a remote wilderness camp in South Africa with all this tension smoldering between us.

"Okay," he says. "Let me know if you change your mind."

His groveling only deepens my resentment. My feelings aren't as fresh, but my tangled emotions of rage and despair remain, and will probably always be there ready to emerge whenever that horrible memory is triggered. So no matter how many times he apologizes, no matter how many times he tries to explain, it won't change a thing.

His justifications fall flat. So what if he'd tried to end his affair with Janice at a coffee shop meeting that very morning? He claims that when he went home to get his forgotten briefcase she followed him to the house. Oh, poor Daddy, pity clouded his better judgment when she begged for one last time together. His excuses only made me want to scream louder. He should take responsibility for his behavior, especially because after Mom threw him out, he went to go live with his precious Jan-Puss anyway.

He should be happy with the way things turned out. He never wanted to marry Mom. He never wanted me either. Now, he's free. My throat constricts. I twist around in the uncomfortable, plastic, airport chair, turning my back to Dad so he can't see the hurt that underlies my anger. So often, the pain hits me when I least expect it. The smell of peanut butter will bring on a memory of Mom, Dad, and me eating a picnic lunch at the park. Or a Disney film that we saw in the theater together will pop up on the TV screen as I'm flipping channels. I'll feel scalded as newfound pain replaces that lovely sense of nostalgia.

"Hey, Claire, check out the differences between the male and female ostrich," Dad says, leaning forward and thrusting the book under my nose to show me the pictures in his stupid, bird book.

His attempts to engage me in conversation throughout the three-hour layover in Botswana have only served to highlight our differences. Dad likes observing deviations in nature— male versus female plumage, an albino peacock, or four-leaf clovers. He's been shoving the idea of majoring in the sciences down my throat since I was in middle school. His dream—not mine. I prefer doing things I can mold and make my own—a block of plain-colored fabric that can be scissored into pieces and sewn into a dress. With fashion, I can make up the rules, but nature does whatever it wants.

"That's nice." I deliver this statement in a deadpan tone, hoping to discourage further discussion.

This airport lacks the frenetic pace of U.S. air terminals. The waiting area only supports about two hundred people and security is lax. No locked doorways. No entrances policed by staff in formal attire. Here, ticket-takers wear bright yellow shirts and rumpled clothes.

"Come on. Look at the ostrich chicks," Dad persists, "brown speckled fluffs of down."

I nod after a quick glance then study a TV screen mounted on the wall by the doors leading out to the tarmac. The show is a tutorial on pie making. The woman is using a cookie cutter to cut heart-shaped images in dough, then layering the pieces over the fruit filling to make the top crust.

Mom loves to bake. If she were here, she'd be staring at the screen. I close my eyes. She hasn't cooked a family meal or dessert since she was served with divorce papers. She doesn't seem to want me around either. That's probably why she encouraged me to go on this trip. That's probably why she let me get a tattoo.

I'm worried about her. Even though Mom's sister will stay at our house while we're gone, I can't check in with her to see how she's doing. There's no Internet connection at the safari camp. And if being cut off from the world isn't bad enough, we're going to a malaria-infested country. When I tried to explain about my fear of becoming permanently sick, Dad's response was that the medicine and immunizations would protect me.

I stifle a yawn. I haven't slept well since he booked my ticket. That's how frightened I am of getting malaria. I don't want to live like Sylvia who relapses with fever and chills every few months. It makes me so angry that Dad brushes off my concerns as if I'm a hypochondriac.

I can't wait until next year when I leave for college— hopefully at Parsons or the Fashion Institute of Technology in New York. Then Dad won't have any say over my life. He has already told me he won't pay for fashion school, but I don't care. I'll take out loans. I'll be free to do as I please.

I close my fingers to cover the tattoo of scissors I had inked onto my index finger three weeks ago. Dad will be pissed if he discovers what I've done and even more angry at Mom for allowing me to do it. I fold my arms tight across my chest, take a deep breath, and sigh.

A woman sitting across the aisle in awesome, brown leather, lace-up shoes glances up and smiles at me. I admire her gold necklace with cool, leopard-spot beads. Her eyes are framed with the perfect amount of eyeliner. She extracts a newspaper from her handbag. The *Ngami Times* is in English, but the logo states that it's a Botswana publication. I gape at the headline: MALARIA EPIDEMIC HITS AFRICA.

The title snatches my breath away. Fear courses through my body. I wrench my eyes from the woman's paper. A sense of foreboding fills me from head to toe. I have to convince Dad. I need to get back on a plane to LAX.

"Dad," I say, tugging on his arm. "Look."

"Beep, beep, beep. Last call for Flight 408 to Gaborone," a metallic voice announces over the intercom. "We wish you a pleasant flight."

My father glances up from his book, sees what I'm pointing at, and sighs.

"Claire," he says, "you don't need to worry as long as you take the medicine."

I took a Malarone pill this morning, but I've done my own research.

"The pills aren't always effective. I can still get malaria," I say. "Dad, please. It's not too late. Let me go home. Daddy, please!"

"Stop it, Claire. You're being ridiculous."

The strain between us is as palpable as my heartbeat. He returns to flipping through his book, but he's not really looking at the pages.

"Ah, honey," the woman says, laying the newspaper on the seat beside her. "Don't look so scared. I've been to Africa three times and never gotten sick."

I half-smile. I know she's trying to be kind, but there's no guarantee that I'll be so lucky.

"Besides," she adds and winks, "I've heard mosquitoes prefer brunettes and you have beautiful, blonde hair."

I tuck an errant strand behind my ear, embarrassed by her praise. I shortened my waist-length hair into a bob right after Dad moved out for good. Most seventeen-year-old girls in my class wear their hair in a sloppy ponytail. But short hair suites me and feels authentic.

The intercom crackles. "Beep, beep, beep. Flight 403 to Victoria Falls now boarding. We wish you a pleasant flight."

"Whoops," she says and stands. "That's my plane. Trust me. Africa's amazing. Relax. Enjoy your trip."

I smile, but after she's gone, I can't stop staring at the newspaper she left behind.

After the throng of people has funneled through the glass double doors and onto a bus, the annoying announcer says it again.

"Beep, beep, beep. We wish you a pleasant flight."

"Yeah, right," I grumble.

Dad shifts in his seat beside me.

"Claire," Dad exhales and closes his field guide. "You are going on this trip. I've invested too much money, so you might as well try to make the best of it."

I stare at him. If I catch malaria, I'll be making the "best of it" my whole life.

He's wearing safari colors—tan khaki pants and a slightly darker brown polo shirt. It's cold in the terminal and he's wearing a leather jacket the color of coffee beans—the coat Mom bought him for his forty-fifth birthday last April. It makes him look handsome, complementing his skin tone and fitting as if it were tailor-made for him. Mom's sense of fashion is impeccable. How could he have left her for frumpy Jan-Puss?

Since that horrible day when I walked in on him and Jan-Puss, I'm as uncomfortable in my father's presence as I've been when on dates with boys where neither of us knew what to say.

I fidget then stand. One wall of the terminal is lined with shops and a snack bar.

"Can I get a bottle of water?" I say. "Didn't you say they take American dollars in Botswana?"

Dad reaches into the money belt tucked under his waist-band. The weight of shouldering the anger that I can't seem to let go of whenever Dad is nearby lifts as I approach the store called Big Five Duty Free. On display is a stack of zebra skins that includes the animals' flattened heads as if the creatures had been run over by a steamroller. Gross. Who would buy that?

A taxidermied giraffe towers over these striped "rugs." I kink my neck to view its head, impressed by the size of the animal. Its skull is tiny in comparison to its long legs and sloped body. A black line bisects the giraffe's eye, making it seem angry at being dead. I scurry by and enter the sundries store.

A case displays cold drinks. I grab a bottled water and a bag of chips. The headline on a stack of newspapers by the cashier bears the same terrifying news about a malaria epidemic. This must be a sign that I should definitely take a second antimalarial pill, even if it isn't quite time yet. The lady at the counter writes down the costs of my items on a piece of paper. She adds the numbers by hand and puts the money into a metal box.

"I wish you a pleasant flight," she says.

I smile and tuck my paper bag under my elbow. A sign pointing to the restroom catches my eye as I leave. I decide I'd better go before we get on the plane. I proceed down a dark hall. Overhead, one small light is suspended by a thin wire from a hole in the ceiling. The bulb is literally dangling by a thread. This is a great metaphor for my life right now.

Midway to the ladies' room I peer at a poster of a grizzled rhino head on black background. White letters next to the prominent rhino horn state "Nobody needs a rhino horn but a rhino." Well, duh!

I move on and duck inside the bathroom, holding my breath. By the time I've relieved myself and washed my hands, my lungs are screaming for air. I'm moving too fast as I open the door, and my shoulder plows into a man with a cane, knocking him off balance. As I reach out to steady him, he grabs my hand.

"I'm so sorry," I gasp as I drag in a lungful of air.

Now that he's stable on his feet, I try to pull away. His grip is strong and he won't let go. He's a lean man with a face as round as a fishbowl. His short hair has tufts of gray, but it's so thin that he's almost bald. His blue-and-white flannel shirt has seen better days. I tug harder to free my hand, but he won't let go. The tattoo on my index finger seems to burn from his touch. I'm so frightened that I've lost my voice.

Is he going to rob me? Or worse? My eyes dart around for

help. We're alone in this dark corridor and I'm trapped. He has big fleshy lips. I cringe and duck my head at the thought that he might try to kiss me.

A voice booms at the end of the corridor, and the man releases me. The heat from his hand lingers as I flee. I sprint past the rhino poster and into the light of the terminal waiting area. I'm breathing fast when I reach my father. I open my mouth to tell him what happened, but he's not even looking at me. He's staring over my shoulder at the stuffed giraffe.

"Isn't that giraffe amazing? I read that the older a giraffe is, the darker the spots," Dad says. "Isn't that interesting?"

He doesn't even see that I'm upset. There has to be a way to convince him that we need to go home. I'm struggling for words as he stretches his arms overhead and gets to his feet.

"Wait," I say. "There was a creepy man. I think he was going to—"

"Watch my bags, okay?" he says before sauntering off toward the restroom.

He's leaving? What if the man is still lurking down that hall? What if he tries to rob him and Dad hurts him and ends up in jail? What if that creepy guy followed me? I scan the terminal, but don't spot Fishbowl Head.

My throat is dry, so I remove the bottled water from the paper bag. I slip to my knees and rummage through my luggage. My hand grazes the vial of my antimalarial medicine. I snatch the pill container and fumble with the lid. Maybe I can't control what happens in a restroom corridor, but I can try to protect myself from catching malaria. I shake out a dark pink pill. The imprint says GX CM3. What does that mean? Is it some warning that I could overdose? Maybe I shouldn't do this. But the image of Sylvia's frail body forms. I can't face a life of sickness. I just can't. I pop the medicine into my mouth and wash it down with water before I can change my mind.

"Beep, beep, beep." I listen to the announcement that follows, knowing it's almost time for us to depart. "Flight 8301 to Kigali, please proceed to the gate. We wish you a pleasant flight."

Not us. Still, I hope that Dad doesn't take too long. What if Fishbowl Head comes back? Several people shuffle past me. I shove the medicine deep into my bag, zip it back up, and settle back into my seat. My gaze flicks in the direction of the bathrooms. Dad reappears but stops at the Big Five store. He's a tall man, but the giraffe dwarfs him. He touches one of the zebra skins with reverence. That is something we agree on. The sale of animal hides shouldn't be allowed. But I wish he would stop dawdling and get back here.

It's only then I remember that Dad asked me to watch his stuff. My pulse quickens when I see the chair beside me is empty. Dad's camera bag is missing. I look left and right hoping to see someone running away, but no one appears suspicious.

Panic envelopes me like a shroud. My eyes dart around in desperation. Whoever took it can't have gone far. Dad is going to kill me. He bought a new telephoto lens for this trip.

"Our flight will be next," Dad says as he arrives.

He looks down at his chair. The shiny, white plastic chair seems to glow with accusation. He peers under his seat then stands at full height.

"My camera," he says, "where's my camera, Claire? Is this one of your jokes?"

I stand, but there's nowhere to run. My lower lip quivers as I shake my head no. My legs surrender under my weight, and I sink back into my chair.

"I'm sorry, Dad. Someone must have stolen it while I... while I was looking for something in my bag."

Dad darts over to a uniformed guard. I hold my breath hoping that this man will fix my screw-up. My father's hands measure out the dimensions of the bag. The officer glances around and shrugs as if it isn't his problem.

When Dad returns, he jerks his Rick Steves bag out from under his seat. I feel so stupid. How could I have not noticed someone making off with that black case? Next to his binoculars, that camera is... was... his prize possession.

"You can still take animal pictures with your phone," I say.

The veins on Dad's fisted hand bulge as he grips the strap of his luggage and pulls it onto his seat. His cheeks are flushed. The air flooding into and out of his lungs sounds like an ocean wave. I hug my arms in close and try to make myself small.

Dad moves his bag and collapses in the seat next to me. He juts his chin the way he does when he's pissed off.

"I'm really sorry," I say in a meek voice.

"Well," Dad says after a moment, "it could have been worse. I still have our passports, and the cash is still in my money belt. I'll buy a new camera when we get to Johannesburg."

I can't bring myself to raise my head and meet Dad's eyes. He asked me to do one simple task, and I failed. A replacement camera is going to be expensive, especially if he buys a new telephoto lens to photograph birds.

Dad takes a deep breath.

"Let's not allow this to spoil the trip," Dad says in a too-cheery voice. "Don't beat yourself up, okay? It might have happened with me sitting here."

If South Africa is a country of thieves and malaria, then we should return to California. I should keep my mouth shut but I don't. Maybe if he actually hears what happened to me, it will finally convince him that we should go home.

"What if this is an omen?" I say, and this time he listens as I explain about the man in the corridor.

"Claire," Dad says then frowns.

Wrinkles appear between his eyebrows, and doubt clouds his expression. He hasn't even looked around for someone matching the description I gave him.

"Is this another one of your stories?"

I cringe. I have told a few lies ever since he moved out. Once, when Mom was having a bad day I told him that Buster had run away. Dad did come home, but he was so mad at me for lying he didn't even notice mom's anguish over the divorce. Another time I told him her car was making a funny noise, and my scheme had the same result. I'm a terrible liar. But this is different. I can't believe he thinks I'd lie about a man grabbing me in the airport. I'm shocked speechless.

"That man was real," I whisper after I finally regain my voice.

"Okay. Even so, he probably held on because he was feeling unsteady. Look, I'm not going to let losing my camera ruin our adventure, and you shouldn't let one minor incident taint your impression of all of Africa. I want to show you what an amazing world we live in. I want to fix things between us. Yes, I messed up. I'm sorry you saw Janice and me together like that. I can't change the past."

No, he couldn't.

"I'm not expecting you to forgive me overnight," he says, "but give me a chance to make it up to you on this safari. This will be an experience you'll remember the rest of your life. Nature can change you in ways you can't possibly predict. You'll see."

My head spins. I don't want to change. I want everything to go back to the way things were. Change isn't always a good thing. Sylvia will suffer from flu-like symptoms whenever another malaria attack hits. Mom doesn't want a new life. She looked so unhappy as I got into Dad's car yesterday afternoon. My lower lip trembles. I'm about to start bawling in the middle of the airport.

Dad must notice that I'm about to cry because he reaches out and touches my arm. I take it away. No matter what happens during this trip, he's torn our family apart, and for that I'll never be able to forgive him.

CHAPTER THREE

S ecurity at the Johannesburg airport terminal is chaotic. Here in the capital of South Africa, there aren't any organized lines for customs. A crush of people has elbowed their way to the counter. Dad is too polite to crowd others, so we are two of the last to get through the process. Because we only brought carry-on luggage, we skirt baggage claim.

A wave of exhaustion hits me as we head toward the exit. My Rick Steves bag seems to have gained an extra ten pounds over the course of our multiple flights. We've been traveling for over twenty-four hours, and I want to collapse into a motel room bed, but our journey into the depths of South Africa isn't over. I dread the long drive to the safari camp that still lies ahead.

A glassed-in area outside of the baggage claim area teems with people. According to Dad, this is where we will meet our safari guide. A dozen or so men hold up placards with people's names. Dad tugs at my sleeve, and I follow him toward a sign where block letters on a sheet of white paper read CLAIRE and JACKSON WOODLAKE. I clutch Dad's shirt to avoid losing him as he weaves through the crowd.

I had assumed that our guide would be dark-skinned and fit enough to outrun a cheetah. He's not. He has lovely olive-tan skin and piercing blue eyes. But he's huge. He'd easily take up two airline seats. People say that Americans are overweight, but this man should seriously consider auditioning for *The Biggest Loser*.

"Hello, Claire, hello, Jackson," the man says, extending his beefy right hand. "Americans can't pronounce my real name and everyone calls me Dugger anyway. I'll be your primary safari guide during your stay."

"*Molo*," Dad says.

The man's eyebrows lift.

"I see you've been studying African languages," Dugger says. "That is a Xhosa greeting. We don't use it here in South Africa."

Dad's cheeks color. I want to melt into the floor. Why can't Dad just say hello like a normal tourist?

After Dugger and Dad shake hands, I extend mine, chagrined to see that my pink nail polish is chipped. Dugger communicates a sense of absolute authority in his grip. And he doesn't mess around. A quick shake and he's done with the formality.

Our guide takes my bag and guides us through glass doors into hot, humid air. I'm regretting my choice to wear a fashionable three-quarter-length-sleeve blouse with a V neckline. A boring cotton tank top would have been more comfortable.

From the outside, this airport looks the same as the ugly, concrete mega-structures we have back home and comes complete with a giant parking lot. We could be in any major city in the U.S.

"I'm surprised you didn't opt for a night stay in a hotel," Dugger says. "Most Americans prefer to get some rest before tackling the four-hour haul to camp."

The sun blazes down on us as we walk to the car park. Or rather, we walk, and Dugger huffs. The heat is stifling. I hope the car has air conditioning.

We arrive at a white van that seems modern enough. After unburdening Dad of his luggage, Dugger climbs into the right front seat. It's the first time I've seen a steering wheel on that side of a vehicle. We are invited into the back and I take the position that would normally be behind the driver. Dad sits to my right, immediately behind Dugger.

A scent of greasy food permeates the interior. I crane my neck to peer up front and see a crumpled red and white napkin from Wimpy Burger on the seat next to our guide. Dugger must have stopped at the equivalent of this country's McDonalds for lunch. My heart thrums in my chest as we pull out onto the wrong side of the road, but I soon realize that this is how South Africans drive.

"Are you called Dugger because of the Cape buffalo?" Dad asks.

Dugger studies the traffic as he shifts lanes and doesn't reply. I can't tell if he didn't hear or didn't care to answer.

Dad turns to me and explains how he'd read in a wildlife guidebook that male buffalo too old to fight for mates go off by themselves or sometimes join up with another male past his prime to live out their final days. These outcasts are called dugga boys.

This was exactly what I was afraid of and one reason I didn't want to come on this trip. Dad's going to shove biology lessons down my throat in an effort to change my mind about my future. But no matter what he says, I'm going into fashion design, not a traditional four-year college to major in the sciences. Dugger still hasn't answered Dad's question, and I'm kinda starting to like our guide.

Dad waits until we've left the city and are traveling along flat, barren land that looks the same as the agricultural fields back home in Central California to repeat his question.

"Dad, that's kind of insulting," I say this time as I smooth the wrinkles from my white capris. "Dugger doesn't look old."

Dugger laughs and studies me in the rearview mirror like he's trying to figure out what makes me tick.

"Well, thanks, Claire. I'm afraid your Dad is right. I got the nickname before I got married, and even though I'm not an old bachelor anymore, the name stuck. I did change the spelling though."

Dad's got this smug look on his face. I imagine a week filled with constant pressure about how many opportunities lie ahead for women in the sciences and that I should enjoy fashion as a hobby but accept that my true calling is biology. My eyes are drawn to the finger where his wedding ring used to be. The gold band is gone. He didn't even wait for the divorce to be final to take it off. I feel anger sprout anew. The words tumble from my mouth before I can stop them.

"Well," I say to Dad, thinking about how he's living with Jan-puss now, "I guess you're not a dugga boy either."

"Claire, now who is being rude?" Dad says.

Dad pinches the flesh between his eyebrows like he's getting a headache. The white tip of my fingernail poking out of my ruined manicure distracts me. The urge to chip off even more of my nail polish overtakes me, and I scrape off the uneven part as my resentment toward Dad festers. What did he do with the ring? Throw it away? Hock it to pay for this trip? My anger morphs into rage.

"You see," I say to Dugger, "my dad is shacking up with his girlfriend."

"Claire," Dad shouts. "Enough."

"Well, it's true, isn't it?" I snap. "Married men run off with mistresses all the time as they get older. Men are all a bunch of horny bulls."

"That's enough, Claire." Dad says in a quiet voice as he turns to Dugger and adds, "I'm sorry."

How easily the words roll off his tongue to a stranger. As far as I know he hasn't apologized to my mother.

"Right," Dugger clears his throat. "Most people are not aware that buffalo are the most dangerous of all African land animals. They will attack unexpectedly. One minute they are grazing by the vehicle, the next they are charging."

Great. More biology lessons. I dig my phone out of my back pocket and check for messages, hoping that Sylvia has sent a text, but I don't have service. I sigh. How am I going to survive a whole week without talking to my friends?

"Will we see any buffalo along this drive?" Dad asks.

"Uh, no. Unfortunately, people have displaced the wild-life. In fact, Kruger National Park is fenced off. Although, occasionally a leopard will escape from the reserve."

"Surely we'll get to see some birds along the road," Dad says, fingering his binoculars. He'd extracted his field glasses from his luggage the moment we landed.

"I'm afraid we won't have time to stop until lunch. I recommend you rest up. Americans have a tough time their first few days after such a long flight. You'll want to be refreshed and ready for our afternoon game drive into Sabi Sands. You'll see many birds then."

Dad leans back in his seat but then lurches forward.

"Oh crap. I forgot to ask earlier. Will there be any place to buy a camera along the way?" Dad asks. "I'm afraid mine was stolen at the Botswana airport."

"You need a new camera?" Dugger says. His eyebrows are knitted together and his cheeks have colored a rosy pink. "You might have mentioned that before we left Joburg. There is a store right by the airport. Now, we will have to go back."

I find it hard to breathe as he swerves into the left lane and skids the van into a U-turn. I grip the back of the seat and suppress a gasp. Duggar's annoyance fills the space in the car. The man is as cranky and unpredictable as his namesake. And he's going to be driving us for the next four hours.

*   *   *

I sulk during our lunch at the roadside café. I'm tired and still reeling that Dad's taken off his wedding ring. Dad doesn't even notice me. He's too busy reading the manual on his new camera.

After we are back on the road, Dugger delivers a safety briefing. He explains that animal behavior is well-understood, and the experienced safari guides at African Trek Adventures are trained to anticipate and avoid dangerous situations. Tourists coming on safari are more likely to be involved in a serious car accident than attacked by a wild animal as long as they follow the rules.

"First," he says, "never ever stand up in a vehicle during a game drive. Ever."

Dad and I are required to repeat the words, "don't run" after every hypothetical animal encounter. Dad plays along, but I feel like I'm in grade school and mumble my responses. I don't see the point. Dugger says we'll always be in a vehicle during game drives, except during sundowners. Sundowners are basically an excuse for adults to drink alcohol while watching the sunset. Nothing about this trip sounds fun to me.

Dugger stares at me in the rearview mirror. I imagine him turning around and snarling at me like the MGM lion.

"Claire," he says. "I can't quite tell what's going on with you. But if you're afraid, I assure you the risk of getting malaria is way higher than being attacked by a wild animal. And catching malaria is easily preventable."

His words hit me with such force that my jaw unhinges.

"You think catching malaria is no big deal?" I explode.

"We're both taking Malarone," Dad pipes up. "We're following the doctor's instructions and started the pills two days ago. But I'm afraid Claire's still overly concerned about catching malaria."

I close my eyes. I wish Dad hadn't announced my biggest fear to this man.

"Right," Dugger says. "Bad example. But catching malaria is rare here. I've been at this camp for three years now. I don't take antimalarial medicine and I have never been sick."

"See, Claire." Dad says. "Nothing to worry about."

He's wrong. There's plenty to worry about. I've probably read enough articles on this subject to write a thesis.

"Statistically," I say, "about two in one thousand people will get malaria even if they take Malarone as directed."

"Maybe that would be true for West Africa," Dugger says. "The number of infected mosquitos in South Africa is much lower."

I shrug, unconvinced. I swear I've just heard the buzz of a mosquito. What if there's one trapped in the van?

"We have another hour to go," Dugger says in a resigned voice. "Why don't you get some rest?"

Dad falls asleep. The lull of the engine makes me drowsy too, but I'm too worried about the possibility of a mosquito bite to doze off.

When we pull off the asphalt thoroughfare onto a bumpy,

unpaved stretch of roadway, the jarring ride rouses Dad.

"Almost there," Dugger announces. He seems less annoyed now that we're close to our destination. "Once we get to camp, you'll have a few minutes to change and wash up, but we'll be heading out to Sabi for your first game ride shortly thereafter. Put on sunscreen, and a hat, and practical shoes. Shorts are fine but be aware that it is spring here and the temperature drops fast after dark."

Our van jostles its way past a campground of green canvas tents, sagging in the center and pitched on the ground. Out front a dark-skinned man is sitting on a stool and picking his nose.

Dad must have read my mind because he leans close and whispers, "Don't worry, we are staying in luxury tents with raised, wooden floors, running water and a flush toilet. There's even air conditioning."

My hand skims away a trickle of sweat from my forehead. If it's this hot in spring, I shudder to think what summer is like in South Africa.

The road gets hummocky and soon my breasts are bobbing up and down. I'm tired, smelly and sticky by the time we arrive at the African Trek Adventures outpost.

As soon as we exit the vehicle, Dugger unloads our luggage. We've parked next to the largest camp structure. To the right, a fire pit is encircled by knee-high cement walls. Beyond that, the tourist accommodations consist of six, large canvas structures raised off the ground. Dirt paths marked off by stones lead to each "luxury" tent. Wooden stairs rise to a small deck in front of each unit.

"Your tent is over here," he says, guiding us toward the nearest structure.

It's one of the larger ones and only about seventy-five feet from the main building. Dugger carries my bag and leaves it on the ground in front of the deck.

"We'll have our afternoon snack in the main building in about fifteen minutes and we'll leave on the game drive within the hour."

My feet are heavy as we climb up the three steps to our accommodations. The wooden deck has two chairs out front. The flap is closed and Dad squats down to unzip it.

He lifts the door with a flourish. "Your humble abode for the next six days."

I duck to enter. It's dark inside. After my eyes adjust, I'm relieved to see that the two twin beds each have mosquito netting creating a white veil that covers the entire mattress. He unzips a second flap at the back of the tent and pulls it aside.

"Here's the shower with hot water just like I promised."

It is far from a five-star hotel, but it's much nicer than I expected. I give Dad a crooked smile.

"It'll do. I guess," I say.

"Why don't you get changed?" he says. "I'll get some photos of the grounds."

I unzip my luggage and pull out a pair of white shorts and a light pink blouse. I kick off my tennis shoes and pull out my camo flip-flops.

"Claire," Dad says. "How about wearing the tan REI pants and matching shirt I bought you? You heard Dugger. It gets cold."

"Tan is sooo boring," I say. "Besides, pink attracts hummingbirds. I'm doing you a favor."

"There aren't any hummingbirds in Africa," he says.

He takes a step toward my luggage like he's going to pull out some clothes. I don't want him to see my medicine vial has too few pills.

"Okay, okay," I say quickly.

I pull out the drab garments and bury the pill container of Malarone under my pajamas.

"And wear your running shoes. And bring a jacket and hat," he says as he goes out the door. "I'll meet you in front of the main building."

I'm annoyed by his bossiness, but I take a deep breath and let it go. I slip into the bathroom and change quickly, but when I go to put on my shoes, sweat dribbles down my temple. It's too dang hot, so I slip on my camo flip-flops instead. I shove my iPhone into my pocket, grab my backpack, and stuff in a floppy hat, a light jacket, my sketchpad, and colored pencils. I exit onto the deck and zip up the tent.

Dad frowns when he sees my exposed feet.

"Claire," he says, "put on proper shoes. Right now."

"Not happening," I say. "It's way too hot."

His jaw clenches and he's about to say more when a dark-skinned woman wearing a black dress comes down the steps of the communal area. I turn my back on my father as she approaches me with a plate of unfrosted yellow cake and a tray of steaming beverages.

Drinking coffee or tea is a bad idea right before a long car ride. I doubt there will be a porta potty out in the bush. But in the end, the lure of caffeine is too great, and I take a mug and move up the stairs away from Dad who has already found a chattering bird to stalk anyway.

The rich elixir slips down my throat, and I close my eyes. I rarely indulge in espressos or lattes, much less standard brews. Exhaustion drains from my body and is replaced by a burst of energy.

"Okay," Dugger says as he emerges through a door at the

back of the main building. "Everybody in the Land Rover."

"Thank you so much," I say replacing the coffee mug on the tray.

Our guide has changed into shorts and a long-sleeved shirt. He still wears a camo baseball cap. But I'm shocked to see that he carries a rifle. We need a weapon? The reality of the danger of seeking out wildlife with claws and fangs descends.

Dad catches up to me as I round the corner. I stop short at the sight of our vehicle. The rifle suddenly makes sense. There are no doors or windows. Four rows of staggered seats, getting progressively higher toward the rear bumper, look like they've been hijacked from a movie theater. Where is the roof? This can't be for real. We can't seek out leopards and lions in an open vehicle.

"What the hell, Dad? We can't roll up the windows or lock the doors."

My father scrambles into the open-air jeep. As far as I can tell, the only thing that it has going for it is the height. The footboard step is about knee-high. Dad grins like a little boy. He's got *The Birds of South Africa* field guide in his hand. It is a hefty book, but even if he hurled it at a charging lion, it would only bounce off.

"Come on, Claire," Dad says. "Get in."

The back door to the main building opens. A young guide emerges from the staff area. He's wearing the same outfit as our over-sized, gun-toting guide, but the clothes make him look rugged and capable. Even in the khaki uniform, his biceps bulge under the short sleeves. I'd like to see him in a tight-fitting black T-shirt. His blond hair glistens in the sun as he saunters toward the Land Rover. He's the opposite of Dugger—thin and fit.

"Hi," he says. "You must be Clar. I'm Diker, but everyone calls me Junior."

He has pronounced my name as if it rhymes with "car." His accent is utter ear candy. It sounds British or maybe Australian.

He's gorgeous—a Disney movie prince—and he's younger than I first thought, maybe even a teen like me. When I shake his extended hand, his touch is electric. Piercing blue eyes travel the length of my body. I'm glad my tan safari shirt has darts that accentuate my breasts.

"You better get in," he says. His head inclines down toward my feet. "Um, do you have any *tekkies*?

"*Tackies*?" I repeat.

Junior points at my flip-flops and says, "I think Americans call them sneakers."

I wiggle my manicured toes and shrug.

"What's going on?" Dugger says.

"Nothing," Junior says quickly.

He tucks his chin to his chest and gives me a look as if he's peering over the tips of eyeglasses, though he wears none. He's covering for me. He just met me and he's already on my side.

I reach out to touch the side of the Land Rover to steady myself. My heart pounds as though I've sprinted across a soccer field. I wonder if he's coming on the trip or just helping people board. I'd rather stay behind and hang out with him.

"I'm not sure I want to go," I say.

"You don't want to be left here." Junior pronounces here like he-yah. "You'll be bored, and your tent will be an oven toward the end of the afternoon—even with the air conditioner."

His accent rolls across my ears in pleasant waves. I could listen to him all day. But my eyes are drawn back to the rifle in Dugger's hand. Our head guide's leather belt contains holes filled with spare bullets and has a walkie-talkie clipped to it.

Junior turns to see what I'm looking at then leans in so that our cheeks almost touch and whispers, "Don't worry. We've never had to shoot an animal. Trust me. Dugger has thirty years of experience. He knows the limits of how close we can get to the wildlife and when to retreat."

He nods toward the Land Rover, where my father sits with his binoculars glued on some twittering little brown bird. He takes my backpack and tosses it inside the vehicle. As he cups my elbow to guide me toward a step stool at the side of the vehicle, his cerulean eyes widen and he takes my hand, rotating it so that he exposes the scissor tattoo between my fingers.

"*Bakgat*," he exclaims.

I pull my hand away, embarrassed. I don't know what that means, but a glint in his eyes suggests that he appreciates my tat.

"Up you go in the Landy," he says.

Landy? Junior's lop-sided grin and his sexy accent have turned my knees to putty.

"Let's go," he says when I haven't moved. "I've got the eyes of a bateleur eagle and I would throw myself in front of a lion before I'd let a big cat touch a single blonde hair on your pretty head. I'll not let anything happen to you."

Did he just say that? I raise one foot to the footboard step as Junior puts his hand on my elbow again. His touch feels like fire. I can't breathe, but somehow my leg cooperates and finds a foothold in the outer design of the vehicle's body, and before I know it, I'm stuck inside the metal death trap.

I'm grateful Dad's flipping through his bird book and ignoring me. I imagine my face has bloomed pink from an unleashed fantasy about kissing Junior. He probably tastes like an exotic spice.

A man and woman appear from around the building. Both are thin and walk with a stiff gait. But when they spot Dad and me, smiles light up their faces. They're wearing identical standard khaki safari outfits. This whole entourage could be a commercial for REI clothing.

They call out an enthusiastic, "Halloo."

"Ah," Junior says. "The English couple is here. That's the rest of our group. You're lucky—almost a private tour."

"What do you want for your sundowner drinks?" Dugger asks.

The English people both want "Cahsel." Dad asks for beer and we find out that Cah-sel is a type of beer. I say I want that too, but Dad glares at me and orders me a Coke.

"You just arrived?" the British woman says. Before Dad or I can answer, she adds. "I'm Phoebe, but everyone calls me Phee, and this is Arden. You're in for a treat. There's a buffalo down. We're hoping the poor creature has died and that the hyenas will come for supper."

My stomach hitches. The sight of blood. And hyenas? Who wants to get close to those vile, spotted creatures?

Junior smiles at Phee and Arden. "You two know the drill, but we have to do this for our new guests."

"I say," says Arden, "it's important."

"What do you do if you see an elephant charging?" Junior says. "Everyone say it together now."

I know what's expected since Dugger briefed us on the drive here. Junior lifts his hands like a conductor. He looks straight at me. His mouth transforms into a slow grin. One side droops slightly, but the lopsidedness suits him. Dimples form as his smile broadens. I find myself saying the words along with everyone else.

"Don't run."

"Leopard rushing toward you?"

"Don't run."

I chime in with such enthusiasm that Dad turns to look at me.

"That's the spirit," Dad says to me.

"Lion?"

"Don't run."

I say it so loudly that my voice overshadows everyone else's response. Dugger puckers his lips to hide his grin. I don't care. Junior's broad smile has revealed beautiful white teeth. I'm amusing him.

"Even if they are coming at you and you see the yellow of their eyes?"

"Don't run."

This time Arden shouts it the loudest and Phee claps her hands. I suspect her husband is not typically that enthusiastic. Junior points to the sky, and Dugger follows suit. I wonder if this is their way of asking God for a blessing to keep us safe.

Dad leans close, "You need to take this seriously. You, of all people, need to heed this advice."

My grin fades. Why does he always have to be a fun-sucker?

"What the hell does that mean?" I say.

"It's what you do, Claire," he says. "Whenever things get tough, you run off. You can't do that here."

I resist the urge to exit the vehicle and return to our tent, which would only prove his point. Instead, I shift in my seat so that my back faces him and I focus on our young guide. Junior nods to Dugger and jumps onto a fold-down seat which projects a couple feet off the front bumper. I've got a bird's eye view of his blond head. His hair is sleek and golden with a bit of a wave. I long to run my fingers through it. If I can ignore all the creatures and focus on Junior, maybe I can find a way to enjoy this trip after all.

The engine roars to life. We exit through a gate and are soon back on the bouncy road. We drive next to a tall fence for about a mile before the entrance to the private reserve appears on our left. We have to wait while Junior takes paperwork into a small office next to the guard kiosk. I stare up at palm trees that look about as out of place as I feel. Then I remember my manners and turn around.

"I'm Claire," I say.

Phee crow's feet crinkle at the corners of her eyes as she smiles. My grandmother had those and told me that old people get them from smiling all their lives. There's a warmth in her hazel eyes.

"Hallo," Arden says.

"Jackson," Dad says.

He shakes hands with Arden and nods at Phee.

"You two must be a bit knackered," she says.

I assume that means tired and suddenly exhaustion threatens to overpower me. I nod.

"Well, once you see your first elephant or leopard, you'll be happy you skipped a nap."

I appreciate the stylish way she tied the beige headscarf around her short, cropped hair. She's in her late sixties, I think. Arden looks maybe ten years older. His hair, whitened by age, is thin. But the wrinkles that furrow his forehead give him a stately appearance. Streaks of gray peek through strands of Phee's brown hair that poke out from beneath her bandana, but the natural look fits her.

"I'd put on a floppy hat if you brought one," she adds. "I turned as red as the guard's uniforms at Buckingham Palace after my first game drive."

I smile and extract the wide-brimmed hat from my backpack and place it on my head, hoping that Junior will approve of the stylish flare it adds to my outfit.

"How long have you been here?" I ask.

"Not long. This is our third night. We're leaving tomorrow. We've seen four of the big five—all except for lion."

"The big five?" I say, remembering that was the name of the store at the airport. "You mean like giraffe and elephant."

She tips her head backward and laughs. "Not quite. Safari companies all claim to be able to show you the big five. But it's not the five biggest animals. It's the most dangerous ones. Want to guess what they are? You already named one."

"Elephant," I say. "And lion and leopard." I hesitate then add in a not too confident voice, "Rhino?"

"Brilliant," she says. "One more. This one isn't obvious, but I mentioned it earlier."

"Hyena?" I guess.

"Nope, try again."

And then I remember what Dugger said during our drive to camp. I am so tired that I'd forgotten.

"Buffalo." I say with confidence.

"Bloody smart, you are," Phee says clapping her hands, which makes me laugh.

I don't confess that Dugger had told me earlier today how dangerous buffalo are.

I turn to look in Junior's direction as he hands a clipboard to Dugger and climbs back up onto his lookout spot at the front of the vehicle. Of all of us, he's the most exposed to the dangers of Africa.

Dugger engages the clutch and we drive through the reserve gates. I expect to see wildlife grazing in full view amidst short, yellow grass. But dead, weedy plants and barren trees with an occasional green, leafy shrub surround either side of the Land Rover. The landscape eventually changes to a plain of green, cropped grasses, dotted with scattered leafless trees with crooked trunks. We have yet to see any wildlife. We'd have been better off going to the zoo.

The sun bakes down on us and reflects off the windshield making me squint. I'm glad for the hat and that I'm wearing shorts. Dad hands me a tube of sunscreen and I slather it on my arms, and face, and exposed legs.

The Land Rover jolts to a stop, and Dugger points at several small, brown animals.

"Dwarf mongoose," he shouts over the engine noise.

We idle next to the frolicking creatures. Dad gives me his binoculars while he snaps a few pictures. He tells me to look at their faces. The animal's twitchy noses are an impossibly bright red—the color of maraschino cherries.

"Zay-brah," Junior says pointing to the left.

His accent electrifies me. As I catch sight of a single black-and-white-striped animal, I'm caught up in the excitement. It has long ears and is smaller than a horse which surprises me.

Junior explains that you can tell the health of a zebra by the way the mane sticks up. A healthy zebra will have stiff, bristly spikes on the neck. He said that last part looking at me. I flush with shyness, hoping my father doesn't notice Junior's giving me special attention.

After a bit, we move on. The Landy jostles along the

rutted dirt road then turns a corner. Behind a bush lies a downed black animal. It's on its side with its knobby legs outstretched. This must be the dying buffalo that Phee mentioned. I stare at its belly, but I don't see movement and I suspect it's already dead.

We leave the road to circle around toward the head. I turn away when I see its sightless eyes. I'm surprised there aren't any vultures circling overhead and relieved that the dreaded hyenas haven't arrived.

"The other animals haven't found the buffalo yet," Dugger says. "Probably by tonight though. We'll swing by on our way back."

As the Land Rover trundles along, Dugger points out a cardinal woodpecker, a blue waxbill, and a brown snake eagle for Dad's benefit. Dad is jotting down the names in a notebook and snapping pictures. Phee and Arden peer through their binoculars and nod, but they don't take photos.

A voice crackles on the walkie-talkie. Strange, unintelligible words hold a tone of excitement. Dugger speaks into it in the same tongue. He shifts into high gear and we are bouncing along at a steady clip. We take a side road and soon see a second Land Rover. Beyond that vehicle, I spot what they've stopped to see. A rhino.

"White rhino," Junior says.

We circle around the large, gray animal and appear to be driving right past, but then Dugger maneuvers our vehicle so that we are in the rhino's path. I clutch the seat as the animal ambles along toward us, its head to the ground, giant horn protruding from its elongated skull. It looks as ancient and exotic as a dinosaur.

There's nothing cute or fuzzy about it. Rather there's something both dignified and stoic about the animal like a wizened grandmother. The dipped head suggests a humble beast. For some reason, the impossible shape of this creature fascinates me.

Dugger inches the Land Rover forward at an angle until we are no longer in the animal's path. Our guide turns around to face us.

"The white rhino is much more docile than the black rhino," Dugger says. "Their eyesight is so poor that I once had a rhino walk into the vehicle. Unfortunately, here in South Africa, three of these animals are killed each day for their horns. There are people who believe that the fibrous material has medicinal qualities. The horn is comprised of material that is equivalent to fingernails, and yet people pay more for it than for gold."

Phee shakes her head and grumbles, "What is wrong with people?"

Now I understand the poster I saw at the Botswana airport that read, "Nobody needs a rhino horn but a rhino."

"It doesn't look real, does it?" I gush.

"No, it doesn't," Dad says.

The shutter on his camera whirrs away.

"Only about three hundred white rhinos are left on our property," Junior adds. "And we have the only two western black rhinos of the *longipes* subspecies right here in this park. They were declared extinct in 2011, but a pair was found in a remote area of Cameroon last year. They were brought to this reserve in South Africa because of our stellar anti-poaching unit. The female is pregnant and both animals are shadowed around the clock to protect them from poaching. If either of these black rhinos die, it will mean extinction of the genetically unique subspecies."

"Can we see them?" Dad says.

"That will not be possible," Dugger says. "Black rhinos are aggressive toward people and vehicles. We can't risk antagonizing the pregnant female by allowing tourists to view them."

Dugger shifts gears, and the Land Rover's engine startles the rhino. The big animal lumbers away, swinging its tiny, rope-like tail across its ample rear end in a way that reminds me of how a horse's braided tail moves when swishing away flies. I'm sad to leave this animal.

"What I wouldn't give to see the last of the western black rhino," Dad whispers.

I nod. There's something magical and goofy and sad about these giants. I would also like to see those two survivors.

CHAPTER FOUR

W e're on the hunt again for more animals, but all around is desolate terrain. Since the rhino sighting, we've passed scraggly bushes and endured bumpy dirt roads. The land is not flat and I've yet to see antelope grazing in open, yellow fields. Where are the giant herds of impala? Where are the grazing giraffes like I've seen on TV? Everywhere dead-looking trees are interspersed with sparse patches of green grass. The South African landscape is not at all what I expected.

The best thing about this game drive so far, besides the white rhino, is that I haven't seen a single mosquito. But the light has started to fade. I fear dusk will probably result in a feeding frenzy. I reach into my backpack, pull out the bug spray, and apply a generous amount.

The Land Rover slows then comes to a complete halt. After Dugger kills the engine, it makes knocking sounds before going silent. He doesn't seem concerned, so I assume these are routine noises for the camp vehicle. My eyes scan the area to see why we have stopped.

"Wildebeest," Dugger announces, pointing to an open clearing.

A brown animal steps from behind a bush. I don't even know how the guides spotted it. It turns its black face our way. Horns sprout out of each side of its head. They curve back toward the skull like an extra set of ears. This odd animal has a black horsehair-like mane and tail. I wonder if they are related to horses, but I'm too shy to ask.

The rich brown tone of its body contrasted against the green grass is stunning. The rumpled coat reminds me of a Shar Pei puppy's wrinkles, and resembles expensive leather. Sylvia often teases me and says I'm obsessed with clothing design, and she's right. I see fabrics and textures everywhere. I hadn't considered that the animals we'd see on safari would be a source of inspiration. But now the image of an ankle-length, suede overcoat the color of deep-roasted coffee forms in my head. A furry black collar of downy material with a belt made of horsehair cinching the waist would be a stunning way to complete the look.

I pull my sketchpad and pencil set out of my backpack, shifting my body so my father can't see my work. I once wanted him to notice my talent, but with college applications looming, it's better to avoid any reminder of my ambition to become a fashion designer.

My heart's desire is to meet Tim Gunn and be on *Project Runway*, not dissect frogs. I doubt Dad has watched this TV fashion show, and even if he had, he'd consider it silly for me to pursue an audition. I can hear him saying that the odds of me making it on the show are next to none.

But I needn't have worried. Dad is busy taking photos and ignoring me as usual. In quick movements, I sketch out the image I see in my mind. My notebook is stuffed away without Dad seeing it.

"Both a blue and a black wildebeest species exist in South Africa. This one is a blue," Dugger says. "In addition to the color, the difference between blue and the black is the size and shape of their horns. Blues are a lot bigger and the horns curve to the side, whereas the blacks' horns curve forward."

The animal stands about three car lengths from us. It nods its head forward and back as it crops the grass like a grazing cow.

"Interbreeding between the two species is a real problem," Dugger continues, "so it is illegal to have both kinds on the reserve. If a black wildebeest were to wander onto the reserve, it would have to be chased off or the owners face a hefty fine."

"I say," Arden says, "that seems extreme."

"Not really," Dugger says in a defensive voice. "We're talking about sparing an entire species from inbreeding and all that goes with that—health problems, genetic disorders, reduced fertility."

When the plane landed in South Africa, Dad had warned me that the main guide at our camp had a reputation for being grouchy. I imagine he thought that this might not sit well with me, so he waited till the last minute to tell me. Dad had been quick to add that this guide had a nose for finding the animals that made him a legend among the guides. Dad said that even if this man was rough around the edges, I should put up with his abrasiveness because he had phenomenal tracking skills. It dawns on me now that Dad meant Dugger.

"You'll often see zebras and wildebeest grazing together," Junior chimes in. His voice is a little too loud, a little too cheerful, like he's trying to diffuse Dugger's irritable nature. "The wildebeest prefer short grass, while zebras eat longer grass so they don't compete for food. They work together watching for predators, which benefits both species."

Dugger starts the engine. He doesn't ask the group if they are ready to go as he has done before, suggesting that he's still a bit miffed by Arden's comment. I resolve not to annoy that man. I wouldn't want to kick that hornet's nest of a temper.

We round a curve, and up ahead, a giraffe stands in the road. It's a fair distance away, but it turns and flees anyway. It's unreal the way this awkwardly-shaped animal runs, both front legs moving simultaneously forward as if tied together, while its extended neck stretches out in front, followed by the seemingly hobbled hind limbs.

It doesn't run far before it stops to nibble on the leaves of a tall tree on the side of the road. Dugger eases our vehicle forward again until we are close enough to get a good look. Dad hands me his binoculars and I zero in on its glorious spotted coat.

I learn from Dugger that it's a female, because the horns are not smooth at the rounded tips. The male's horns get worn down during battles with other males. He adds that the giraffe's eyelashes are the longest of any animal. My blonde eyelashes are as thin as spider webs. Mom says that it's just as well because dark eyelashes would detract from my aquamarine eyes. But I think my blue eyes would look spectacular highlighted by thick, black lashes.

"Look over here," Dugger says, pointing to a small red antelope about the size of an Irish setter. "A bushbuck."

I study the curve of Junior's neck as Dugger explains how dangerous this little horned animal can be and how the male will gore you if you get too close. I shudder, vowing never to get out of this vehicle. A hawk flying overhead startles the bushbuck and it runs off.

Junior's eyes connect with mine. I offer a lopsided smile. I want to tell him that seeing the white rhino took my breath away, and he's lucky to have a job which includes tracking a giant creature that doesn't look like it belongs in this millennium, and how watching a giraffe run is a privilege few people on this planet get to experience.

I wonder if he'd be impressed that I plan to find a fabric the same texture as the wildebeest's wrinkled skin, and that the animal inspired a coat design. Or would he think clothing design is as frivolous as my father believes?

I hate to admit it, but most of the animals have inspired fashion designs. I could make an entire collection... Wait. That's a brilliant idea. My creations would feature all aspects of the safari, from the green of the grasses to the textures and colors of the animals.

Junior nods and launches off of his lookout post on the vehicle. Wait. What's he doing? Aren't we all supposed to stay inside? I turn to see if Dugger is alarmed. He's explaining the differences between rhino and elephant poop and is watching Junior without emotion. I'm appalled when Junior picks up a chunk of orange, elephant dung to show us. Junior is risking his life to show us poo? I look around, but I don't see any animals and both Junior and Dugger are calm as the elder guide describes the animals' diets.

For a moment, I fear that Junior plans to hand the excrement over to us to pass around like show-and-tell for kindergarteners. But he only pulls it apart so we can see it is lightweight and loosely formed, as opposed to the dark brown spoor of the rhino.

My fantasy of holding hands with Junior as we watch the sunset evaporates. I hope he washes his hands before he handles our drinks and snacks.

The radio crackles, followed by excited chatter in a foreign tongue. Junior drops the poop, dusts off his hands, and scrambles into his jutting seat. The Land Rover circles around to head back the way we came.

"Hold on," Dugger shouts and he doesn't sound the least bit miffed anymore. "It's time for Ferrari safari. There's been a big five sighting."

Phee leans forward and says, "They don't tell you which animal in case it moves on. They don't want to disappoint you. But I really hope it's a lion."

Dugger wasn't kidding about the speed. I grip the back of the seat in front of me and plant my feet on the floor of the vehicle as we career over the rough road. We are jarred by ruts and bounced airborne. Junior manages to stay in his seat by reaching behind to grip his seat back. There isn't a roof overhead or any seatbelts to keep us from flying out of the vehicle. Still, I can't help but grin. This is almost as much fun as the Indiana Jones ride at Disneyland.

Up ahead, a Land Rover holding another tour group moves slowly in our direction. Dugger decelerates as he pulls up beside their vehicle. The other guide and Dugger speak in their native Afrikaans language. After Dugger pulls away, he explains that the leopard disappeared into some thick brush, and it won't be possible for us to track it down.

"How disappointing," Dad says.

But I'm relieved. If we're going to observe big cats, I want windows and doors.

The sun's descent seemed to have accelerated during our wild ride. The sky is now layered with blues and pinks with puffs of white clouds sprinkled throughout. Dugger and Junior engage in a discussion as we putter back to the main road. I get a wisp here and there of their conversation and gather they are debating the best place to have sundowners.

Dad points at a herd of orange antelope with horns twisting up in lazy concentric rings toward the sky. Black markings outline the contours of their hind ends. He asks

Dugger to stop, but either Dugger doesn't hear or he chooses to ignore my father. He accelerates past the herd and they charge off.

"We don't want to miss the sunset," Junior says by way of explanation. I suddenly feel sorry for him. He is saddled with a grumpy boss. "Impala are common here. We'll see many, many more under better light for photos."

The radio crackles and Dugger brakes to answer. I study the crooked curves of the branches on the tree next to the Land Rover. The upper limbs grow parallel to the ground in a tangled mass like a mushroom cap made out of gray thread.

"What are these trees called?" I ask Dad.

"Acacia," he says.

I'm not surprised that my father knows. He bought a stack of field guides about both the animals and plants of South Africa. Dugger creeps around a curve and stops.

"Kudu," Junior announces, pointing ahead to where two large animals graze on a dead-looking shrub.

Dugger shifts gears and takes the Land Rover off the dirt track. The vehicle jostles and bounces us once more. Dugger stops about twenty-five yards from the duo.

Kudu resemble a cross between camels and antelope. Their spines round up near the forelegs and they have tapered hind ends. A series of white stripes descends from the back as if someone dribbled white paint to add interest to their otherwise drab brown coat. One of the animals turns its head in our direction, and for the first time I see the horns. There is an artistic flair to the spirals that remind me of blown glass.

"Blimey," Phee says.

"I say," Arden says, "those horns are brilliant, eh?"

"I understand that the kudu horns are used as a wind

instrument in African music," Dad says as he leans across my lap to take a few photos.

"Right, everybody out," Dugger (AKA Mr. Grouchy) says. "Time for sundowners."

Steps have been carved into the vehicle's exterior for shorter people to lessen the distance to the ground when exiting. The seats behind us, where Phee and Arden are located, share the same steps as the row I'm in. Dad has already hopped out on the other side, but I wait for Phee and Arden to exit so I'm the last one inside. I smile as Junior squirts hand sanitizer onto his fingers. I'd have no problem at all now if Junior wants to hold my hand and inspect my scissor tattoo. None at all.

As I swing my leg over to get out, Dugger glances up from where his is setting up a tray for our snacks.

"Agh, shame," he says as he turns to Junior. "Didn't you help her into the Landy?"

Crap. My painted pink toenails glisten in the waning light. This is about my shoes. I don't see what the big deal is, but Junior bites his lower lip, looking uncomfortable. He nods.

"And did you see what was on her feet?"

Dugger is both big and loud. Arden and Phee have backed away and stand toward the bumper.

"Yes, but..." Junior begins.

Dugger's face blooms the color of the reddening sky. Junior slouches and drops his chin to his chest. This is my fault.

"You realize she's going to have to stay in the vehicle, right?"

"Hang on," Dad says. "This isn't Junior's fault. I told Claire she needed to put on better shoes and she refused. She has to suffer the consequences."

I appreciate that Dad is defending Junior, but he's embarrassing me in the process. Why couldn't he have waited so that I could confess? I feel like a small child who has been given a timeout. Anger bubbles to the surface. The only time he pays any attention to me is when I screw up.

"I don't care if I have to stay in the car," I say, glaring at my father. "I never wanted to come on this trip."

Dugger shakes his head and stomps away. Junior busies himself by passing out beers to Dad and Arden. Dugger bends over and places his hands on his knees. I suspect this is how Dugger calms down when his temper flares. Then he takes in one giant breath, grunts, straightens, and walks back to the car. He peels plastic lids off containers in quick, angry movements. The smell of bacon makes my stomach rumble.

Dad wanders away with his beer to snap more photos of the kudu. Phee and Arden stand with linked arms, enjoying the sunset. Dugger grips a food container and frowns. His green eyes connect with mine and he shakes his head. Now I see resignation, rather than annoyance, in his eyes.

"Right," Dugger grouches. "Since the others are more interested in the kudu and the view, I guess you can be the first to enjoy the appetizers."

Dugger hands one of the containers to Junior who has rummaged through the cooler and is now holding my Coke Light. Dugger fills a clear plastic cup with white wine and approaches Phee.

Junior approaches my side of the vehicle and offers me a snack. I peer inside and smile. Tiny corncobs like the ones Tom Hanks nibbles on with his front teeth in the movie *Big* are stacked in neat rows. Each corn is wrapped in bacon and skewered with a toothpick. I take one and say thanks.

"I'm sorry I got you in trouble," I add.

"Clar" he says, "the only thing I'm worried about right now is that your Coke is getting warm."

I reach down to take the offered drink. My fingertips connect with Junior's and he doesn't immediately release the can. His eyes sparkle with mischief which makes me grin.

"Dugger is right to make you stay in the car though," he adds in a low voice. "Baboon spiders can deliver a painful bite. Not to mention the scorpions. I should have been more insistent that you put on proper footwear."

"Junior," Dugger barks, "how about passing the food around to our other guests?"

Junior jumps as if he's been caught doing something wrong. He releases my drink so suddenly that I almost drop it. Without responding to Dugger, he walks over to where my father stands.

Of everyone in our group, Dad is physically closest to the kudu. I wonder if Mr. Grump will ask Dad to move back so as not to scare them away, but Dugger returns to the Land Rover. He extracts his own camera from the cab. It has a giant lens. He's a serious photographer. I can tell by the way he is making minute adjustments before snapping a shot. He doesn't even bother to get closer to the animals.

"That's quite a camera," I say.

Dugger grunts, but his expression changes, turns kinder somehow.

"I—I'm sorry about my shoes. And... and thanks for showing us the rhino."

He lowers his camera to look at me. Astute green eyes study me and I shift in my seat. There's a reason he's good at spotting wildlife. It's clear he doesn't miss much.

"So you liked the rhino, huh? I probably have thousands of rhino photos. But I believe you can't take enough rhino pictures. Hell, there can't be enough of kudu either. Someday soon these digital images may be all that is left of African wildlife—especially the rhino. Those amazing animals are being killed for the horn at a rate that they may be extinct in my lifetime."

There is a façade in his manner that makes me think he goes about pretending to be grumpy, but underneath all the gruffness is a guy who probably loves to play with kittens.

"Check this out." He clicks through a bunch of photos then tilts the camera screen toward me. "Can you believe how small those eyes are?"

A little black bead of an eye lies above bags of wrinkled, gray flesh. It makes the rhino appear tired and a bit sad, as if it knows that there are people out to kill it.

"These animals have giant skulls and two massive horns," he continues, "but still, there was plenty of space to have given these guys bigger eyes."

I can see he's working hard to be professional and do his job, but I get the sense he'd rather be taking more photos than dealing with a rule-breaking teen.

"You know, everyone loves the big cats." He sighs and shakes his head as if I represent all the dumb tourists of the world. "But the rhino is my favorite. It is a real privilege to see all the animals though. Enjoy this night. Each safari drive offers new experiences. But the world is changing. Someday, you'll reflect on the gift of this moment and all you will see is regret that you were more interested in disobeying your father than enjoying this safari."

I suspect he's right, but my anger at my dad is too fresh.

"You don't know what he's done," I say.

"Maybe not," Dugger says, shaking his head, "but you may only be in Africa this one time. Don't squander this precious experience."

I locate where my father stands alone. He's not taking pictures. Dad is sipping his beer with an enamored expression. I don't know if Dad is enchanted by the blazing red-orange sky surrounding the sun or by the presence of the kudu. But he seems to have forgotten my existence. The gulf between us feels bigger than ever.

CHAPTER FIVE

The kudu wander off behind a teepee-shaped mound of earth as the sun descends toward the horizon. Junior explains that termites have created this structure. It's at least as tall as a one-story house and as wide at the base as an elephant. Hard to believe insects could create such an enormous home for themselves.

I'm relieved the mosquitoes haven't arrived. At the moment, the sun appears to be perched on top of a barren acacia tree. A glowing orb about to try to play hide and seek—an impossible feat given the big sky that dominates the African plain. But the yellow ball will eventually drift out of sight, it will win the game, a feat possible due to the curved surface of the earth.

"Time to go," Dugger announces.

The others gather around the Land Rover waiting for their turn to climb into the staggered seats of the vehicle. Dad stands next to our seat row with that hangdog look he gets after we fight.

"Some people have seeing an African sunset on their bucket list," Dad says as he climbs up and sits beside me. "Even though you aren't interested in the safari animals, I hope you can at least enjoy this part of this trip."

I glance at Dugger to see if he's watching. He raises his eyebrows at me, so I bite back a snarky reply. When I was younger we used to have monthly family meetings—my mother's idea. We could say anything. Complain about

Mom's cooking, reveal how sad I felt after friends hurt my feelings. But the person speaking had to offer up a possible solution. If I didn't care for the lasagna we'd had for dinner, I could request that Mom make spaghetti next time. If Mom resented how many times I asked her to drive me to friends' houses or requested rides to the mall, she would ask me to help put the dishes away or some other chore to make up for the extra time and work that my social life demanded. Mom and I made an effort during these family meetings. Dad never had much to say. Mom always wanted Dad to work less. But he didn't embrace any of her suggestions. The family meetings stopped two years ago when Dad said he would make an effort to spend more time with Mom, if he had more time, and one way to have more time was to stop attending these family meetings. Dad wasn't trying back then, but he is now.

"The sunset is amazing," I say. What I want in return is a possible solution to help me let go of my anger. I know that it's big and he's not going to like it. I take a deep breath. "I'll make an effort to enjoy this trip. I'll wear the proper shoes. But you have to promise I won't have to spend time with Janice when we get home. We can meet for dinner, but I don't want to step foot in her house."

Dad looks as if he's been slapped. He must have hoped I'd come around and accept his mistress. That isn't going to happen.

"Claire—"

"My terms," I say.

Dad frowns. He picks up his camera and starts reviewing the photos he has just taken, making it clear he's not interested in my offer.

I shrug and turn away. I shouldn't have mentioned the

footwear as part of the deal. I'd planned to wear the sneakers anyway to avoid getting Junior in trouble again.

As soon as everyone else is loaded inside, Junior extracts a large spotlight from a storage box at the front of the Land Rover and turns it on. He aims it toward the ground.

Dugger clears his throat and addresses us all. "Junior won't be shining the light on any of the ungulates, I mean antelope-type animals. The light can blind the impala and the kudu for up to forty-five minutes and that can leave them susceptible to predators. It isn't fair to the animals to endanger them so you can have a better view. You might think we didn't see the wildlife, but I assure you, Junior is one of our best spotters."

I smile at Junior. Dugger doesn't seem like the kind of guy to give praise. That means Junior must be top-notch.

Behind me, Arden and Phee are so quiet that I sneak a peek. She gazes in the direction of the last ebb of orange light but seems to be peering beyond the horizon into some distant, happy memory, her wedding day perhaps. Phee nestles herself against Arden, and he drapes his arm around her. He bends down to kiss the top of Phee's head. They appear so content and it gives me hope that all marriages aren't destined to end the same way my parents' did.

Dad fidgets in the seat beside me.

"This discussion isn't over," he says. "You will be spending the night at Janice's."

"You can't make me," I hiss.

"I say," Arden says, "can't you two discuss this later?"

I turn around. Phee sits up straight in her seat, no longer cuddling against Arden.

"Sorry," I say, before facing forward and slumping in my seat.

"I apologize, too," Dad adds.

I almost hope we see a lion as we head back to base camp. I want Phee's final impression of her last safari night in Africa to be so spectacular that she'll forget about the American girl and her father who couldn't get along. But the reality of our exposed vehicle makes the idea of wishing to encounter a big predator seem ludicrous.

The Land Rover claws its way through the rutted road. Darkness sets in fast and with it cool air. We retain some visibility because of the nearly full moon, but there is something primeval in traveling in an open-air vehicle under the cloak of night in Africa. I feel an odd sense of wonder, until I remember that there could be lions and leopards around the next curve in the road and shudder.

Overhead, a few stars twinkle in the deepening blackness. Inspiration hits out of nowhere as I combine this sky with the unique animals we've seen today. I could design a black dress featuring African stars on a moonless night buried in the silhouettes of giraffes and rhinos. I could superimpose these images in a variety of background colors. I could do the same thing on blouses. Africa has opened me up to all kinds of creative ideas. And I realize with a start that I haven't seen a single mosquito.

Dugger studies Junior as he drives, like a defense lawyer might examine a juror looking for clues to see if they believe a defendant is guilty. Junior leans forward and trains his beam toward a small shrub. Dugger takes the cue and stops.

I don't see anything at first but then I see a white-striped, furry blob resembling a stubby-legged house cat. It starts to run through the short grass, lifting its black, fluffy tail like an agitated skunk about to spray.

"Honey badger," Junior announces and then hoots. "First

time I have seen one in this reserve."

"Great spot," Dugger says after he switches off the engine.

"Yes!" Junior's voice has raised a full octave.

He throws his free arm up in the air in a half-victory pose and pumps his raised fist.

"Bloody good eyes," Arden adds.

Dad's snapping photos as usual and grinning. I don't see what all the fuss about this animal is, but I keep my opinion to myself for Junior's sake. The animal scrambles into the cover of some low-lying shrubs, and Dad lowers the camera. In the distance, I hear a deep rumbling noise. It is an eerie sound, and I wish Dugger would restart the car.

"Hear that?" Junior says. "Lions. Across the river. Their vocalizations can be heard for miles. I'm afraid those guys are too far away, or we'd try to locate them."

Phee sighs, and I turn in time to see Arden plant a kiss on her head. I stare at the windowless, doorless vehicle and feel only relief that those big cats aren't close by. It would be bad enough to encounter a lion in daylight. At night, well, I don't even want to think about it. The image of a pride of lionesses stalking us makes me shudder. When Dugger starts the car, I exhale unaware until just then that I'd been holding my breath.

Dugger guns the vehicle through a rutted section of the dirt track. The jarring makes me squirm. I should never have had both coffee and a diet soda. The men had gone off to "water the plants" during sundowners, but Phee had declined the option of squatting in the bush. Even if I'd been allowed to get out of the vehicle, I would've opted to wait too.

Mercifully, the car slows, and my bladder settles. The sweeping arc of light illuminates the dark landscape.

The white beam captures the glowing eyes of an occasional deer-like creature, but the light is quickly pulled away. Junior gestures at Dugger by patting the air as if pushing the oxygen into the ground. This must be safari sign language, because Dugger stops the vehicle. Junior then directs the light into a tree. I see the sparkle of reflected dots of light skittering from branch to branch.

"They are hard to see," Junior says, "but those little glowing dots are caused by the eyes of two bush babies."

Flashes of gray fur appear as Junior bobs the light from place to place. He seems to understand where the creatures will jump next. Dad leans across me to snap photos, but I imagine the photos will show a giant blur. I glance over my shoulder wondering if lions or leopards might be hunting these furry little creatures. I'm relieved when Dugger starts the engine.

The road has leveled and we drive fast, until Dugger abruptly slows. Junior only directs the light to the right now. I remember that the plan was to return to the dead buffalo. My stomach lurches, and I turn my head away. I don't want to see a hyena feeding on a carcass. My mind conjures up intestines strewn about, the vile creature panting, its mouth dripping blood, and I shudder. Dad nudges me with his elbow.

"It's okay, Claire," he says. "You can look. Nothing's eating the buffalo."

I take a peek through squinted eyes. The spotlight illuminates the bulky, black belly of the immobile animal lying on its side. No rips or tears on the skin. There's not even a foul odor. The buffalo could be sleeping. I barely have time to process this scene before we race away.

Arden leans forward and explains that the car has to exit

the park by six p.m. If we don't make it, the guides will have to pay a fine. It is clear Dugger doesn't plan on arriving late. I hold tight as we buck and dip our way towards the reserve gate. I cross my legs and resolve not to drink a full soda during the next sundowner.

The wind makes me shiver. I pull my lightweight jacket from my backpack and put it on. I wish I'd brought a warmer coat tonight.

We make it to the gate before six. I adjust my posture trying to relieve the pressure. I silently scream as Dugger slowly makes his way back to camp. My bladder feels about to burst. I clutch my flashlight and slip my backpack on so I can be the first one out after the Land Rover pulls up to the main building. Dugger hasn't even cut the engine before I hop to the ground and bolt toward our tent.

After fighting with the outer zipper, I curse that I have to contend with a second zipper. But somehow I manage to make it to the toilet. I've relieved myself, washed my hands, and zipped the bathroom door before Dad arrives a few minutes later. When he enters the tent, I can tell he's angry that I hadn't re-zipped the tent flap after I came inside. He flips on a lamp then places his binoculars and camera on the bedside table with deliberate movements.

"Can't you follow the camp rules?" His measured tone makes me cringe. "Do you want scorpions crawling around in here?"

I blow air through my nose and place my hands on my hips.

"Yeah, Dad, that's exactly what I want," I snarl.

I click off my flashlight from where I tossed it on the bureau. A mosquito hums near my ear and I jump up and down as if I've stepped on a bed of hot coals while slapping at the air around my head.

"There's a mosquito in here. Get it away from me," I screech.

"Yet another reason to zip the tent flap closed."

Really? Great hindsight. I whack at the air with more fervor.

"Geez, calm down, Claire," Dad says in an exasperated voice.

When I finally stop moving, a speck of gray buzzes near my arm. My hands clap together. I examine my palms and discover there's only a squished, black body. No blood. I've killed this one before it bit me. But how many more followed me in?

I tilt my head and listen, but don't hear anything. At least the mosquito netting over our beds will protect me as I sleep. Even if I let a few bugs in.

"Just be more careful," he says. "Okay? Can we agree to always zip the tent?"

But if I had taken the time to secure the tent, I would have left a puddle where he's standing. I'm too embarrassed to explain.

"I'm not stupid," I say.

"Claire, don't you dare disrespect me."

What? Disrespect him? He's the one trying to force Jan-Puss on me. He's the one who brought me to this place. He's the one who never wanted me in the first place. And how hard is it to figure out that I might need to pee really, really bad? The unfairness of it all explodes inside me.

"Disrespect YOU?" I shout.

"Claire—"

"You're the one treating me like a moron."

"Claire—"

His face has turned scarlet and for a moment I think I might have gone too far. It scares me, but I'm too upset to reel in my anger.

"I also heard Dugger say it wasn't scorpion season," I say in the snottiest tone I can muster. "Did you?"

Dad takes a deep breath. He runs his hands up and down the front of his thighs. He closes his eyes, but when he opens them, he appears visibly calmer.

"We have about ten minutes until the *braai*," he says in a weary voice.

What the hell is a bry? Probably some lame touristy show.

"I'm not going to some kind of dumb demonstration of African dance."

"No, Claire. It's a barbeque."

He spells *braai* out for me then proceeds to describe this South African custom as if he's instructing a toddler. I stare at him while he explains that it's like a combination pit fire and barbeque.

"Wow," I say. "Thanks for the lecture."

I wait for him to react, but I only hear him suck in air. It's quiet, and I swear I can hear him counting to ten.

"Are you hungry?" he asks softly.

"Like you care," I mutter under my breath.

"What did you say?"

"Hungry as a bear."

Dad's eyebrows furrow, and I know he doesn't believe me, but he doesn't say anything. The temperature has dropped lower, even inside the tent. Goosebumps sprout on my arms as all the anger drains from my muscles.

Dad's chin rests against his chest. I know he feels bad. But he won't back down. He'll still insist on doing things his way. This is how we always deal with conflict. Never finding middle ground. Never appreciating the other's point of view. Maybe if we could talk to each other, he wouldn't brush off my feelings. He might begin to understand how utterly terrified I am of getting malaria. How uncomfortable and embarrassing it is to be a woman who needs to pee. Maybe I could tell him I know he never wanted me and how that knowledge makes me feel. Even before Jan-Puss, we didn't know how to relate to each other. It's even harder now. He doesn't look up, and I don't say anything. The air in the tent is still weighted with tension, and there's an awkward silence. Nothing has changed between us.

I pull off my lightweight jacket and replace it with my black fleece coat, and even though I really want to wear the khaki skinny jeans that show off my curves, I can't bear to spend more time in this cramped tent with Dad. I pull on black sweat pants over my shorts. As much as I don't want to hang out with the other tourists, I have to get out of here. I stride to the tent and unzip the flap, reminding me what started our argument in the first place.

"Don't worry. I know what to do," I say quietly.

I hear a low whistle. When I whirl around after zipping up the tent flap, Junior is standing at the bottom of our deck. By the bemused expression on his face, I know he's been there long enough to hear the argument. I want to slink back inside, but it's too late for that. So, I straighten my spine and smile.

"So what's for dinner?" I ask in a cheerful voice.

Junior doesn't reply until after I've descended the three stairs to the ground. He's still in his khaki clothes and he looks so adorable that I go weak in the knees.

"Don't worry, all our food is *lekker*," Junior says as he falls in step beside me.

"*Lekker*?" I say.

He smiles. Dimples form and his eyes squint together. I grin, relieved he isn't holding my outburst with my father against me.

"It means good. Or tasty," he says.

Our tent is the closest to the main camp area. Already I hear the crackle of burning wood and the quiet voices emanating from the fire pit area. I want to keep Junior all to myself, so I stop and look up, but the stars are cloaked by the steady moonlight. A bird interrupts the quiet with a haunting imitation of the whip-poor-will's call. I couldn't admit this to my father, but there is something exotic and thrilling about Africa.

"It's still early enough," Junior says edging closer, "but after the *braai,* you'll have to be escorted back to your tent."

The air between us seems charged with desire. Yeah, Africa definitely has some perks. He hasn't answered my question about dinner. I don't care what's being served, but we are alone for the moment, and the temptation to flirt is strong.

"Come on," I say, smiling and elbowing him. "What *lekker* food can I look forward to eating tonight?"

Junior grins. "Right, Clar."

My knees wobble at his pronunciation of my name and I almost stumble. I could listen to him all day long.

"Here's a hint," he continues. "We South Africans love to grill meat."

I fantasize about a juicy steak. But it occurs to me that he hadn't said beef. He'd said meat. A horrible thought forms. I think about the impala and the zebras we saw today.

"You aren't going to feed us game animals, are you?"

"No," Junior laughs. "Most tourists would probably starve

themselves if we did. A lot of people don't want to eat these beautiful creatures. Beef and chicken are the only meats we serve here."

He sidles even closer and leans in, like he's coming in for a kiss. Behind us, the distinctive sound of a zipper separating pierces the air, announcing that my father is emerging from our tent.

"We do serve some traditional food though." Junior moves to create distance between us and speaks in the professional voice he uses on safari.

He heads toward the fire pit. I walk alongside him, hoping Dad will have trouble closing up the tent.

"There's bibotie, which is kind of like American lasagna and curry with no pasta. We're having that tomorrow night."

Our hands brush against each other's and his breath hitches.

"Hey, Junior," Dad calls. "I was hoping I'd get a chance to ask you about the bird call I heard while we were looking at the bush babies."

Junior stops to wait for my father. I don't want to, but I plant my feet too. Really? He has to ask this now? Can't he let me have some time alone with Junior?

Dad hands me a nerdy headlamp when he catches up to us. He's already got one strapped to his head. I take it to avoid another argument, but I don't put mine on.

As Dad starts to imitate a bird, I pick up my pace and arrive at the outdoor dining area ahead of them. Chairs have been set in a circle around the fire. In front of each foldout seat is a small plastic table just large enough for a dinner place setting and a drink. The hum of conversation disappears, and a stillness descends.

I scan the faces, wondering what's going on. Four new

tourists have arrived: an elderly couple who I presume are Americans and two Japanese women in their thirties who look so much alike I suspect they are sisters. Phee and Arden look embarrassed and glance away. Had they been talking about Dad and me?

"It's so quiet," I say to break the silence.

The Japanese women glance up at me at the same time. Now I see they are dressed in the same outfit. Both wear white short-sleeved blouses and red capris—colors we've been advised not to bring to camp. They have the same round faces and identical haircuts; their black horizontal bangs extend to their eyebrows and straight shoulder-length locks are cut perfectly even. They must be twins.

I slide into one of the two empty chairs. Arden and Phee are seated across from me, separated by the fire pit. Phee has donned blue jeans and a practical, tan-colored sweatshirt with some sort of mountain formation on the front. Arden wears a matching outfit, which I find both adorable and corny. I'm beginning to think traveling partners were asked to dress alike, but Dad and I missed the memo.

"We were just talking about how sound carries out here in the wilderness," Phee says, and her words seem to shrink the distance separating us.

My eyes flicker shut as the obvious dawns on me. These people must have heard my father and me fighting. I feel embarrassed that Phee and Arden have been subjected to yet another father-daughter argument. I straighten my spine, determined not to let embarrassment ruin the whole evening. Junior finally arrives with Dad who takes the seat to my left, while Junior wanders off and disappears into the main camp building.

I turn my back on my father to face a gray-haired man

dressed in a Hawaiian shirt that must be blue, but in the yellow glow of the fire, his garment looks green.

"I'm Claire from California," I say.

"John from Alpine, Texas," he says.

He goes on to explain how he and his wife Sandra drove to Midland International Airport, then flew to Dallas, had a five-hour layover in London and landed in Joburg yesterday afternoon. Next to him, Sandra engages the two Japanese women in rehashing the highlights from their game drive in Kruger. Dad leans across his table, invading my personal space, when Sandra mentions elephants.

"I swear there had to be at least fifty of them elly-phants," Sandra says.

She yells this as if increasing the volume of her voice might overcome any language barrier. I cringe. No wonder the rest of the world thinks Americans are loud.

"And then we went across this concrete bridge," Sandra continues, "and boy those skeeters they was eatin' us alive. I thought mo-skeeters were bad in our big ole state, but y'all shoulda seen 'em tonight."

I hadn't seen any mosquitos during our drive, just the one inside the tent. Then again, I had coated myself with bug repellant. We hadn't been by water either. Even here at the campfire, I don't see or hear any of those malaria-toting insects.

"But the best part, oh Lordy, I think John took hisself a zillion photos—that was at Lake Panic. It was a croc that dun it. We got 'em in Texas, honey, 'cept we call 'em gators and I ain't never seen one do this. It leapt itself right up out of the water and snagged a goo-lie-ath heron that was flying by. That sure was sumpthin' to see. Y'all seen one of them big red birds yet?"

"You saw a Goliath heron?" Dad says, leaning across my little TV dinner tray. "That's one of the birds I'm dying to see. Is it really five feet tall?"

"I couldn't say fah sure," Sandra says. "But it sure 'nough was mighty big from where I stood."

Junior reappears and enters the inner circle of chairs and, starting with Phee and Arden, proceeds to take drink orders. This quiets Sandra, and we all listen to the sound of hyenas laughing in the distance. When Junior gets to us, Dad asks for a Castle beer that he pronounces (Caw-sill) like a regular South African. I request water.

"Still?" Junior asks.

I had a diet soda for sundowners. What does he mean still? Does he expect me to order alcohol? I hadn't looked into the drinking age in South Africa. But before I can ask for a beer, Dad interjects.

"Carbonated," Dad says.

Two things register: the nature of Junior's question and Dad's wrong answer. My head turns to stare at my father. How dare he order for me. In fact, fizzy water makes me pee. It's the last drink I'd want to have before bed. I'm about to correct him, but Junior places a hand on my arm and says something.

I try to recall what he has asked, but all I can focus on is the gentleness in his touch. He could probably tame a hyena with those hands.

"Is that what you want, Clar?' he says.

He smiles and I feel my heart yawn open like I've stretched my arms apart to invite his embrace. I start to nod, but then remember I want regular water. I shake my head side-to-side, unable to find my voice.

"So, still then?"

I nod, and Junior moves on to take another order.

Dugger appears from the main building. He asks how we want our steaks cooked. Dad wants his rare. I want mine well done. The sight of blood turns my stomach. Sometimes I think we have nothing in common.

Soon the smell of sizzling meat permeates the air. My stomach grumbles, and I'm happy when Junior appears with a plate of those delicious bacon-wrapped mini-corns that we had during sundowners. I take two when he offers the appetizer plate to me. But he lingers in front of me. My face flushes with warmth under the intensity of his gaze. A silence falls over the group and Junior quickly moves on.

I see Phee whispering to Sandra who shoots a glance in my direction. What was she saying about me? Was she warning Sandra about the difficult American girl who can't get along with her father? Or making a comment about how I seem smitten with Junior? I don't want her gossiping to bother me, but it does.

A log shifts in the fire pit and sparks shoot into the air. An animal barks, and I wonder if it could it be a wild dog. Of all the animals Dad talked about possibly seeing on this trip, I hope we'll encounter the wild dog. They're about the size of a small wolf so they don't seem scary. With their big rounded ears, splotchy bodies, and white-tipped tails, they remind me of a red merle Aussie mixed with a cardigan Welsh Corgi. But Dad cautioned wild dogs are rare—only about five hundred are left in Kruger National Park and I shouldn't hold my breath.

The animal barks again. Wild dogs run in packs, but this is a lone dog. Perhaps one of the guides owns a domestic dog.

"We saw a honey badger," Phee pipes up to fill a gap in

the conversation. "It was sooo cute."

"Cute, huh?" Dugger says, then grunts. "In Africa we have a saying, 'tough as a honey badger.' That little animal is both mean and fearless. It will take on cobras, lions and pretty much any creature, big or small. Once, one charged our Landy with its fangs bared and it punctured the back tire with its teeth. I had the rifle out in case it decided to try to crawl into the vehicle. This animal is as dangerous as a leopard on LSD."

"Oh really?" Arden says.

I frown. One more reason to stay in the vehicle during sundowners. I sneak a peek at Junior. He's clutching a meat fork and nodding in agreement.

"Dugger's right," Junior says. "That animal's claws and razor teeth can slice open the thick skin of a lion to lay open its intestines. There isn't anything cute about it."

Junior looks straight at me as if to reassure me he won't let one of these animals get near me.

"I fancy another," Arden says, raising his empty beer bottle, "if it's no trouble."

Junior passes by me probably to get another beer for Arden. My heart flutters at the lithe, cat-like way he moves. Dad sees me staring.

"I see you've found one animal you enjoy watching," he says.

I can't believe my father said that loud enough for everyone to hear. Junior hesitates and raises his eyebrows. My face flames hotter than the fire.

I'm so mortified that I'm about to bolt for our tent, but then Junior looks askance and winks at me. Oh, how those blue eyes sparkle with promise and desire.

After he's gone inside, a mosquito buzzes by my ear. My

heart roars in my chest. I paddle at the air, grateful that Junior isn't there to witness my panic.

"Claire," Dad says. "Settle down."

I slap and miss then nail it on my second try. I wipe my hands on my pants, pull my coat up to my ears, and hunch down in my chair. Maybe I can trust Junior to ward off attacking honey badgers. But no one, not even Junior, can protect me from contracting malaria.

CHAPTER SIX

Dugger leans against the buffet table, chugging a beer. Junior still hasn't reappeared with Arden's drink order. It sure is taking him a long time. The fire pit makes this trip seem more like a Girl Scout outing than a fenced-in campsite surrounded by African wildlife. The air smells marvelously of charred beef and I've grown too crazy hungry to worry about animals that may be lurking nearby. This will be our first decent dinner since we left the States.

A middle-aged man I haven't met appears on the deck of the main building where breakfast will be served tomorrow. I can tell he's the boss by the way Dugger suddenly walks over to talk to Phee and removes the seemingly permanent scowl from his face.

"That was some sunset tonight, wasn't it?" Dugger says to Phee.

Arden pushes up the sleeves of his tan-colored sweatshirt then places a hand over Phee's. He leans back in his chair with one ankle hooked over his knee. They seem so content together. He offers a rare smile to Dugger.

"Truly," Arden says

Arden appears to be a man of few words, but Phee compensates for Arden's limited vocabulary. The English seem so reserved on television, but she is quite talkative.

"And how!" Phee exclaims. "All those orange and yellow

tones. They remind me of the orange oxtails growing in my flower box back home."

"Oxtails?" Dugger says then chuckles. "We once had a tourist who had visited Botswana before coming here. He told us he walked into his hut and saw what he thought was an oxtail hanging from the thatched roof. He thought the natives had placed it there for good luck," Dugger says shaking his head. "It wasn't until the black mamba fell onto his bed that he realized it was a snake."

Dugger doesn't seem to notice that Phee's face has faded to a pasty white, or that I'm gripping the table in front of me.

"Mambas hang out in trees growing out of termite mounds in Sabi Sands," he continues. "And they're fast. They can travel up to twelve miles per hour. You don't want to mess with them. Their bites are often fatal."

Phee gasps.

"Snakes?" I say to Dad. "You brought me to a place where there are dangerous snakes?"

Dugger finally seems to realize that Phee is mortified. She looks ghost-like in the firelight. I imagine I appear just as pale.

"Oh, don't worry," he quickly adds. "We keep antivenom in camp and in each vehicle. We've never seen a mamba." Dugger pauses as if remember something. "Though we did see a spitting cobra in the road last week. If the venom hits your eyes, you could be blind for the rest of your life."

Phee picks up her wine glass and drains it. I glare at my father. Now I have to worry about catching malaria, going blind, and dying.

Dugger must have realized he'd said too much because he hurries on to chat with the Texans. Bossman is too far away to have caught exactly what was said, yet he must sense something is amiss because he descends the stairs and heads toward the group. Except for the moon, the sky above us is dark now. As he steps inside the circle of chairs, the firelight highlights Bossman's standard khaki-colored clothes with a hint of orange. He scans his guests and zeroes in on Dad and me.

Dad leans close and whispers, "No drama, okay?"

I shrug noncommittally. Bossman playfully punches Dad's shoulder. This man is not particularly tall, but the dimples that form when he smiles remind me of Junior and that makes me like him immediately.

"Denvin," the man introduces himself while holding out his hand to Dad. "And you must be Jackson. So, we meet at last."

Dad shakes Denvin's hand and lifts his beer in the man's direction. I'm trying to process Denvin's statement. I thought this safari trip was a spur of the moment decision. What does he mean by "at last?"

"Can I buy you a beer?" Dad asks.

Denvin shakes his head no then tilts his head to the side like a curious puppy.

"So what happened? You were supposed to come two years ago with the wife."

Two years? I stare at my father. I'd never heard about this plan. Why hadn't my parent's gone? Were they having problems even then? Or maybe Mom had refused to go. Africa isn't exactly a destination she would have picked. Before Dad has a chance to answer, Denvin turns to me.

"Welcome, Claire."

I'm surprised he knows my name. His accent is not nearly as strong as Junior's. He seems pleased to see me. I suspect Dugger hasn't briefed his boss on the problem American tourist. Denvin moves on to greet the Texans, and Dad takes a long drag from his beer.

"You were going to drag Mom here?" I say. I'm stunned. "She would have hated this place. Why didn't you offer to take her to the Greek Isles or Paris?"

Dad won't look at me. He shifts in his seat. He's uncomfortable even beyond his normal awkwardness. Beads of sweat sprout on his forehead.

The truth hits like a rhino ramming into me. He wasn't planning to bring Mom. He'd planned to bring Jan-Puss.

I stand up so fast that the chair falls backward. Anger buzzes in my head like a swarm of agitated hornets. The others fall silent. I sense everyone staring at me, but I don't care. Junior emerges from the building with a beer in hand and freezes.

"Janice," I shout. "You were going to bring Janice here two years ago, weren't you? Exactly how long have you been cheating on Mom?"

Somewhere in the distance I hear the grating, chuckling sound that I recognize as a hyena. Dad gazes at me with a pleading expression. Guilt oozes from his brown eyes.

"How long?" I demand.

"Sit down, Claire," he hisses. "Now is not the time."

I'm beyond caring if Junior is appalled at my behavior or if I'm embarrassing myself. The firelight feels sinister as if it's there to burn someone at the stake.

"How long?" I repeat.

"Sit down," Dad says.

I don't move. We stare at each other until Dad looks away.

"Since you were ten," Dad whispers.

Seven years? I stagger backward, reaching down to steady

myself on the tray table with trembling fingers. I can't seem to catch my breath. My emotions teeter on a precipice, and if I give in I'll start to bawl. I grip my anger and pull it into a coiled knot.

"Mom's right," I growl. "You are a bastard."

I back away, clenching my fists to my chest, before whirling around to sprint toward our tent.

"Clar, wait," Junior calls.

I can't wait. Not even for Junior. I run. As I sprint in the direction of our tent and leave the light of the fire, darkness closes around me. I can't see the ground under my feet because I've forgotten to bring my stupid headlamp. I'm disoriented under the cloud of emotions and blackness that fills the path before me. But I can't stop.

Something grazes my elbow. I run harder. Oh god. A hyena. I'm going to die in this awful place. Then the thing closes onto my arm and I scream.

"Clar," Junior gasps. "Stop."

And the next thing I know I'm on the ground.

"It's dangerous to run here. You almost plowed into an electric fence," he gasps.

Junior's grip is strong and reassuring. My thoughts tumble over themselves. Everything is happening too fast.

"Ag, shame," Junior says, sitting up. "Your father. I—it isn't right."

Junior pulls me into a sitting position beside him and puts his arms around me. I lean into him, and as I catch my breath, my panic eases.

"Okay, okay," he whispers.

His voice is so soft and warm and filled with caring. So, in that moment when the world is tilting and I have lost myself, I reach out and wrap my arms around his waist. I breathe in his scent. A mix of campfire smoke and sweat.

I tip my head up and lean close until my lips find his. He tastes of an exotic Indian curry. My blood seems to fizz like champagne bubbles, and my skin shivers all over. I want to surrender myself into this kiss so I can forget the pain and shock of the depth of my father's betrayal. I part my lips and probe with my tongue. For a split-second I feel him respond, feel him draw me close. I don't want this kiss to end, but he pushes me away.

"Not like this," he says in a husky voice. "I can't. Not like this. Not when you're so upset."

I scramble to my feet, ashamed and angry at his rejection. He bolts to his feet too, blocking my path, as if anticipating that I might run off. His fingers encircle my wrist. I struggle to get free, but his grip is strong. He waits until I stop resisting then draws me close. It feels so good to be held.

"I'm sorry," I say at last. "I shouldn't have done that."

"I didn't say I didn't like it," he says, and bumps his shoulder against mine, which makes me smile in spite of everything.

He's made it all right. I'll be able to face him in the morning.

"Are you hungry?" Junior asks. "You can eat in the kitchen away from your father."

"No," I say. "Thanks, but I've lost my appetite."

"I'll take you back to your tent then," he says in a gentle voice—one I imagine he would use if he were cornered by lion. "You can't run around out here. Not after dark," he says as he cups my elbow and guides me towards the tent I have to share with my cheating father for six more nights.

"Do you think I could get my own tent?" I ask.

"I'm sorry, Clar. Uncle Denvin told all the staff yesterday that we're fully booked for the rest of the month."

Uncle? That's his uncle. But as I think about it and remember the dimples, I'm surprised I didn't make the connection immediately.

When we reach the deck, Junior ushers me up the stairs. His touch makes me feel safe. I want to thank him for coming after me, but then Dad's chuckle filters through the night air from the direction of the campfire. It feels like a slap in the face. He's laughing as if nothing happened. This is his big, bucket-list trip, and he's not going to let me ruin it. I'm afraid if I speak now, I will dissolve into a crying mess.

"I'm going to let go now," Junior say, "so I can unzip the tent. Okay? Don't run. Okay?"

I nod. He releases me and stoops down to unzip the tent flap. Dad had left the lamp on, and the inside of the tent is awash in light.

A mosquito buzzes by my ear as Junior lifts the canvas. I slap at the air, then duck inside the tent. The whir of the zipper secures me inside. I'm glad he was quick. I don't want the bugs that are attracted to the light to follow me inside.

I put my face close to the fabric where he stands on the other side. The canvas is rough against my skin. I don't want him to go.

"Rest up," he says. "Your wakeup call will be before sunrise. If your Dad tries to come check on you before dinner is over, I'll tell him not to, that you have gone to bed."

"Can you... err... apologize to the group? I hope I haven't ruined their evening with my outburst."

"Trust me," he says. "Some people party late into the night. I've seen much worse drunken behavior. But I'll relay your message."

Junior's kindness makes me want to pull him inside the tent, if only to feel his warm arms around me once more.

It seems unlikely that I'll be alone with him again during this trip. The camp schedule is rigid. Get up before dawn's light, have a small snack, go on a three-hour excursion, eat breakfast, take a nap, have a late lunch, depart on a second game drive around three, sundowners at sunset, drive back in the dark, end with dinner. All there is to do is eat, sleep, and try not to be eaten by wild animals or bitten by mosquitos. Then I remember the lumbering rhino and the impossibly shaped giraffes and think safari life has its perks.

"Good night," he whispers.

"Good night."

On the other side of the tent flap, I hear Junior move toward where I stand. He's handsome and kind and so very sweet. It's stupid to be falling for someone who lives all the way across the world.

"If you change your mind about food, I'll be sitting at the foot of these stairs."

I suspect he's issuing a warning: Don't try to run off again. As Junior's boots clump down the stairs, the enormity of Dad's secret life sinks in. My whole life has been one big lie. I collapse onto the bed, pulling the mosquito netting into a protective shroud.

I rub my arm. No, no, no. A raised welt has formed. A mosquito has bitten me. I suck on my skin trying to extract the venom like I've seen done for snakebites in old Westerns. Dumb. It's already too late.

I rush to my suitcase and take out the vial of Malarone. I shake out a pill. I dry swallow the medicine before I can change my mind then crawl into bed, scratching at my itchy flesh. What if I get malaria? What if I've poisoned myself by taking too many pills? I hug myself, rocking from side to side. When I become aware of the tears wetting my cheeks, I bury my face into my pillow so Junior won't hear me cry from his perch on the steps.

CHAPTER SEVEN

When I awake, it's still dark. A dog barks in the distance. I'm confused at first, thinking I'm at home and Buster is making the racket. Then I remember I'm on safari. Then I remember all that happened last night. I feel my arm and can't find the raised flesh caused by the mosquito bite.

In the twin bed next to me, Dad rolls onto his back, snorts, then relaxes once more into a steady snore. I flip onto my side so my back is to him. I wonder if he'll agree to send me home on the next flight? Surely, he can't expect me to smile and forgive him in the morning.

Darkness shrouds the tent, but the white mosquito netting that drapes over my bed glows from the moonlight seeping through the zippered door. I notice the fabric doesn't quite seal at the headboard. What if one of those bloodsuckers slipped in? I run my fingers along my face and shoulders, searching for more bumps. I find two new welts. My breath hitches. This can't be happening. It only takes one infected mosquito to pass on malaria. I wish I could call Sylvia. She'd said she wished she'd taken more Malarone than was prescribed. But how many can I safely take? Doesn't matter anyway, my cell phone is useless.

I slip out of bed. I don't care if it isn't time for more anti-malaria medicine. I'm taking another Malarone pill.

I tiptoe to my suitcase. Using a flashlight, I find my Malarone pills and select a safari outfit.

I shiver. I hadn't imagined Africa could be this cold, especially during their spring season. The clock on the nightstand indicates that it is 4:40 a.m. Our morning wake-up call is to be at 5:15. I'll go on the game drive and apologize to Junior, but I won't sit near my father. And when we get back, I'll see if I can change my return flight to later this afternoon.

I creep to the bathroom and see Dad has zippered the opaque bathroom flap partition as well as the outer zipper. I tug on the zipper at a snail's pace to avoid waking him then close the barrier behind me.

I brush my teeth. Goose bumps rise on my arms. I fumble until I find the light switch, then click off my flashlight. A quick swig from my bottled water and the small, pink pill slips down my throat. Now for my shower. I remember Dugger said that it takes a while for the hot water to arrive, so I turn the knob.

The shower isn't like the one at my house. There are two separate knobs. I twist the hot water on, wait a few minutes for steam to rise, twist on the cold a bit, and step into the cascading water. It feels good to warm up. But as I lather my hair with shampoo, the water turns icy. I jump to the side and turn up the hot water, but nothing changes. I turn both knobs off completely and start over. This works, but after my hair is rinsed, the cold water returns. Dad promised me hot showers. I should have known not to trust anything he says.

I forgo conditioner and towel myself dry. Shivers course through my body, so I quickly dress. All I want to do is to crawl back under the covers and stay there until we leave this awful place.

When I unzip the separating flap, Dad is still snoring.

I've just hidden my pill vial in my suitcase, when I hear footsteps outside followed by the creak of stairs.

"Rise and shine," Dugger says.

"I'm awake," I say.

Dad stirs then stretches. I turn on the light, and he winces at the brightness. He rubs his eyes.

"Great, you're up," he says.

My nerves bubble up and transform into anger. I wait for him to apologize, but he only rubs his eyes and stretches.

"That's it?" I say. "That's all you have to say?"

"Claire," he says, ignoring my tone. "I'm really sorry about how you found out about Janice. It's really complicated, and I don't want this to be a rushed conversation. Let's talk after the morning drive, okay kiddo?"

"I don't want to hear your lame excuses. I want to go home," I say. "By the way, the shower sucks. The hot water comes and goes."

He sighs.

"You'll warm right up after you put a cap on your head," he says then shudders. "You'll need one this morning."

"I didn't bring one," I say.

"Claire," he groans. "We went over the packing list. What else didn't you bring?" He sits up. "Let's go through your things. There's a store in Kruger. We can buy you a hat and whatever else you forgot."

I step in front of my suitcase and put my hand on top of it, like a guilty child hiding a stolen cookie behind her back. I can't let him see inside. What if notices how empty my Malarone vial has become? My heart pulses in my ears.

Dad pulls back the covers and heads toward me. He's only wearing boxer shorts. The image of his naked chest reminds me of that horrible day when everything changed.

"Dad, can you pah-leez put some clothes on?" I snap.

"Good grief," he says. "Since when…"

I hear it in his voice. He's remembering what I can't seem to forget.

"I have everything else on the list," I say. "I didn't bring a wool hat because I thought Africa would be a sweltering desert. Okay?"

"All right, honey," he says. "Let me get ready and we'll grab a bite together, okay?"

I jerk the zipper closed on my suitcase in one angry movement. I close my eyes. He really thinks everything can go back to normal? Just like that I'm supposed to get over that he cheated on Mom for years?

"I don't want to eat breakfast with you," I say.

I don't even yell. I'm too tired, too disappointed in him.

He goes into the bathroom without a word.

I grab my iPhone and my backpack. Maybe we'll drive somewhere where I can get service. The sun is cresting as I fling open the tent flap and step into the crisp morning air. It's light enough that I don't need an escort.

The smell of coffee hits me as I approach the communal area. Like our tent, the main building's foundation is raised off the ground. I take the stairs up. It is an open-air structure with a veranda with a few four-seater tables. A wainscot-height wall separates the indoor space. A wrap-around leather couch with a coffee table occupies the front of the structure, while inside tables and a breakfast nook inhabit the far back.

I'm the first to arrive. I head straight to the square-like cookies in the glass container with a screw top. I'm not sure if these will taste sweet or savory, but I take a handful. A dark-skinned woman bustles in and sets down a bowl of fruit.

A yellow and green scarf covers her hair and the tips of her ears. She wears a plain, olive green shirt, and a white-and-avocado-colored, striped skirt. Her flip-flops match her shirt, too. She's put some thought into her appearance, which makes me smile.

"Nice outfit," I say as I take two bananas from her bowl.

I've gobbled down the cookies and am in the midst of inhaling the second banana when Junior appears. I quickly finger-comb my wet locks.

He wears a black baseball cap with the company logo—a running cheetah. His plaid, long-sleeved, flannel shirt acts as a jacket to his khaki shirt. His smile widens when he sees me. But I remember my brazen kiss and feel my cheeks warm despite the cool air.

"Hey," he says. "Feeling better today?"

I nod, though it's not really true.

"You're going to have a great drive. My uncle has a surprise in store for you and your dad."

"What's that?" I say.

"You'll have to wait and see," he grins.

Two large coffee pots arrive. Junior pours a mug then sits at one of the tables. I visit the breakfast nook for my own caffeine fix. Junior bites into an apple and stirs cream into his coffee. He pats the chair to his left.

"Might as well get cozy," he says. "It's only you and me and your dad this morning. We're going to Kruger to hunt up some hippos. The other guests will head into Sabi Sands to see what, if anything, is left of the dead buffalo."

I consider asking if I can go in the other Land Rover to get away from Dad, but then I'd be separated from Junior. And the idea of looking at a dead animal being eaten by vultures makes my skin crawl. If we have the whole vehicle to ourselves, I can sit in a whole different row in the Land Rover.

The six other guests arrive together, chatting and laughing among themselves. All of them wear khaki and big floppy hats. They look and act like a single team, as if they all went shopping together and I wasn't invited.

Arden grabs a cup of coffee. He starts to head toward me, but Phee clasps her husband's elbow to guide him to a different table. When Dad appears, I turn my back on him. I hear him approach from behind and my shoulders stiffen. All I want is for him to leave me alone.

"I figured you forgot to take your antimalarial," Dad walks around the table to face me and places a pill in front of me. "I brought you one of mine." He glances at my banana peels. "Good, you ate. You might get nauseous if you take it on an empty stomach."

I don't tell him I've already taken my Malarone. The pill sits on the table like an unopened invitation.

Dugger enters the room and announces he heard over the radio that the buffalo carcass is nearly gone and the last few hyenas are drifting away, so the guests going with him should grab a quick snack.

"I'm ready," Dad picks up his backpack and starts to follow.

Phee's shoulders slump, and Arden glances away. The other six guests scramble to their feet. Seating in the Land Rover isn't reserved, and while they may all be vying to get a front-row view, it's just as likely that they are only eager to get away from the toxic father-daughter duo.

"Uh," Dugger says. "Guess Junior hasn't told you yet. You're going into Kruger today. With Junior. A private tour for the two of you."

Phee stands and rushes after the others, leaving Arden to scurry out of the room after her. Dad's smile falters. He's dressed like a total nerd with binoculars and a giant camera dangling from his neck. A white splotch of sunscreen dots one ear where he didn't rub it in. His water bottle is clipped to his belt loop, as if we're going on a hike, not sitting in a car.

Dad settles down on the other side of Junior with a banana and a cup of coffee. Dad appears stricken. His disappointment is palpable. Too bad. He doesn't deserve to enjoy this trip. He's ripped apart my life. And for what? Stupid Jan-Puss.

"What's going on?" Dad asks.

"Err... Um..." Junior chews on his lower lip. "Ah, here he is."

Denvin emerges from the kitchen and approaches my father. Junior jumps to his feet.

"I'm going to get some blankets to bring along," Junior says. "You can come out to the Land Rover whenever you're ready."

The camp owner takes a seat on the opposite side of the table from Dad and me. He clears his throat.

"Look, I don't know of a nice way to put this, but the other guests have complained that the drama between you two is ruining their safari experience."

I suspect it is probably Phee who has made the biggest fuss, but whatever.

Denvin shrugs. He has the same thick hair as Junior, but rinsed gray, not blond. He's handsome in a rugged kind of way. And his tone is like melted chocolate, smooth and creamy. But Dad isn't happy.

"I see," Dad says in a tight voice. "Does that mean that

every time there's a sighting or the animals are doing something interesting, we'll be excluded?"

"Not at all," Denvin says. "In fact, we have a better experience lined up especially for you. After your Kruger drive this morning, you're in for a treat. We operate a bush camp inside Sabi Sands. Very exclusive and normally twice as expensive. There weren't any existing reservations through the rest of your stay, so I am giving you your own private guide and cook. We're going to treat you to the experience of a lifetime. It's why I wanted to send you into Kruger today, because it will be your only shot at seeing hippos. After the drive, you can collect your luggage and we'll move you to the bush camp. You'll probably see some animals during the transfer, so you'll even get a bonus game drive out of the deal. Now, how does that sound?"

Dad grins. But I'm panicking. Junior has been the best thing about this trip and now I'm going to be separated from him.

"Wow," Dad says, "Thanks. That's amazing."

Dad loves a good deal. He loves one-on-one attention. This sounds like the trip he'd first envisioned, but as he'd explained on the plane, the cost of the divorce had been too great, so he'd had to settle on a budget trip.

I'm twisting my napkin under the table, barely able to contain my fury. Nobody has asked how I feel about this change of plans. The only place I want to go is home.

"Or maybe we should just go home," I snap.

"Claire," Dad barks.

"The bush camp is almost identical to this one, only smaller." Denvin smiles like a car salesman about to seal a deal. "And you don't have to get up so early since you will be in the heart of the wildlife reserve. I think you are going to prefer the smaller venue. In fact, if you truly hate it, you can transfer back to the main camp tomorrow. But I'm betting you will want to stay."

"Are there showers?" I ask. "Hot water? Flush toilets? What about the tents? Are they raised off the ground or do I have to worry about snakes?"

"Claire—" Dad says with a sigh but stops when Denvin raises his hand.

"Yes, there are showers and hot water and normal toilets. Junior is going to be your full-time guide, so there's nothing to worry about."

Our own private camp with Junior? Denvin knocks on the table twice like a judge making a final statement with a gavel. Then he rises.

"You better get off to Kruger," he says. "Hippos await!"

Dad jumps to his feet, but I hesitate.

"Come on, Claire," Dad says. "Take your pill and let's go."

Anger swells in my chest. He just presumed I hadn't taken my medicine. I'm about to tell him I've already taken one when a bite on my arm starts to itch. Every time I get bitten, the odds go up that I'll catch malaria, so I pick up the dark pink pill and pop it into my mouth.

*　　　*　　　*

The Land Rover for our Kruger game drive is bigger than the vehicle we rode in yesterday. It has a canvas top and iron doors. There's room for twelve. Lots of space to avoid my father. I clamber into the second row of seats, expecting Dad to take a front row seat, but he climbs in beside me. I scoot over to get as far from him as possible. Junior explains that lots of safety rules at Kruger don't apply to private reserves. I think roofs and half doors are a great idea, but I don't say anything. Windows would be even better.

I endure what Junior calls "the safari massage." The bumpy road causes the vehicle to buck like a rodeo bronco all the way to the main thoroughfare. After we reach this flat road, he accelerates. The open sides allow cold air to whip my wet bangs into my eyes. I wish I'd packed that wool cap.

It takes thirty minutes to get to the Kruger Park entrance. I scrunch under the blankets to avoid any possibility of a conversation with Dad. I don't want to make another scene in front of Junior. My emotions are stretched as taut as an overinflated balloon.

The open-air drive has turned my fingers blue with the cold, despite huddling under the blanket. We soon cross a concrete bridge that spans a river. Giant rocks litter the meandering curves of the waterway. Grassy clumps of vegetation wave in the light breeze. Green trees border the wide, sandy floodplain. This beautiful landscape isn't at all how I pictured Africa.

"Look," Junior says as he stops the vehicle.

Below, two elephants emerge from a clump of trees. Both have large, white tusks and swing their trunks as they walk. They stop when they reach the river's edge and seem content to stand with their front feet in shallow water. It's magic to watch these huge creatures roaming free.

After Dad takes about fifty pictures, we drive on toward the front gate. Junior cuts the motor and hops out to go inside a building to deal with the entry fees and paperwork. A statue of Paul Kruger's head draws my attention. A slab of concrete gives the impression that this man had massive shoulders. Beneath the faux upper body are multiple stone pillars.

Except for the intricate carving of the face and head, the structure has an unfinished feel. Kruger's wavy hair frames his face and the undulations of these locks connect to a full beard. I swear he looks like a male lion.

Dad isn't facing the tribute to the founder of the park. His field glasses are glued to the shrubs at the edge of the clearing. What a birdbrain.

"Wow," he gasps. "It's a sunbird. I think it's a white-bellied. Such a busy little bird. They have curved bills and occupy the same niche as the North American hummingbird."

He whips the binoculars off his head and offers them to me. "Want to see?"

I look at his hand and think how these same fingertips have touched Jan-Puss. For. Seven. Years. Does he think I can forget that?

"No," I snap and turn my head away.

Fortunately, Junior arrives from the office with papers in hand. A plastic divider between the driver and the tourist seats has helped shield us somewhat from the wind, but now Junior rolls the opaque sheet up like a window blind. Then he climbs into the driver's seat and we continue on. I still can't get used to the driver on the right.

"Kruger is 19.485 kilometers squared." Junior is using his official voice, which is deep and resonates with professionalism. He sounds both capable and charming at the same time. "Sounds like a lot, right? It's still impressive in American terms. 7,523 miles squared. I'm told that it is bigger than your state of New Jersey."

Dad whistles through his teeth. I don't really care what facts Junior spews as long as he continues to keep looking in my direction.

"The park opened its gates in 1927, shortly after gold was discovered in Johannesburg."

Gold? I knew about blood diamonds from Africa, but the continent has gold, too?

"Kruger currently is home to an estimated twelve thousand elephants," Junior continues, "and one thousand leopards and twenty-seven thousand buffalos. You can see all of the big five here."

"But we probably won't see hyenas feeding on buffalo," Dad grumbles under his breath.

I twist my body so I face the brush and trees whizzing past. I scratch at my mosquito bites. The radio crackles, and Junior speaks into it. After some back and forth discussion in Afrikaans, Junior calls back that three lionesses have been spotted. He wants us to think about whether we want to Ferrari safari to the lions, which is deeper in the park than he's ever driven, or whether we want to visit Lake Panic to see crocodile and water birds.

I don't want to see an ugly reptile or any stupid birds. Lions might be cool to see as long as we don't get too close. Besides, a lake means more water and that means more mosquitoes.

"Lake Panic," Dad says at exactly the same time I say "Lion."

Junior's shoulders stiffen. I imagine he's regretting asking our opinion. He'll have to select my father's choice anyway, because Dad is the paying customer.

"Um, well, either way," Junior says, "we're going to have to cross a bridge over the Sabie River, so we'll stop to search for hippo first since this will be your only chance to see them. You can decide after that."

Then we're going to Lake Panic, I think bitterly. I slump

in my seat. The blanket isn't helping to warm me much. I wish I'd brought mittens. Dad glances at me, then whips off his hat and offers it, but I shake my head. I'd rather freeze than accept any show of kindness from him.

By the time we reach the hippo bridge, a light drizzle dampens the air. I can't feel my nose, and my fingers are tingly. When I'd packed for Africa, I'd imagined sweat dripping from my armpits and off my forehead, not rain.

"My photos aren't going to come out in this dim light," Dad says with a sigh.

I massage my numb fingers and don't respond. We are crawling across the narrow bridge when the vehicle lurches to a stop.

"There," Junior says. "A mama and a baby hippo. Do you see them?"

The river surface is calm. I see two black blobs. Each has knobby ears and protruding eyes with bumps of nostrils clearing the surface. The baby's head is about a third of the size of mama's.

"Hippos can weigh up to two tons and run up to thirty kilometers... sorry, I forget you are American. I mean nineteen miles per hour, which means it can outrun a human. It is considered one of the most dangerous animals in Africa, because of its nasty temper. It is the third largest mammal in Africa behind the elephant and the white rhino."

I think about the gray, prehistoric-looking animal we saw yesterday. It's weird how there's something about the rhino that enchants me. It is not cuddly or cute like a teddy bear. And then it hits me. Rupert! A memory surfaces of Dad reading to me. I might have been five or six. He'd found an old childhood book of his in the garage. It was called *Rupert the Rhino*. I can't remember the story now, but the front cover showed a rhino wearing eyeglasses and roses tied to his tail. I swallow hard as emotions fall over each other. How I want to be that little girl again. A child who could cuddle on her father's lap and feel his love. I know I'll never blindly trust him like that ever again. I hate that I can't. Tears threaten to spill, so I turn my head, pretending to be interested in the hippo.

"I read that they come out of the water at night," Dad says.

"A-ya," Junior says. "Hippos are only semi-aquatic. They spend most of their time submerged because they sunburn easily and need to stay cool. But they emerge from the water at dusk to graze. This baby will have been born in the water. In fact, some scientist think hippos are closely related to whales."

Dad is reaching across my lap to take photos. I smell his aftershave. I used to find comfort in that scent, but now it nauseates me. His hand touches my shoulder, though he keeps his eye trained through the camera lens, he has stopped taking pictures.

"Did you know that your mom wanted to birth you in the water? She would have too, if you hadn't been breech. You were such a beautiful baby with those bright blue eyes."

As he leans back, he lowers the camera. His expression is so filled with pain that I suck in my breath.

"Claire," he whispers. "Let's figure this out, okay? I can't change what I've done. But I swear I never meant to hurt you or your mom."

I glance in Junior's direction, but he's busy scanning the area for wildlife with his binoculars. I glare at my father. All the pain and anger rise to the surface.

"You ruined everything," I say. "We were a happy fam—"

"Claire, that is not true. Your mother and I, well, it just wasn't working. We fell out of love a long time ago."

He's right. We haven't been a happy family. I think about what I overheard during their fight. Did he ever love her? Did he marry her out of a sense of honor because she got pregnant?

"Tell me the truth," I say quietly. "I overheard what you said when you were fighting about only marrying Mom because she was pregnant. Did you ever want me?"

"Oh, Claire. Oh, baby."

He takes my chin and turns my face. Our noses are inches apart. Our eyes connect with an intensity I've never felt from him.

"I. Have. Always. Loved. You." Dad's voice cracks.

His words don't matter. The timber and pitch communicated raw emotion. The world goes blurry. My throat is cinched tight. I don't want to dissolve into a blubbering idiot in front of Junior, so I twist away from my father and turn to watch the hippos again.

Dad pats my leg. He used to do that after he'd read me a bedtime story. I'm standing on the edge of a meltdown. I reach deep for my anger, but all I find is sadness. He's right, he can't change the past. The bad parts or the good parts. But I can't see how to move forward.

"Junior," Dad calls. "Let's go see those lions."

I'm so surprised that I actually gasp. I wipe my eyes, take a deep breath, and glance at my father. He winks at me. I offer a crooked smile. My chest aches with nostalgia.

"I was a cute baby, huh?" My voice is coated with emotion.

"The most beautiful baby in the world."

CHAPTER EIGHT

W e traverse the remainder of the hippo bridge on our way to see the lions. For the first time I think forgiving my father may be possible, that maybe this trip wasn't such a bad idea. But then a mosquito lands on my sleeve. I swat it dead before it bites. Fewer of the disease-infested creatures lurk about than I would have expected given how close we are to water. Perhaps this frigid weather is too cold for them to be active.

I'm glad we're going inland away from Lake Panic. I hope the lions are sleeping and lounging around. The cowardly lion in the *Wizard of Oz* had always been my favorite character.

The bridge is about a quarter of a mile long. It would be an exaggeration to call the waterway below us a river—more like a marsh with scattered vegetation and sandbars. The cerulean blue water reminds me of Junior's eyes. He's been the best thing about this trip.

I stare at the back of Junior's head. It would be a romantic place to hang out with him at sunset. I haven't had a serious boyfriend, and given what I've seen of my parent's relationship, I don't know if I'll ever want one. But if I'm stuck here over the next few days it would be nice to have a short fling with him.

I remember something Mom said to me when she told me Dad had filed for divorce. She said her therapist had a framed quote on her desk that Mom was supposed to repeat every morning before she got out of bed. "Reinvention lies on the cusp of unwelcome change."

Can Dad and I reinvent our relationship? Dad's decision to forgo watching birds at Panic Lake to defer to my desire to see the lions could start the healing process. We are almost off the bridge when a giant, feathered creature emerges from behind a clump of reeds on the shallow riverbank. A similar bird follows it out of the greenery.

"Stop," Dad yells and adds, "Wow. Storks. Two of them."

The vehicle comes to a halt.

"Fantastic. An adult and a juvenile," Junior announces, while staring through his binoculars. "One of the Big Six birds."

It figures birders would outdo the big five mammals and have one more special species. Bird enthusiasts like Dad seem to take everything to the extreme.

"Two down," Dad says as his camera shutter whirls. "We saw the martial eagle, yesterday, remember, Claire?"

"Yeah," I say, without enthusiasm.

I don't add that I only remember it because I admired the white legs speckled with brown spots. This pattern on its plumage will make a great pattern for a faux mink stole.

I sit up then. Surely, another one of the Big Six birds should inspire my collection. But the whine of a mosquito buzzes in my ear. I slap at it and miss. It hovers near my face and I flick it away. I don't care about fashion now. All I want to do is flee from the water.

"Can we go?" I say.

"Just let me get a few pictures," Dad says.

When no more mosquitos appear, I glance at the birds. The younger stork struts through the water close to the bridge, while the adult forages further away, both occasionally using their prominent bills to pierce the water for food. The beak is tricolored. A black stripe bisects the red tip and the yellow bill close to the eyes. I don't care about birds but I'm impressed.

"The juvenile is a male," Junior announces. "See its black eyes? Females have yellow eyes."

A mosquito the size of a housefly lands on my hand. I whisk it away, paddling the air around my head. I reach into my backpack and take out repellent and spray my clothes and exposed skin. The creatures retreat now that I emit a toxic aura. But I don't think they'll stay away long.

"Dad," I say. "Come on. Let's go. The mosquitos are biting me."

"Of course, of course. But would you look at that?" Dad exclaims. He has flipped though his bird book and points at the picture of the saddle-billed stork. "The illustration doesn't even show the juvenile plumage. That's how rare this bird is. I can't believe this. There are only about fifty of these birds in Kruger."

Fifty? Now I sort of understand why Dad and Junior both seem so excited.

"Ay-ya," Junior says, "you are more likely to see cheetah or wild dog than one of these colorful storks. It's your lucky day."

These birds will definitely have to inspire my safari clothing line. It would certainly make a good story during a *Project Runway* critique. Maybe I could even impress judge Nina Garcia. I've read that she loves nature travel.

I study the black-and-white-feathered creatures with renewed interest. They both have stilts for legs with bulbous orange knees and red feet. The contrast of colors strikes me most. On the adult bird, a white belly underlies a uniformly gray back except for a patch of white at the base of the neck. On the juvenile, the gray is splotchy and dull. The adult plumage is bold and commands attention and the colors of the yellow and red bill add contrast.

I pull out my sketchpad onto the seat once again turning so my body blocks Dad's view, but in such a way that he'd think I was watching the birds. I draw a man's gray business jacket and speckled gray pants. I make a note in the margin that wool would be perfect to provide a representative texture. A white shirt with a red-and-yellow handkerchief in the jacket pocket would capture those striking bill colors.

Sketches of the final details in my fashion journal are complete when Junior starts the engine. I ease the pad back into my backpack, excited by the design I have developed and grateful that I decided to come on this game drive.

*   *   *

It isn't long until we turn off the smooth asphalt and traverse bumpy, dirt roads. Junior drives past the game we encounter without stopping, but when we see a herd of about twenty zebras huddled together and staring in the same direction, he pulls over.

"Do you think Junior spotted the lions?" I whisper to Dad.

He shrugs. He has his binoculars trained on the herd. One of the striped animals opens its mouth and calls. It sounds like a cross between a barking dog and braying donkey. The others startle, turn, and run in the opposite direction. They emit a strange whistle-like noise.

Junior scans the area with his field glasses. Dad's back is ramrod straight as he performs the same sweeping survey. In moments, the zebras have disappeared into the brush.

"Huh," Junior says. "I can't find what spooked them. The grass is pretty tall. I was hoping for a lion or a leopard. Could have been anything though. A snake or a hyena. Unfortunately, we can't leave the road to investigate. We best get on our way."

"Wait," Dad says, pointing at a cloud of dark specks flying overhead.

Junior lifts his binoculars. After a pause, he says, "Red-billed quelea. Dugger once told me he saw a flock which darkened the sky for two hours. They are a big problem for farmers."

I glance at the moving blob headed away toward where the zebras had stood. All of a sudden, as if a gust of wind had pushed them, the amorphous fluttering collection shifted direction as a group.

"Did you see that?" Junior says. "A single bird can influence the flight path of the whole flock."

"Amazing," Dad says.

Junior starts the car. The noise flushes one of the zebras out of the brush, and the herd emerges for a moment before disappearing from view again.

"Do you know what a group of zebras are called?" Junior yells over his shoulder as the vehicle moves on. He doesn't wait for an answer. "A dazzle."

This makes me smile. I think about my safari clothing line and wonder how I can fold this knowledge into my description.

"Tell me more animal group names," I say.

Dad raises his eyebrows and smiles.

"Ay-ya," Junior shouts to be heard over the engine. "There's a journey of giraffes, a crash of rhino, and an obstinacy of buffalo. One of my favorites is a parliament of mongooses."

Then Junior hears something on the radio. He tilts his head then calls back to us, "I've been told the lionesses are on the move and we need to hurry. Hold on. It's Ferrari safari time."

Junior's acceleration flushes a bunch of birds resembling miniature turkeys with blue heads. Dad gawks but doesn't ask Junior to stop. We turn off dirt road after unmarked dirt road. How will Junior be able to guide us back to the entrance to Kruger?

He slows and picks up the radio. I wish I knew how to speak Afrikaans so I could eavesdrop. He replaces the radio mouthpiece and accelerates.

"Good news. The lions have stopped to rest," he calls over his shoulder.

We round a corner and slow to watch a single zebra mill around an impala herd. Junior points out an injury on the zebra's rump. The gash isn't big—about the size of my hand, but the pink flesh underneath is exposed. I shudder as if a thousand ants have crawled across my spine.

"I suspect that one of the lionesses is responsible for that injury," Junior says. "We must be close."

Now, I'm regretting my choice. Why had I asked to see the lions?

"Will it die?" Dad asks.

"Not likely. A healthy animal's wounds heal surprisingly fast in the bush."

Junior shifts the Land Rover into gear. Our view expands as we emerge from a patch of thick brush lining the road. A jeep lies ahead. It's rare to encounter other tourists. I suspect this is a sign that interesting wildlife is nearby. Junior coasts forward.

"I see them," Dad exclaims and points.

Sure enough, three large yellowish cats lie in the brush off the side of the road. Junior eases the car to a halt about two car lengths away. Good, he's keeping some distance. And they're resting. That's good.

But then the largest of the three lionesses hauls her body into a sitting position using her front legs. The two other big cats stir, but merely stretch their bodies out without lifting their heads from their prone positions. The lead lion tenses and stares across the clearing toward grazing warthogs that appear unaware of the big cats. The lioness hasn't looked in our direction. Her laser focus is on her prey and not us. My pulse slows a notch.

"We've come just in time to watch them hunt," Junior says. "I don't believe it. This is turning into the best game drive ever."

Wait. What? Junior's eyes dance at the prospect. And suddenly I find myself grotesquely intrigued. The two smaller cats contort their bodies and rise to their feet, apparently sensing the change in their leader. These two spot their prey and creep forward as one cohesive unit, while the bigger cat heads in the opposite direction. Junior whispers that they are creating an ambush—that the largest cat will chase the mother warthog and her four young straight in the direction of the other two cats.

OMG. I'm watching lions hunt. I'm fascinated in the same conflicted way I am when I go to a horror movie. I want the lionesses to succeed, yet I don't want to see an animal die.

Dad's camera shutter is clicking like an automatic

machine gun. And for a change, I want him to take pictures. Lots of them.

The lionesses move quickly. In a matter of seconds, the chase is on and the unsuspecting warthogs head straight toward the two crouching lions, but it is over almost before it starts. The pig-like animals with their knobby knees are amazingly agile and dodge out of harm's way before any of the lionesses can pounce.

"Wow," Dad says.

"Yeah," I say.

I feel excited, relieved, and disappointed all at the same time. I'd forgotten to be scared amidst all the action and the rush has left me intrigued about what game animal we'll encounter next.

"It was a good choice to come out here," Junior says. "Not many tourists get to witness that."

The big cats have moved far from the road, perhaps off to search for other prey. With his binoculars, Junior searches the area.

"I have a hunch where those Three Stooges might be headed," Junior says.

"Three Stooges?" Dad asks.

"We name all of our lion prides," Junior says.

"These three bungle their hunts more often than not, hence the name. One of them has been known to chase her tail. They may not be great at catching game, but they are entertaining to watch."

He makes a three-point turn on the narrow, brush-lined road, and turns back in the direction that we came from. I suspect he is going to see if the lionesses will return to hunt the injured zebra.

We round the curve, but the zebra and the impala have

fled the area. Junior drives at a snail's pace. We approach a fork in the road, and he veers the car in the direction of a grove of scrubby trees. The road curves, and Junior hits the brakes. On the barren ground about fifty feet in front of our Land Rover, two of the lionesses walk like princesses with their heads held high, as if they meant to let the warthogs live another day. I imagine if the cats could talk they'd say: "I meant to miss, thank you very much."

Their hind ends sway as they pad softly forward. The third big cat trails behind these two on the lip of an embankment that borders the road.

"That's Curly Jane," Junior says as he pulls the vehicle right alongside the lagging animal.

Dad's eyebrows rise in alarm. I scoot as far away as possible, keeping Dad's body aligned between the lioness and me. But the big cat seems completely at ease with our presence even though we are so close that Junior could almost reach out and pet her.

I'm speechless with awe. These yellow felines move like regular house cats. The one beside the Land Rover turns her head toward us, and I peer right into her yellow eyes. She is beautiful and wild. She radiates primal instinct. I can't believe that I'm here sharing this nonverbal exchange.

The two lionesses in front twitch their tails as they amble along. I blink twice. The sun is bright, but I could swear these cats' fur sparkles as if they've been showered with glitter.

"Are their coats always this... this shiny?" I ask, though I'm sure that what I'm witnessing can't be possible.

I close my eyes and open them again, but the animals' fur still shimmers.

"They are very clean animals," Junior says. "They use

their tongues to keep their fur clear of dust and debris. The spines on the tongue are nasty and could remove the skin from your hand with a few licks. But after a kill, their paws and muzzles will probably have blood on them."

Junior closes the gap so that now there are two cats walking along in front of the bumper and one walking beside the Land Rover. Now, I only see normal, yellow-brown fur. It must have been a trick of the light.

Dad snaps pictures like crazy. Then Junior slows to a stop. The lions keep heading straight, but we can't keep following them because the road has narrowed. Still, we linger and watch them until they disappear from sight.

*   *   *

The drive back is like heading to school, something you have to get through before the weekend. But it isn't long into the jarring, bucking ride that my vision blurs, and I feel as if my head has been plunged into ice water. And though the Land Rover moves fast, it happens in slow motion. Something is wrong with me. Really, really wrong.

Junior stops to point out blue-headed birds like the ones we flushed earlier.

"Helmeted guineafowl," he announces.

The birds shift in and out of focus. Unease has settled in my throat like a bite of stale hamburger bun that I can't seem to swallow. Small puddles of rainwater on the edge of the road catch my eye. I see rainbows in them. Not ordinary sheens, but bright colors of turquoise and pink and Barney-colored purple.

I nudge Dad and point.

"What's up with the water, here?"

"What do you mean?" he asks.

"The colors. In the puddle. Pink and blue."

Dad's forehead wrinkles together and he frowns. "You feel okay?"

I nod. But inside I'm freaking out. He doesn't see what I see. Just like Junior hadn't seen sparkly lion fur. I close my eyes and count to ten, but when I open them, fluorescent blue, magenta, and neon green rivulets reflect off the water's surface.

I'm relieved when Junior drives away, but in a few minutes, the trees that zoom by are a bright Kelly green. The color is all wrong. I've seen plenty of this shrubby, weedy-looking foliage and it's always been olive green. The trees aren't a uniform color either. At first, they're yellow ochre then as we pass, the branches become brighter and brighter. I gasp as one tree even turns blue.

"Claire?" Dad says. "You're so pale. Here. Drink some water."

"Thanks." I take a small sip and smile.

I sniff. The air reeks of rubbing alcohol. I want to cover my nose, but when I look at my father, he seems unaffected by the acrid scent.

"Don't you smell that?" I whisper to Dad.

"Smell what?" he asks which is enough of an answer for me.

Something is really wrong with me. I can't confide in Dad though. Or Junior. They'd think I'm crazy.

I close my eyes and breathe from my mouth. I let my chin drift toward my chest so Dad will think I dozed off. The smell is stronger now, but at least now I don't have to look at blue trees.

*   *   *

By the time we get back to camp, I've convinced myself that I'm seeing things because I haven't eaten a full meal in over two days. Once I fill my belly, I'll stop seeing weird colors and smelling things that can't be real.

Breakfast is laid out buffet-style when we enter the main building. The table bursts with sweet rolls, and cereal, and ham, and tomatoes, and eggs, and toast. A feast worthy of kings and queens.

The Texans, Japanese guests, and Dugger occupy one dining room table. The Texan lady gives me a wary glance as I pass. The only place with open seats holds Arden and Phee. Dad and I will be forced to sit with the English couple.

Junior waits till we have filled our plates then says he's going to skip breakfast to pack for bush camp. He escorts us to our seats before heading out. I admire his cute butt as he descends the steps of the main building.

Phee has changed into regular clothes. Her white, sleeve-less top matches her white shorts. Her jade necklace brings out the green in her hazel eyes. Arden continues to embrace the khaki look even though they're heading to the airport.

"Are you sad to be going home today?" Dad says, nodding at the luggage stacked to the side of the table.

"Yes," Arden says.

Phee sighs. "I wish we could stay a few more days." Her eyes study my plate brimming with pastries, meat, eggs and toast and shakes her head. Her expression is one of longing rather than disapproval. "It gets my goat how young people can scarf down whatever they want and stay slim."

It is a lot of food. Way more than I'd normally consider eating, but if the world will return to normal if I stuff myself, then I'm all in. I pick up my fork and spear a piece of ham.

"Claire has a healthy appetite," Dad says. "But she works out, too."

Dad's coming to my defense? I'm not all that surprised. Something shifted between us on the hippo bridge. With time, I think I might be able to come to terms with all that's happened. I'm feeling better too. The table is brown, my plate is white. The world seems to have shifted back to normal.

"I say," Arden says, winking at me. "It is hard to resist, isn't it? The food is so scrummy here."

I'm grateful that he seems not to be upset with my drama last night. Phee, though, chews on her lower lip as her eyes dart back and forth between Dad and me. She appears to be anticipating another argument.

"Well, I swear I've gained half a stone on this trip," Phee says.

"That's about seven pounds." Arden chimes in. He reaches over and gives his wife a peck on the cheek. "Now, Phee, you know I don't care about all that. You're perfect just the way you are."

I hardly hear him. I'm freaking out again. I had taken a piece of pink cake from the buffet, but what's on my plate is a yellow slice. How is that possible? It was pink. I know it was pink. I take a deep breath to steady my nerves.

"Well, I fancy I'll call up a personal trainer when we get back," Phee says, pronouncing "call" as "coal."

"Did you see anything interesting on your game drive?" Dad asks Arden.

"I say," Arden says, "the dead buffalo was a disappointment. A few vultures and bones were all that remained after last night's hyena feast. Pretty amazing though. How such a big animal can be stripped down to a skeleton overnight."

I imagine Phee would be green with envy if she knew we'd seen lions. I'm glad Dad hasn't mentioned it, and that neither Phee nor Arden has asked what we saw.

I munch on a piece of toast as I glance around to make sure the interior of this building is as I remembered it. Yellow walls, brown floors. No bright colors. And outside, the safari bush grounds appear in ordinary, natural colors. When I look down at my plate, the cake is pink again.

My heart rate slows, and I settle into eating. I'll be fine with a full stomach. The alternative is too frightening to consider. I chow down as if someone might take my food away if I pause for breath. It doesn't take long for me to consume the contents of my plate. I lean back in my chair, suddenly tired. My hand covers my mouth as I yawn.

"This little lady looks about as knackered as I feel," says Arden.

Dad mops his face with his napkin.

"A good day to go home," Dad says. "It's going to be a scorcher."

"It does feel a smidge hot," Arden says.

He's right. Already, sweat prickles my neck, and it isn't even ten-thirty. The clouds have disappeared. Now the sun beats down. The temperature must have increased twenty degrees since my plate hit the table.

Dad pushes a water glass toward me. He keeps pestering me to drink, but I don't want to have to pee during our drive to the private bush camp.

Chairs scrape the floor as the other guests push away from the table behind us. Dugger cradles his ample belly and groans. Do the guides feel guilty about their gluttony? I've seen the bloated bellies of African children starving to death on television. No leftovers remain on my plate. I resolve that I won't leave a scrap of food behind during the rest of this trip.

Denvin ambles up the stairs to the building and spots Dad and me.

"Junior said you had a *lekker* morning, yes?" he says as he approaches us, smiling. "I hear you saw lions today. That's good news since we don't see many of them at our remote bush camp."

I cringe. We'd managed to keep quiet about it to avoid upsetting Phee until now.

"Lions?" Phee says. "You saw lions? Arden, I knew we should have gone into Kruger where we were scheduled to go."

Phee glares at me. Oh, geez. She had changed their game drive plans to avoid dealing with my drama. She could have seen a lion today, and now they're leaving and it's too late.

"Now, Phee," Arden says and moves to her side. "Let's go back to our tent and make sure we didn't forget anything."

He takes her arm and leads her away. I nibble on my fingernail.

Denvin clears his throat. "I understand you saw a saddle-billed stork too. Those are only in Kruger."

"It was a fantastic game drive," Dad says. His face gleams with excitement. "We've already seen three of the big five. Four if you count the dead buffalo, but I'd like to see a live one. And now I've seen two of the Big Six birds."

"Plenty of live buffalos roam around Sabi Sands. Those are hard to miss. And there's no guarantee, of course, but I'm pretty confident you'll get to see all of the big five. Sabi Sands has the highest leopard population in the world."

"What about mosquitoes?" I say. "Will there be more of them there?"

"There may be some. But we have netting over the beds, just like this camp, and bug spray will protect you. Now, let me introduce you to the staff who are going to be at the private bush camp."

"Puja," Denvin yells in the direction of the kitchen.

A dark-skinned woman with a yellow and red bandana tied around her head pokes her head shyly into the room. She has a wide smile and puffy cheeks. Her gray dress with white polka dots is simple and functional. It reminds me of a gray shift that my grandmother used to wear with those wide shoulder straps.

"Puja will be your housekeeper," Denvin says, "Puja, is Kago out back? Can you get him and send him in?"

She nods her head and disappears into the kitchen like a turtle retreating into its shell.

"Kago's going to be your cook and he's an experienced guide," he says. "That man's ability to grill a steak is unmatched. And he's one of the best birders on the staff."

"Well, then," Dad says leaning back in his chair, "now you're talking."

Kago appears. I cringe at his outfit—a pink-and-blue-striped polo shirt paired with pants that are a rich, reddish brown. He dresses more like that golfer John Daly than like a skilled guide. He has squinty eyes, a wide flat nose, and a welcoming smile. He pulls his lips inside his mouth, which gives him an air of self-consciousness that is absolutely endearing.

"Hi, Kago," I say.

He dips his head and starts to chuckle. He grins at me as if I've told him the best joke and he can't stop laughing. His good humor is infectious even though I have no idea what's funny.

Dad jumps to his feet and pumps Kago's hand, "You know birds."

"Ay-ya," Kago says.

When Dad releases his hand, Kago waves, shakes his head, still chuckling, and leaves.

"Kago has the best sense of humor," Denvin says then grins. "All you have to do is smile and he'll be bent over clutching his stomach."

"We also have two permanent staff at the bush camp. We want to get you settled, transfer the food to camp, and still leave enough time for your evening game drive. Are you packed up yet?"

Dad nods. He tilts his head. Some kind of bird is squawking outside. It sounds like a group of old women engaged in high-pitched laughter that morphs into a musical crescendo.

"Do you hear that?" Dad says and stands up.

I roll my eyes.

"Arrowmark babblers. They are rather dull in appearance except for their golden eyes." Denvin says. "Witch doctors, I mean natural healers, believe that the babbler's claw is a talisman for protection."

I smile. Even though I don't care about the birds, I'm impressed that our hosts are never at a loss for trivia.

"I need to get my things together," I say.

"Okay. You should plan to head out in a half hour," Denvin says.

"Great," Dad says. "I'll bring my bag over now then I can snap some photos of the babblers while she gets ready."

Dad's bird-watching obsession is coming in handy for a

change. I need to repack and I don't want Dad seeing how few pills are left in my vial.

CHAPTER NINE

A wave of hot air escapes as I lift back the tent flap. I let Dad go in first to get his bag. I can't believe my fingers felt on the verge of getting frostbite a few short hours ago and now the back of my shirt sticks to my shoulder blades and sweat moistens my armpits. As I enter the sauna-like atmosphere, Dad flips on the wall unit air conditioner.

"Turn that off before you leave," he says.

I nod. I stare at the multiple chips in my fingernail polish as I wait until Dad has collected his luggage and exits. I hadn't been able to pack nail polish remover since Dad had insisted that we not check our luggage, but I did bring polish. I dump the entire contents of my suitcase onto the bed. The burnt-orange vial of Malarone rolls off the pile and onto the floor. I scramble to retrieve it. It looks visibly empty. If Dad notices, he'll know what I've been doing.

I scratch at welts that have bubbled on my forearm. I touch my neck and feel swollen skin where three more mosquitoes have injected their venom. Oh no. No, no, no. I can't live with frequent chills, fever, vomiting, and headaches. I have to do something. I claw at the bites. I grab the pill container. I'm so frantic that I fumble with the child-proof lid. At last I get it open and shake a pill into my palm. Water. I need water. I swear as the zipper catches on the tent flap that separates the bedroom from the bathroom. I lunge inside.

I turn on the tap, but the reflection of myself in the mirror stops me cold. A crazed expression haunts my eyes. What am I doing? What if the Malarone is causing the hallucinations? Can you overdose on this stuff? I've already had three pills in less than twenty-four hours. I'm not thinking straight. The coating from the pill is melting from the sweat on my palm. I look back at the girl in the mirror and touch my face. My nails are a ruined mess and my hair sticks up in a cowlick in the back. I'd never have gone out in this condition back home.

I turn off the water and duck through the doorway to return to the bedroom. I put the pill back in the vial and sink down onto the bed next to my suitcase. I take in a lungful of air and let it out slowly as I stand to refold my clothes, tucking the medicine at the very bottom of the pile.

*   *   *

Dad and I climb into the passenger seats closest to the front as our luggage, boxes of food, and a cooler are loaded into the third and fourth rows. Denvin mills around the open-air Land Rover like a nervous parent sending his kinder-gartner off to the first day of school. His cream-colored safari vest and matching shorts appear to have been ironed. Ankle-high hiking boots and calf-high socks complete his safari outfit. This is a man who knows how to dress—even at a remote, dusty camp.

Kago has changed into the standard khaki uniform. He tells us Puja will join us tomorrow. Kago is to be our driver, while Junior occupies the spotter's seat. Dreadlocks cascade neatly over Kago's shoulders, while Junior's blond hair is in disarray as though he just woke from a nap.

Two rifles lie on the front seat. Why do we need two weapons? I turn to face my father.

"Is this bush camp safe?" I ask Dad.

"Of course," he says. "But we'll be staying inside the reserve. They want to take proper precautions."

"Wait. What?"

Somehow it hadn't registered that we would be sleeping inside the wildlife sanctuary. Are these people nuts?

"Claire," Dad says. "Good grief. These guides are professionals and the camp is protected by electrified fencing."

"Kago will do the safety briefing," Junior says as he tucks the rifles out of sight in a storage compartment.

"I will not run, I will not bolt, for if I do, the leopard will too," Kago says and slaps his knee. "That is all you need to remember."

My nerves are as taut as violin strings. I have a bad feeling. A really bad feeling that sinks all the way into my bones. My leg muscles quiver. Junior smiles at me, which settles me enough that I don't bolt from the vehicle.

"Ready?" Kago says. He tips his head and guffaws. "We have big adventure. Okay?"

I find his broken English endearing and he oozes charisma. Kago has dark, kind eyes and straight, white teeth that seem to glow against ebony skin. He would make a great runway model. He has a reassuring presence, too. Dad's probably right. Our guides won't let anything bad happen to us.

But as we pull away, I turn around. Denvin's arms are folded across his chest and his brow is furrowed. When he lifts his hand and waves, it feels as if he's saying a final farewell.

*   *   *

Dad is in heaven. Kago stops at each bird sighting because we are the only two tourists and we are in no particular hurry. So far we have seen a blue waxbill, yellow-billed hornbill, and a Wahlberg's eagle.

It goes like this: Dad shouts, "stop." The Land Rover comes to a halt. Dad points out the bird. Sometimes he will identify it as an eagle or a woodpecker and sometimes he knows exactly what it is even before the guide identifies it. I'm a little impressed by that. Okay, I'm a lot impressed. But I won't let him know. He'd probably start giving me bird field guides as Christmas and birthday gifts.

It's so dang hot. I wish this vehicle had a canopy. Every time we stop, the heat descends and it's as if I've been shoved into an oven.

"African green pigeon," Dad shouts now, pointing excitedly at several green birds in flight. "African green pigeon."

I hope the birds keep flying. At least there's a cool breeze when the vehicle is moving. But two of the green birds split from the flock and land at the top of a barren tree. Kago rolls to a stop a short distance away. My eyes are drawn to the bright red bill and feet that contrast with the breast feathers that are the color of an artichoke. Africa paints everything in bold colors as if the creatures are in competition with the amazing sunsets.

"There aren't too many bird species with blue eyes. I don't think there are any in the States," Dad sputters the words because he's so excited.

The burning sun makes me feel like I'm the Wicked Witch of the West and have been doused with water. But when Junior turns around and smiles, I melt even further into my seat though that has nothing to do with the weather.

Dad's taking photos so he doesn't see when Junior winks at me. A strange shyness overwhelms me. My lips twitch into a smile as I glance at the two green birds, pretending that's what has amused me.

"These are quite common," Junior says, "but a favorite of tourists. You often see them hanging upside-down on fruit trees. Figs in particular."

"Whoa," Dad says. "Would you look at the bright yellow feathering on the legs! This bird looks even more magnificent than its picture in the guidebook." Dad hands me the binoculars. "You've got to see this for yourself."

I groan but I lift the field glasses and zero in on the one perched closest to us. The bird seems to peer down at me through eyes the color of blue topaz. I wonder if I would think I was hallucinating if Dad hadn't described the bird's coloration. He hadn't mentioned the plum-colored accents on the bird's wing. Calling this bird a green pigeon is an injustice to its beautiful plumage.

The colorful feathers inspire a fashion idea. *Project Runway* often has a kid challenge. For that outfit, I could use all these hues. I imagine a little girl's dress layered with lace ruffles, each made of one of these colors, starting with a strip of red that will include shoulder straps. Under the cheery cherry base, I'll place a stripe of sunflower yellow followed by green, blue and finish with purple. Not quite a rainbow, but close. I hand the field glasses back to my father.

"Pretty, cool, eh?" he says.

I smile, grateful he insisted that I take a closer look. But the heat is overwhelming and I'm relieved when Kago engages the clutch and we move on.

I take out my sketchbook and draw the child's dress, holding the pad so Dad can't see. When I finish, I fan my face.

"Can I see what you drew?" Dad says.

Crap. We're finally getting along and now he's probably going to realize that I'm still planning to apply to fashion colleges. What if he blows a gasket? All the progress we've made will disappear. I don't want to get into another argument, especially in front of Junior.

"It's not very good," I say, shoving the sketchpad into my backpack.

Junior has turned around to see too. My stomach lurches without warning. My mouth fills with saliva as though I'm about to puke. Beside me, Dad takes a swig of water. He offers me some, but I'm afraid if I take a drink, I might throw it up and Junior's attention is still on me.

"You need to stay hydrated," Dad insists.

"I have my own," I say.

My head feels fuzzy. Is that a sign of dehydration? Maybe I should have some water. I rummage through my backpack, searching for my stainless-steel water bottle. Leaning over makes me feel dizzy, so I straighten up.

"Stop," Dad says. "STOP."

Dad is tense. This isn't another bird sighting. I can tell by the tone of his voice.

He whispers, "Oh. My. God."

Kago hits the brakes. My head snaps forward before swiveling in the direction my father is looking. Dad shifts position to block my view.

"No," Dad says. "Don't look, Claire."

Junior reaches back and lifts one of the rifles out of the storage area behind his seat.

"What the hell is going on?" I say.

Dad puts his arm protectively over my shoulder. I clutch the seat and duck low. Up in the sky, large black birds circle overhead in a tight spiral like water swirling down a drain. More vultures lurk in a nearby tree, cane-shaped heads extend out to peer at the ground at something I still cannot see. My father isn't even looking at these ugly birds, further confirming something has gone terribly wrong.

"Dad?" I whisper. "What's going on? Why is everyone so quiet?"

"Shush," Dad whispers back.

The engine idles. Kago hasn't turned it off this time. When Junior sets the rifle on his lap, it's clear that we're not in immediate danger.

I sit up and try to lean around Dad to see what he's looking at, but he senses my intention and moves with me, shielding my view. Kago lifts the radio and speaks into it in staccato spurts of Afrikaans. Panic laces Kago's statements. Then I hear a crackling response in what I think is Denvin's voice.

"Base camp here." A string of rapid Afrikaans words follows.

"Dad, what is it?" I say a little louder and more insistent.

"Shh. Hang tight, honey," Dad says. "Everything is going to be all right. Trust me and don't look, okay?"

Trust him? This from the man who had a secret affair for seven years. How can I trust him? I close my eyes and hug my arms into my belly. What is he trying to hide from me this time?

Kago's tone takes on a new urgency. I have to know what's happening. I just have to. My eyes open and I do what you are never supposed to do on a game drive. Predators don't recognize humans as prey as long as we stay sitting, but it's the only way I'm going to find out what's happening. I stand so that I can see what my father is trying to protect me from.

"Sit down, Claire," Dad hisses, grabbing my shoulder and pushing me backward.

My knees had given out anyway. This can't be real. A male lion lies on the side of the road, gnawing on a severed human arm. I want this to be a hallucination like the rainbows in the water and sparkly lion fur, but I know it's not. This time everyone is acting weird. And Kago isn't laughing.

My stomach lurches. I try to push the image out of my head, but the sight of bloodstains on the fur around the lion's mouth has been imprinted on my brain. I start to shake.

"Claire," Dad says, wrapping his arm around my shoulder.

I take in deep breath after deep breath. The skin on the human arm is black and the hand has the thick fingers of a man.

Junior glances back at me. A panicked look haunts his eyes. We must be the first tourists to see the aftermath of a lion mauling a human. He doesn't seem to know what to do or how to act. Probably he has been trained how to handle charging elephants, unexpected leopard appearances, and failing Land Rover engines. But not this.

"Is he dead?" I whisper to Dad.

"I don't know. Maybe not. The man might have only lost a limb. There's not a lot of blood on the ground."

I hope that a man is dangling from a branch of a tree somewhere nearby, clutching the stump of his arm. Despite my quick glimpse of the lion, I'd noticed how its belly bulged. The lionesses we'd seen earlier today had appeared thin. This lion has eaten well. I had a sinking feeling that this animal had consumed most of the person elsewhere. It must have then carried the arm away with him for a snack.

Kago is now madly radioing people. Dirkus. Dika, James. He's probably trying to find out whose arm that is. A guide? A camp worker? What poor soul had the bad luck to encounter the lion on its own turf? Kago's shoulder muscles relax every time someone responds on the radio.

"We have to get out of here," I say, my voice raspy and filled with panic.

Daddy hugs me tighter.

"Can't we move on?" Dad asks Junior.

"Not yet," Junior croaks. He shakes his head from side to side. "Denvin asked us to wait here. He says the game reserve manager will want to try to retrieve the hand. It will have fingerprints. I'm sorry you have to see this. It shouldn't be too long before an anti-poaching unit responds."

"Thato?" Kago says on the radio.

"*Hallo,*" a male responds.

That simple response must mean that Thato still has two arms.

The hand Junior keeps on the rifle shakes.

"Devin's going to try to organize a search party," Junior tells us. "Following the lion might be the only way to find the man in this vast wilderness. I'm so sorry, but we have to stay here."

His eyes find mine. Is he thinking, as I am, that sitting in a seat that juts out from the Rover—a vehicle that has minimal protection as it is—is not a good profession to be in? Is he thinking that could have been him?

The lion flops onto its side and groans. I glance over before I can stop myself. His belly is so full that one of his back legs is pointed skyward. On the Animal Planet channel, they show a lion successfully hunting zebras, impala and wildebeest. No one ever shows a lion chasing a human.

I recognize Denvin's voice on the radio. Kago replies to him, speaking loudly enough for all of us to hear. "The reserve warden is delayed, and the anti-poachers are at the far end of the reserve with the rhinos, so Denvin is coming. He was taking Arden and Phee to the airport and he's the closest vehicle. It shouldn't take long. We need to sit tight a short while longer."

Phee can see a lion after all. If she's brave enough to look, that is. I'm sure this isn't what she had in mind.

"Anyone need a water or soda?" Junior asks. He turns to my Dad, "Or a beer?"

"Yeah, a beer." Dad's face is ashen. "Are they in the cooler? Should I help myself?"

He asks me, "Soda? Water?"

I shake my head, no.

"Junior? Kago? Can I get you a drink?"

"Water, please," says Junior.

Kago declines with a shake of his head. "Bango?" He hears a response and continues his radio inquiries.

After Dad passes the water to Junior and twists off the cap of a Castle, Dad forces his water bottle into my hand.

"Honey, you need to stay hydrated."

I don't want to argue, so I twist off the lid and take a small sip. I press the cool container against my forehead. Will Denvin ever get here?

A witch-like cackle erupts from nearby shrubbery.

"Babblers," Dad says.

"Ay-ya," Junior says. "Probably a snake has upset them,"

Snakes? Goosebumps sprout on my arms despite the heat. I shove Dad's stainless-steel water bottle at him and the metal clinks against Dad's camera. It makes a loud hollow sound and the birds fly off in a ruckus of movement, leaving an eerie silence in their wake.

Kago sets down his radio. He must have run out of guides to check in with. The engine's tick fills the silence.

A sliver of sweat trickles down my neck. The sun has created an oven-like shroud. I listen for the sound of an approaching car, but don't hear one.

In the distance, two giraffes walk in their stiff-legged, graceful gait. They enter the road and turn so that they face us directly. One of them must sense the lion's presence because it immediately turns and starts to run. The second animal joins it. I shift in my seat. It's too quiet.

"A journey of giraffe," I say.

Junior glances back at me. And then he nods, like he remembers the answer to a quiz question in his guiding test.

"Right," Junior says in his guide voice. "Giraffes can run fifty-five kilometers per hour. Sorry, err… about thirty-two miles per hour. A giraffe can reach seventeen feet in height and weigh almost two tons. And if you get close to them, they have a tobacco smell."

"No kidding," says Dad with false cheer. I suspect both of them are trying to distract me. "Like a lit cigar?"

"No. More like chewing tobacco."

For some reason, this sets off Kago. He snorts then starts to laugh. His guffaws break the tension in the car. Even the corners of Dad's mouth stretch a bit.

Behind us, I hear the rumble of a car engine. Junior lets out his breath. Kago pulls out his binoculars. We wait. The lion hears the car and rolls over onto its belly like he's doing a sphinx pose in yoga. His head pops up and with his legs stretched out, it reminds me of the statue in front of the

Legion of Honor museum in San Francisco. I swear those yellow eyes peer straight into me. I inch closer to Dad.

I wish Kago would start the vehicle and back up. I don't want any of us to be the next human filling this animal's stomach. But Kago doesn't do anything.

"Denvin will make a plan," Kago informs us.

I wonder if he'll shoot the lion, but I'm afraid to ask. Either outcome is unpleasant. Either the lion will die or a man-eating lion will be on the loose.

The engine noise increases. The white van that Dugger used to pick us up from the airport appears from around a curve. Denvin pulls off of the dirt track and drives up beside the Land Rover. He frowns at the lion.

He talks for a while in Afrikaans. Kago listens. Junior sits up straight and purses his lips. I can't tell if he likes Denvin's plan or not.

Kago asks a few questions. Junior nods and asks another question. Then both men nod.

Denvin turns his attention to us. "Well, first let me apologize. This is certainly a first. A rather unpleasant situation. But it is much too dangerous to try to retrieve the... the arm. So, here's what we will do. We'll back up a safe distance where you and your father can safely transfer into the van with Phee and Arden. Their flight out of Joburg isn't for two days and they have agreed, under the circumstances, to go to the bush camp."

The bush camp? He can't be serious? I turn to my father.

"Can we go home now, Daddy? Please? Or can we at least go back to the base camp?"

"Honey. Right now, we have to do what these men tell us. They need to figure out if there's an injured man out here. His life may be on the line."

"Your father is right," Denvin says. "You'll need to spend the night there tonight. But don't worry, you'll be safe with Junior. Kago and I can track the lion. We've confirmed that the local guides are all accounted for and we believe this man was here illegally. Probably a poacher. But we still need to do a sweep of the area in case the man survived. Now, let's transfer you to the van."

The idea of getting into a vehicle with doors and windows and a roof sounds great. But we will have to step out of the Land Rover to get there. Haven't the guides emphasized that we are never to get out of the vehicle? That as long as we stay sitting, the big cats don't see us as a threat?

Denvin and Junior converse in Afrikaans. When Junior nods at Kago, the man starts the engine and backs up all the way to where the road curves. We can still see the lion but from a safe distance. Denvin also reverses and pulls up beside us.

The lion licks its paw and ignores the moving vehicles, but Junior raises the rifle and points it at the large animal anyway. Devin exits the van, circles around back. Kago joins him and the two men transfer our luggage into the van, while Junior stands guard.

The lion's tail flicks, but then the big cat flops onto its side. Denvin slides open the side van door and using his body as a shield, first ushers Dad then me into the van.

"Denvin," Junior says.

The lion raises its head and looks at us.

"Don't you shoot that lion," Denvin says to Junior. "Don't you dare."

Now, I know the lion's fate. It won't be killed. Denvin climbs into the Land Rover next to Kago, while Junior scrambles into the driver's seat of the van with the rifle in hand. They both are back in their vehicles before the lion has managed to get up on its feet. The big cat's yellow eyes are trained on us now. We've gotten situated just in time.

I glance into the back seat of the van. Phee's widened eyes say it all. Her hand grips Arden's.

"Denvin told us not to look," Arden says.

But I can tell by Phee's shocked expression that she has ignored the advice. Both Arden and Phee now have their heads turned away from the lion and the human arm. But like me, Phee will have seen something that won't be easy to forget. I wish I had listened to my father.

CHAPTER TEN

We coast past the lion. Junior apologized but said it was unavoidable, because it was the only way to get to the bush camp. The impulse to take another peek as we pass proves too strong. The lion holds the man's limb between its forepaws, gnawing like a dog chewing on a bone. My stomach rolls. I cannot believe this is really happening.

"Can't they take it away?" I say to my father.

I don't care if that man was a poacher or an awful person. His remains shouldn't be left as lion food.

"Oh, honey," Dad says. He takes my fidgeting hands in his own. "The best thing to do now is put this ugly business behind us."

I close my eyes, and as a distraction think about the contents of my sewing kit: design rule, seam gauge, press cloth, pins, tape measure pod, chalk, and my purple rabbit's foot that I tossed in there one day and never took out.

"We're not far from the bush camp," Junior says from the front seat of the vehicle.

"I'm sorry about this," Phee says.

I turn, and her eyes hold mine for a moment. I smile my thanks as the van picks up speed. Behind us, Denvin and Kago's Land Rover veers off the road beyond the lion's prostrate form.

Dad releases my hands and reaches across my body to buckle my seatbelt. As if being strapped in would make me feel safe. But Junior smiles and buckles himself in, too. One good thing about all this shuffling around is that Junior is now secure inside a vehicle, not sitting in that open on a seat that juts out in front of the Land Rover.

"Will we still be able to do an evening game drive?" Dad asks Junior.

I stare at my father. Has he lost his mind? A man-eating lion is on the loose.

"Of course," Junior says without hesitating. "There's no reason not to. This was probably an opportunistic kill. It's unlikely that it intentionally hunted down this man. Your Hollywood would probably want to make a horror film about this big cat and turn him into a crazed man-eater now that it has tasted human blood. But that's not reality. Lions are hard-wired to hunt herd animals."

I turn to Arden and Phee. "Do *you* want to go out on another game drive?"

"Why not?" says Phee. "We're safe in the vehicle."

Arden pats her hand. He'll do whatever she wants. I pull air into my lungs and catch a whiff of a pungent masculine-smelling soap. Does this calm man of few words ever break a sweat?

No one has asked me what I want to do. If someone did, I'd say that I want to check into a hotel with deadbolts and windows and no wildlife. I want this nightmare of a trip to end.

Half an hour passes before we arrive at camp. The entrance gate resembles an old fashion hitching post for horses, consisting of a single metal bar about breast height. The rest of the area has an eight-foot cyclone fence with barbed wire, but the gate doesn't appear to be secure at all. Ample space exists for a man-eating lion or leopard or hyena to slip underneath.

"Really?" I say to my father.

Dad shifts uncomfortably in his seat. I suspect even he is nervous about the camp conditions. I turn around to see if Arden and Phee share my reservations, but they seem unperturbed.

"Not to worry," Junior says when he catches my eye in the rearview mirror. "The fence is electrified. Dangerous animals don't wander inside the camp."

Junior exits the vehicle. He fusses with a box, which I assume disengages the electricity. He lifts up the metal bar, returns to the van, and drives into the camp.

The metal hinge clangs the gate shut, locking us in as Junior closes the meager barrier. I linger inside the safety of the van as the luggage is unloaded, but it's soon too hot, and I reluctantly get out.

Denvin's description of the accommodations was accurate. The tents are on raised decks and about the same size as those at base camp, but only three tents occupy this small camp. An eight-foot, electrified fence topped with three strands of barbed wire surrounds the campground. If only the gate were as secure.

"Keep your eyes open for monkeys," Junior says. "And sometimes I've seen some of the smaller antelope species graze right outside the fence."

"Where there's prey, there are predators," I whisper to Dad. "Didn't Dugger say that?"

He grunts. But I can tell he doesn't think there's a problem. He's scanning the trees with his binoculars.

"Yes," Dad exclaims.

He points at a tree, central to our campsite, and sure enough several gray animals with long tails are perched on the branches. Obviously, the fencing doesn't keep all the wildlife out.

"When you were little," Dad says, handing over his field glasses, "you loved the monkey exhibit at the zoo. Now you can see them where they actually live. Isn't that amazing?"

It is. Kinda. Their faces are black and barren of fur except for a strip of white fluff that stretches above their eyes like a unibrow. Amber eyes study us with apparent curiosity. Behind one of them, a petite replica of its parent nibbles on leaves. For a second I forget where I am.

"Oh, Dad," I say. "Look at the baby. It's so cute."

He whips out his camera. Whir. Click. Whir. Click.

Junior unloads our luggage. He points to the tent furthest away from the front entrance. "That one is yours," he says to Dad and me.

"Phee and Arden, you'll be in that one." Junior points to the nearest tent.

I wonder if Phee is concerned. Any lion or leopard crawling under the gate will encounter the English couple's tent first. Junior says he'll introduce us to the maintenance man and his wife who live year-round at the camp. I assume that all the staff share this third and largest tent. I smile realizing Junior will be sleeping close by.

Our luggage is lined up on the ground next to the car. Dad retrieves his belongings, so I follow and grab my own bag.

As we make our way to our tent, I note how compressed the camp is. The main structure, a smaller version of the base camp common area, houses a sitting area and dining tables. A raised deck near the dining area is furnished with two Adirondack chairs and a short, rectangular table. And that's it. There isn't much to this place.

At least our tent is made of the same thick canvas material

as the accomidations at base camp. I put down my bag, while Dad deals with the tent zipper, which is giving him trouble. I move a few dozen paces then climb up three steps to check out the communal deck area.

The camp is perched on the edge of a ravine. It's a good fifteen-foot-drop down. The slopes rise up from a dry drainage bed at about a forty-five-degree angle. Dugger's words echo in my brain. They call these site features predator alleys because the big cats use them as corridors. By walking below ground level, they can hide their scent and ambush prey that might be wandering along the banks.

I blink, not sure that I'm comprehending what lies before me. My eyes dart around. Fence. Fence. Fence. No fence. My breath comes in ragged gasps. No barrier secures this side of the camp. What kind of operation is this? How could they have left a portion of the camp unprotected? The part that abuts a predator alley no less. WTF?

Dad places our luggage inside the tent and wanders over to join me. He smells of sweat and bug spray.

"Great, isn't it? Real Africa right outside our tent. Did you ever in your life think you'd get to do something like this?"

I turn and stare at him open-mouthed.

"Dad, look," I say pointing. "No fence. No effing fences."

"Claire," he says. "Do not use that language around me."

He's lucky I didn't use the curse word on the tip of my tongue. I hug my arms to my chest, expecting a leopard to appear around the bend down below at any second.

"Fine," I say. "Send me home and you won't have to hear one more cuss word. But our effing tent is next to this effing predator alley and there's nothing cool or great about that. As we witnessed today, lions will eat humans. I want to go home. I want to go home now."

"Claire, do you really think this outfit is going to put the lives of its guests in danger? Look at the angle that a big cat would have to clear to get into camp. It's perfectly safe here."

"Is there a problem?" Junior jumps onto the platform from the ground.

He'd been over by Arden and Phee helping them with their luggage. I'm pretty sure he must have overheard me, but he's pretending otherwise.

"What do you think?" he says, "Amazing, huh?"

Amazing—everyone's word of the day. Before I can protest and point out what I think is an obvious design flaw in the camp setup, Junior cups my elbow. The warmth of his hands ricochets into my heart, and I start to feel silly worrying about the fence when Junior is watching out for me. I do believe this strong, agile boy would never let harm come to me. I imagine him sitting out on the small, raised deck in front of our tent with a rifle in his lap.

"I want to show you something," he says. He glances at Dad. "Okay if I steal her for a minute?"

Dad nods with apparent relief.

Junior adds, "Hey, can she borrow your binoculars?"

Dad raises an eyebrow and I fear he's going to ask to come along and see whatever it is Junior wants me to see. But Dad hands over his field glasses then turns away to stare down predator alley. Probably he's hoping to spot a leopard.

Junior guides me into the main building. He's giddy with excitement and it's contagious. There can't be wildlife lurking inside so maybe he's going to give me a Wi-Fi password or show me that they have satellite television here.

This communal area has an open-air design with a couch and coffee table littered with animal guidebooks. A chest-high table with two tall-legged chairs are positioned near the sole window. At the back of the structure is one long, dining room table for meals. A ceiling fan offers some welcome relief from the heat, but there's no TV screen anywhere in sight.

He leads me to the tall, circular table. No coveted electronics here. Still, he must have something special in mind. He's acting like a boy about to enter a circus tent.

"Sit, sit," he commands, motioning at one of the barstools. "I spotted them when I was here a few days ago."

Then he stands behind me. The feel of his body heat radiating off him and his breath tickling my ear are electrifying. He smells musky with undertones of sunscreen. It's not at all unpleasant. His chin rests on my shoulder.

I become as pliable as a bungee cord under his touch as he twists my body so that I sit facing the glassless window. The view isn't spectacular. A roof overhang shades the side of the building that I assume houses the kitchen and pantry. There are no windows. Only brown wallboard.

"There," he says, pointing.

A tangle of grasses that I assume is some kind of bird's nest hangs from the eaves. A small, brown bird has arrived with twigs in its beak.

"Quick," he says. "Check it out through the binoculars."

I want to groan. A bird. He has brought me here to see a tiny, feathered creature. A dull-brown bird no less. He should have brought my dad.

A second more colorful bird arrives. This impossibly small creature belts out a long, passion-filled, twittering song that seems to go on and on. I lift the binoculars to my eyes. This one, presumably the male, is gorgeous with a white belly, a glossy green back and head, and a cobalt blue chest.

It's similar to a hummingbird, but it moves more slowly and has a curved beak. I draw my vision down to the apex of the nest where the female clings to the outside, stuffing small pieces of grass this way and that which makes me smile.

"You know," Junior says, "everyone comes here to see the big five. But African wildlife is so much more than large, dangerous animals. Watching the smaller ones going about their daily lives is what I most enjoy."

I nod. Even though he has shown me what we have come to see, he hasn't taken his chin off my shoulder. I'm glad that I skipped taking the Malarone dose. If that's what caused my hallucinations, I would be wondering if this were real. I'm afraid to move even an inch. I want Junior to stay close. But then Dad comes clomping into the room, and Junior moves away.

"Hey," Junior says. "You'll want to see this, too."

Dad rushes over. "What've you got?"

"A white-bellied sunbird making a nest," Junior says.

It seems strange that the bird has been named for the most non-descript color on its body. Junior makes room for Dad near the window, increasing the distance between us.

The smell of brewed coffee wafts from the next room, which must be the kitchen. I hand over the field glasses, but right as Dad gets into position, both birds fly off.

"Darn it," Dad sighs. "But I added this one to my life list when I saw it at the Kruger gate anyway."

"Don't worry," Junior says. "They'll be back."

"Does the male help with the nest-building?" I ask.

"Nope," Junior says. "He only sits around and serenades her."

Typical male, I think. Probably flies off once the eggs are laid. The undercurrent of anger I feel for my father rises without warning. Male sunbirds are just like Dad. Running around with Jan-Puss instead of helping Mom raise me. Junior must sense my mood swing, because he takes a deep breath.

"Well, I'd better finish unloading the van," Junior says.

I don't want to be left alone with my father, so I announce that I'm going to go search for monkeys.

"Wouldn't mind a quick look myself," Junior says.

I hide my smile as my heart leaps that Junior wants to hang out with me longer.

"Yes, yes," Dad agrees. "Go. Have a good time."

A blast of heat hits as I step outside with Junior by my side. The building interior isn't all that cool, but it's better than full sun. I wipe away a trickle of sweat.

"There they are." Junior says. He guides me to the same tree where we'd seen the primates earlier.

"Vervet monkeys." He announces in his deep, official voice. "We have two species of monkey in South Africa, but this is by far the most common."

Phee and Arden recline in the chairs on the communal deck. The English couple fan folded newspapers in front of their faces. It's hotter here than at base camp.

"Let us know if you see anything of interest," Arden calls to Junior as we pass.

I feel special. Technically, this is time off for the guides. But he's still pointing out wildlife. Is that because he likes me? He must, based on the way he was resting his chin on my shoulder earlier.

"What's the best thing you've seen on a drive?" I ask.

"Easy," he says without hesitating. "I watched three lionesses take down a young elephant. That's pretty much unheard of. The predators are usually pretty careful to take prey that they are confident won't hurt them. An injury to a lion can mean the difference between life and death."

I imagine the yellow cats clinging to the elephant's hide like ticks. It seems impossible that they would have the strength to bring down animals so much larger than themselves.

"Wow," I say. "That must have been something to see."

I follow Junior to the van, which is one of the few places that's private and out of immediate view of the tent or community deck. He stops short then moves in front of me as a male antelope-like creature with two giant black horns steps from behind the vehicle. The horns are about a foot long and are anchored between the ears where they curve outward before twisting into a spiral. White spots interrupt its otherwise vibrant red coat.

Junior stands rigid. He has not turned on his guide voice to spew facts. It's the first time that I've seen him truly nervous.

"Must have jumped the fence," he mutters under his breath.

A black stripe bisects the animal's red face. White splotches on either side highlight its black nose. It doesn't seem threatening. Its thick, bushy tail resembles a feather duster. A strange-looking animal, but stunning, too. I make a mental note that this shade of red with black and white lace pockets and sleeve cuffs would make a wonderful woman's blazer.

The animal's big, black eyes hold no malice. We could be watching a horned Bambi. Except Junior seems agitated. I suck in my breath as it dawns on me what kind of animal this is. A bushbuck. Dugger had warned us bushbucks are aggressive and prone to gore people. No wonder Junior is so tense.

A gash traverses the animal's back leg. It's wounded and we're too close. It has a stiff-legged walk as it takes a tentative step in our direction. It freezes, nostrils flaring. Junior shifts position so that his body still shields me.

"Hey now," Junior whispers to the animal.

The bushbuck vocalizes. Its hoarse bark makes me jump. We're in real trouble.

"I say," Arden calls, "is everything all right over there?"

Junior doesn't respond.

"Clar," he whispers, "start moving backwards. Real slow. Make sure that you keep my body between you and the bushbuck. When you get to the front of the van, go around the far side, ease open the van door and hop in. You'll be safe there."

I want him to come with me, but I don't argue and retreat as he instructs. The bushbuck keeps his gaze on Junior. It's as if he has hypnotized this animal. When I'm inside the van, I peer through the back window to watch. Junior makes a low whistle noise and backs up. He's following the same path I did, except that when he gets to the front of the van, I open the door for him and he crawls in beside me.

The bushbuck flicks its tail, snorts then ambles back toward the gate as if nothing bothered him. It easily clears the five-foot high barrier, despite its injury. Why wasn't this gate as tall as the rest of the fence?

"You okay?" he asks, gazing deep into my eyes. "The fence usually keeps them out, but whatever hurt it probably chased it into camp. When they're in danger, they jump higher and run faster than normal."

Junior's stare unnerves me. His hip is pressed into my

thigh, his face mere inches from mine.

I think about the seventeen-year-old boy who was killed by a tiger after it escaped the San Francisco Zoo. He and two friends reportedly harassed the poor animal into a frenzied state until the animal launched itself out of its enclosure. Could lions and leopards scale this fence if they became agitated enough?

Beads of sweat dot Junior's forehead. His calm demeanor has been ruffled, but he seems more concerned about me than his own near miss. I feel emboldened, so I lean toward him. He takes his thumb and runs it along my chin, his eyes taking a measure of me. My knees feel jittery as he kisses my nose. I want more, but he pulls away.

"Well, this will be a day to remember, huh? I know that this trip isn't exactly what you bargained for. Especially after what you witnessed today. But I have never had so many things go wrong on one safari."

As he speaks, he tucks a strand of my hair behind my ear. I smile. He bends closer, and my lips part. I want his tongue to probe and explore. I want to fall into those dreamy, blue eyes and forget about near misses with bushbucks and man-eating lions and predator alleys and fences with big gaps.

Junior's head inclines. He's about a foot taller than I am, even when sitting. He mesmerizes me. The world slows as he comes closer. He's going to kiss me. He's going to kiss me. It seems as if my heart will explode with the anticipation and then... and then... the radio in the van crackles. A slew of words in Afrikaans punctuated by static makes Junior whip around.

"Agh," Junior grumbles as he lunges for the receiver.

He answers in Afrikaans. I recognize Denvin's voice when he responds. His intonation is one of disbelief. I hope that means that they have found a one-armed man alive.

Denvin delivers a long monologue. That isn't unusual. Denvin loves to talk, so I don't know how to interpret this. Finally, there is a pause. Junior asks a question. He takes in a deep breath and seems relieved. Then he signs off.

"Well," he says. "They found the... err... kill site. Kago recognized the victim."

I shudder, realizing that means that the head was found.

"He was a notorious poacher,' Junior adds. "I can't say I'm sorry the man is dead. South Africa loses three rhinos every day to poaching. This man is rumored to have been responsible for butchering twenty rhinos in the last three months. I'd say justice was served today."

I don't know what to say. I'm glad the man can no longer kill rhinos, but I want him locked up, not dead.

"Now for the good news. Denvin has arranged for a special event when we go out on our evening game drive."

"Denvin's going with us?" I say.

"No. He has to deal with the authorities back at base camp. But Denvin's going to drop Kago off in a bit. He'll take the van so that we can have the Landy."

Wait. What? He can't be serious. We can't go out there tonight. Not after the bushbuck and the lion. We should all go and hide in our tents until this awful day is over. Then I think about predator alley, so maybe we are safer in a vehicle.

"Why isn't there a fence next to the gully?" I ask.

"Oh, that bank is too steep for the big animals like rhinos and elephants. The cats are only going to stay in the bottom of the ravine. There's no need for a fence there."

I'm about to point out that an injured bushbuck could lure a big cat into camp, but Junior interjects.

"Devin asked me to check if Arden and Phee still want to spend the night here or if they want to go back to base camp with him."

I want to leave this unfenced place, too. But Dad would never consider it. And now I don't want to leave Junior.

"What about that awful lion? Is it still out there roaming around?"

Junior's eyes narrow. "Awful? As far as I'm concerned, it did the wildlife of this reserve a favor. Who knows why it attacked that poacher, but we don't need to worry about it stalking us."

"How can you be so certain?" I say.

"Listen, I wouldn't let a tourist get in a situation where they faced a lion on foot. I wouldn't put myself in that kind of danger either. But if it were to happen, all you have to do is make yourself as big as possible and hold your ground. Don't run. I repeat, don't run. Most lions will bear down on us as a threat without intending to attack. This poacher probably turned and ran. Stay put and you can survive a leopard and even an elephant charge. I know that's opposite of what a panicked person wants to do, but not running is the number one rule of the bush."

I doubt I'd have the courage. I hope I never have to find out.

"Okay, then. Sorry." Junior gives me a sheepish smile. "Uh, that was an intense lecture. Don't worry. You won't have to face down a big cat. Not while I am your guide. Okay?"

I nod, hoping its true.

"Want to come with me to ask the English couple what they want to do? Then I'll walk you to your tent? I imagine you're worn out after all this excitement."

I am tired, but how will I ever be able to sleep in a tent that lies on the precipice of a predator alley?

"Hallo," Arden calls when he sees us approach. "What was that strange noise? Did we miss anything?"

Junior shrugs and smiles at me.

"Nope. You didn't miss a thing."

"I've heard from Denvin," Junior adds. "He is planning to drop off Kago, so you and Phee have the choice to return to base camp or spend the night here. Denvin has arranged a special surprise for the bush camp guests, so I recommend that you stay."

"Oh, I don't want to miss the surprise," Phee says. "Our flight isn't for two days and we're not that keen on seeing Joburg."

Arden pats her hand and nods agreement.

"I'm so glad," Junior says. "We want you to end with a positive experience."

Junior turns to leave, and I fall into step beside him. The hair on his arm brushes mine and it sends a tingle straight into my heart. I believe he will do his best to keep me safe. But will his good intentions be enough in this unpredictable and rugged land called Africa?

CHAPTER ELEVEN

The first thing I realize as I wake is that I actually fell asleep. It takes me another moment to remember that we're at bush camp. And one more beat for fear to wedge its incessant nattering into the core of my being.

The mattress on my bed sags in the middle. Its frame is only about three feet from Dad's. He reclines on his bed, his hands laced behind his neck, elbows jutting out like bird wings. *The Birds of South Africa* book is splayed face down on his chest.

A small air conditioning unit hums and puffs cool air into our tent. The glow from the little lamp on the bedside table barely illuminates the small room. We're in a miniaturized version of our base camp accommodations, down to a compressed version of the adjoining bathroom. I wonder if this shower works any better, or if it will spew out alternating hot and cold water, too. I sit up and stretch.

"Hey, Sunshine," Dad says. "Good nap? I was about to wake you. It's four p.m. and about time for our evening game drive. I heard the Landy arrive a little while ago and the van drive off. "

I roll my eyes at his use of the guide's term for the Land Rover. I want to pull the sheet over my head and go back to sleep, but no way am I staying behind by myself when this place is only fenced on three sides.

"This area is supposed to be flush with lilac-breasted rollers. And there's a good chance we'll see African Hoopoe.

I know today has been traumatic, but let's make the best of the rest of the trip, shall we?"

"I want to go home," I say.

"Oh, Claire, that lion isn't coming to get us."

"It isn't just that," I say, trying to keep my voice steady. "It's dangerous here."

"Claaaire," Dad says, stretching my name into two syllables.

I glance at my suitcase. I want to take another Malarone, because even if the big animals don't kill you, the mosquitos will. I'm not quite due to take another pill, not till tomorrow morning, but why take chances?

"It's true," I say.

I tell him about the bushbuck encounter, leaving out the part about the almost-kiss.

"Well, I'm glad nothing happened, but this company has an outstanding safety record." He looks askance at me and grins. "And I think as long as Junior is around, someone will be watching your every move."

My face flushes. I can't believe Dad said that.

"If we don't leave, one or both of us is going to end up dead," I say. "So, I'll go on this one last drive, if you'll agree to leave with Arden and Phee tomorrow morning and go with them to the Joburg airport."

Dad sets the bird book aside and stands up. His shoulders, taut with tension, flex as he unscrews the lid to his water bottle, then fills it from a pitcher on the bureau.

"Claire—"

"Seriously, Dad. We can still make it out alive. Please, Daddy. You can come back another time. Bring Janice. Don't you want to show her all the birds? If we leave tomorrow, I promise I'll be good back in California. I swear. I'll study and apply to whatever college you want. I'll even be a model tourist on this last drive. But please, let's leave in the morning."

"No, Claire. I've sunk my bank account into this trip. And with what I've set aside for your college expenses and the divorce costs, there won't be another trip. This is it. This is our chance."

"Your chance, not mine."

He shakes his head. He's got that look—the one where his teeth clench and his chin is tucked to his chest—that tells me he's not going to back down.

"Okay, okay," I say. "If you want to stay, let me go to Joburg. I'll wait there."

"No way," Dad says. He puts down the water pitcher and turns to face me. "Joburg is a hell of a lot more dangerous than this bush camp. It has the highest incidence of rape in the world. I'm NOT going to let you stay there by yourself. That is NOT an option."

Rape? Dad's probably exaggerating. I scratch at a bug bite from last night. The thought of raging bouts of stomach flu for the rest of my life spurs me to action. I can't do anything about fences or lions, but I can protect myself from the malaria-infected bugs that will appear at dusk. I roll off the bed and head toward my suitcase.

"This trip has had a rocky start," Dad says. "So, it can only get better. You enjoyed seeing the rhino, right? Maybe we can ask Junior to try to find more of them. How's that?"

"Sure, Dad," I say sarcastically, as I rummage through my clothes until I find the pill vial. Then I realize Dad will see what I'm doing. I pick up insect repellent instead. "Whatever you say."

"Can I fill your water bottle for you?" he asks.

I don't want his help. I want him to leave so I can take a pill.

"No, I'll take care of it."

Dad collapses onto his bed. He closes his eyes, then exhales. I pick up the bug spray and coat my legs, hoping the smell will make him get up.

"They called us over for a snack about five minutes ago," he says. "You hungry?"

This is my chance to get rid of him so that I can take another Malarone.

"Yes," I say. "Grab me something. I'll meet you by the Land Rover. I need to change."

Dad rises to his feet. He squints at me as though he suspects that I'm up to something. I peer into the mirror over the small dresser and finger comb my hair as if everything is normal.

"It'll get cold when the sun goes down," he says at last, "bring a jacket."

He unzips the tent and leaves. The moment he's gone, I put on khaki pants, which will be an added layer of mosquito protection. I spray the outside of my outfit with repellent. The Malarone pill container lies on top of my jumbled clothes.

I remove the childproof cap, shake a pill into my hand, and replace the vial under my clothes, but then I hear the zip. Crap. I grip the pill in my closed fist as Dad unzips the tent door and pops his head through the flap.

What am I going to do? Dad will lose it if he discovers that I've been double dosing.

"Come on, Claire. Everyone is waiting," he says. "I brought you a muffin. Oh, and can you grab my water bottle?"

"I still need to fill mine," I say.

"Don't worry about bringing yours, I'll share."

Crap. Now what? Dad's water bottle is on the bureau. He forgot to replace the cap after he filled it. I use my body as a shield so he won't see me slip the pill into it. It is stainless steel and even if the Malarone doesn't dissolve, he won't know it's there. Then I twist on the lid and hand it to him.

I pick up my backpack, walk to the door, and step through the tent flap. I won't mind sharing his Malarone-laced water. Not at all.

As I walk up, Junior grins wide like a model in a dentist advertisement. Dad was right. The van is gone and has been replaced by the Land Rover with no roof. I'm probably the only one who would have preferred windows and doors.

Junior shifts from one foot to the other in impatience as we load into the vehicle. Kago is already behind the wheel. He seems no worse for wear. Whatever he witnessed after he and Denvin left us has not fazed him.

I clamber into the first row next to Dad to show him that I meant what I said about being good and trying to enjoy this drive. Arden and Phee have taken the row of seats behind us. Phee's wearing pale-pink lipstick and a bit of blush. Her collared-shirt appears freshly ironed. I suppose that makes sense since she thought she was going to the airport. Junior hops onto the spotter's seat and turns to face us.

"Denvin was so upset at what you all saw today that he has arranged the impossible," Junior says with a smile broad enough for his dimples to show. "Arden and Phee, you are going to be so glad you decided to stay for this drive." He winks at me. "You all are in for an experience of a lifetime. You'll have a quite a story to tell your grandkids."

Grandkids? I don't plan to even have children, so how

will I have grandkids? The thought of stretch marks and screaming babies makes me shudder.

"Does this surprise have feathers?" Dad asks as he hands me a muffin wrapped in a napkin.

I gobble it down since we can't take food on a game drive. The sundowner snacks are secured in a cooler until the guides deem that we are in a place where the food won't attract predators. A rifle is tucked into the seat next to Kago and this time I'm relieved to see it.

Dad checks and double-checks that he has both his binoculars and his camera. He clips his water bottle onto a belt loop on his pants then pats his geeky wilderness vest that has a gazillion pockets until he locates the one that fits his field guide. The bulge reveals that he has not forgotten his most revered safari item.

"I'm not going to answer any questions, and we aren't heading there quite yet. I've been told there's a herd of elephants headed toward a watering hole near here. We're going to check in on them first. Everyone in?"

Junior's blue eyes meet mine. Underneath his excitement, I see desire. His tanned face gives him a rugged cowboy look. He should be in chaps and a brimmed hat. He should be a runway model. He should—Dad shifts on the seat beside me. My father grins at me, and I look away.

We round a curve, and Kago hits the brakes. I lurch forward. My breath catches when I see why we've stopped. Next to the road, three elephants whip their trunks from side to side. I'm stunned by the sheer size of them. My mouth has dropped open, but I clamp it shut before Junior sees. The ones we saw at Kruger were far away. I'd been closer to these huge beasts at the zoo, but now Kago inches forward until we are only about thirty feet away.

"Do they have names?" I ask.

"No," Junior says. "There are just too many these days."

The two bigger ones dwarf our Land Rover, but even the smallest is as big as a rhino. The mid-sized one has a broken tusk. I name them Big Mama, One-Tooth, and Rhino. Kago cuts the engine. It's surprisingly peaceful here. None of the elephants seem at all concerned by our presence. Their trunks twist around barren branches sprouting new growth, snap them off then cram their prize into V-shaped mouths. These browsing animals don't mind us watching, and we don't have to worry about being eaten. This is my kind of safari.

A bird calls, and Dad gets distracted by a black-feathered creature. He's such a nerd.

"I say," Arden says, "was that middle one victimized by the ivory trade?"

"No, actually," Junior says, "here in South Africa we have waged a fairly successful war against ivory poaching. In fact, we have a different elephant problem—too many. Currently, Kruger Park and Sabi Sands have twice the carrying capacity of elephants. And the situation is worse in areas of Botswana where the elephant population is three times normal. Some of the elephants there are suffering from poor nutrition and have weak tusks."

"Why haven't we heard about the overpopulation problem?" Arden asks.

"It's the rhino in the room as you Americans say," Kago says.

As usual, he slaps his knee before erupting in laughter. I can't tell if he was making a joke or if he doesn't know the saying is "an elephant in the room."

"A few years back there was a plan to cull the population," Junior adds. "But it was the year of the Soccer World Cup. That worried the politicians." He shakes his head. "Too much concern about bad publicity and international outrage, so the plan was cancelled."

"They tried a different plan," Kago adds. "They took down fences between Kruger and Sabi Sands to give elephants more room. But it did not work."

"Why not?" Phee says.

Junior shakes his head. "It still isn't enough room. Ellies used to migrate long distances, so the trees and shrubs had time to recover, but now too many people and too many road barriers have isolated them. They are such voracious eaters that they are creating massive habitat changes. It affects all the grazers and so it affects the predators such as lions and leopards that are dependent on the smaller antelopes. Too many ellies cause many problems."

I like the way Junior calls them ellies. He catches my attention and smiles.

"So why don't they feed the females some kind of food with birth control?" Phee asks.

"It has been tried and it has failed. They've talked about relocation. Both solutions are incredibly expensive. The elephants would have to be helicoptered out, and even then, they have been known to return. South Africa has so many expensive human problems to tackle, too. It's a big issue."

"So, the only choice is to kill them?" I say.

The words are weighty and a somber silence falls on the group. The mood in the Land Rover has transformed from excitement to disillusionment.

I stare into Big Mama's eyes and envision a park ranger aiming a gun at her. The image makes me shudder. As she lumbers away from us, her low rumbling vocalization sounds like a growl. In the distance I hear a gravelly response.

I shrink back in my seat. It occurs to me that Big Mama could easily turn around and charge us, hook her tusks under the bumper, and roll our vehicle. But she continues to move away from us, and my fear subsides.

"That call," Junior says, "is how the ellies communicate with other members of the herd. She's telling them of her intention to leave. Essentially, she is saying to the others 'I am here' and the others are responding that they hear her. She'll call again after a few seconds to let them know that she heard their reply."

"Like texting," I say.

"Except the survival of the elephant depends on group dynamics. They actually have a complex language. Like humans, they can communicate danger or urgency by their tone. They have many vocalizations, including snorts, barks and, of course, trumpeting. I should warn you that their trumpets are incredibly loud."

Branches crack and snap. Dad finally loses interest in the bird and lets his binoculars dangle around his neck. He turns his head to watch. Moments later, two more elephants emerge from the thick brush and join the first three gray beasts. One of them is smaller than One-Tooth and I immediately dub him "Wannabe." The other one is a baby.

Dad lifts his camera and starts taking photos. The elephants flush a flock of small birds, and Dad immediately releases the camera in favor of his binoculars.

"That new arrival is a teen girl," Junior says, "probably a sister to the little one."

Her wrinkled skin resembles conditioned leather, and my mind imagines elephant-inspired ensembles. I pull out my sketchpad. I draw a tunic fashioned after the crinkly skin—

long tube sleeves extend beyond the fingertips. I add details until a ready-to-wear, gray sweater with an expansive cowl neck that covers the shoulders fills the page. I envision the loads of wool fabric that will be needed so that the material can bunch up at the hips. I'm completely in love with this idea. And then a second inspiration forms: a light-gray, plain cotton top with a torn neckline, the same dropped sleeves, but shorter. Starting at the bicep, I'll sew on a black-and-white knit with African symbols, elephant heads mixed with black-and-white triangular patterns, abstract but carrying the flavor of Africa. Centered near the elbow, a pop of color, the South African flag, will complete the look. The sideways, green Y-shape will be outlined in white and yellow. There are red and cobalt blue on their country's banner too. A girl could wear pants in any of these colors with this top and be stunning. My fingers itch to add more details on the paper, but Dad loses interest in the birds and I quickly return my drawing pad to my backpack.

Now, my eyes turn to the elephants. The two new ones pass across the road in front of us. Wannabe stops and turns to face us. She flares her ears and lifts her trunk.

"Elephants are incredibly protective of their young," Junior whispers. "But they have terrible eyesight. We are upwind and she doesn't really know that we're here. She senses something is wrong, but she isn't sure what the threat is or where it lies. Watch this."

Junior nods and Kago starts the engine. Wannabe trumpets, and Junior is right. It's as loud as a tuba in marching band. She hustles across the road to join the other three. The little baby hesitates. Then he runs a few steps to catch up, but when he reaches dead center of the road, he stops and turns to face us. When he lifts his trunk and attempts to trumpet, it's the cutest thing I've ever seen. The noise he makes is like a middle-schooler practicing the horn for the first time. It's so nonthreatening that I actually giggle.

The Land Rover creeps forward, and the little guy bolts to catch up to his family. We pass a clump of thick brush and find six more of the giant animals calmly munching on beleaguered-looking shrubs. A tiny ellie stands next to its mother. Toppled trees and shrubs stripped of all foliage surround this group. There can be no doubt that there are too many elephants. But how could anyone possibly shoot one of these beautiful beasts?

These new ellies are not at all pleased to see us. The four mid-sized males immediately form a circle, encasing the youngest member in the center for protection. All have their ears fanned out to make themselves bigger.

Kago stops the car, but this time he does not cut the engine.

"One of the worst things you can do is to get between a mother and her young. And these musth teen boys, you have to watch out for them, too."

"Musk?" Dad says.

"No, m-u-s-t-h," Junior says. "It is a gland secretion in males. See that wet streak above and behind that one's eye?"

I do see discoloration between the eye and the ear. If the tearing were below the eye, I'd think the animal was crying, but it's in the wrong spot to be tears.

"This is a sign that this male is primed to mate," Junior continues. "He gets cranky. It is physically demanding to maintain the body in musth condition. It is nature's way of making sure only the strongest bulls will mate."

Junior gestures, and Kago moves on.

"Around this curve is a watering hole," Junior adds. "If

we get lucky, we might see some elephants spraying water over their backs like in *The Jungle Book*."

Water. That means mosquitos. I pull my jacket out of my pack and put it on. It's not cold yet, but I want to shield my bare arms from the malaria-carrying bloodsuckers.

The elephants flare their ears, shifting to face the car as we pass by, while making sure the young elephant stays in the center of their barricade. But then one of the musth males breaks formation. It trumpets so loudly that I scrunch up close to Dad. He has the video going on his camera and he elbows me aside so that I don't block his view. He's grinning—enthralled by this experience. Junior is smiling, too. I glance over my shoulder, and Phee grins behind her camera. I'm the only one freaked out as the animal barrels down on us. Kago hits the gas, and at the last moment, the elephant falters and turns in the opposite direction.

My heart thuds in my chest. I swallow hard as I stare over my shoulder to make sure the elephant doesn't decide on a repeat performance. Dad's got the camera on replay to see if he captured the experience. Why would anyone want to relive that?

We round a corner and the Land Rover lurches to a halt. Before us, a large bull elephant stands in the road, blocking our path to the now empty watering hole. Junior holds very still. The ellie is a good twenty feet away from him, but way too close. I expect Kago to reverse, to get us the hell out of here, but he doesn't. We sit with the engine idling.

The spread of the bull's ears is wider than the front end of our vehicle. It lifts its trunk then drops it. The circumference of each tusk is as big around as a salad plate and the length must be at least four feet.

Junior sits as still as a statue. Perhaps we all realize that we could die if this animal charges, so no one moves. Dad doesn't even lift his camera.

The elephant's tail swings back and forth, but this is not the happy wagging of an exuberant puppy. I imagine this bull reaching out his trunk, plucking Junior from his seat and crushing him with one of its big stump-like feet.

My throat has gone dry. How long will this stalemate go on? Then, the ellie turns his head and lifts his trunk, waving his appendage back and forth like a banner. I hope he'll turn his body now and wander off. But he only shifts his head toward us again, looking straight at us, still twitching that trunk like a teacher waggling an index finger at a naughty student. He lifts his trunk even higher, but my eyes focus on the thick tusks. I imagine how easy it would be to gore through a human stomach—Junior's stomach. I want to duck down, but any movement is a bad idea. It could endanger everyone, especially Junior.

The elephant must have tired the muscles in his trunk because now he drapes it across one of his tusks. It almost seems like something you would see in a circus act, designed to elicit laughter from the crowd. But this is no show. This is real life.

Kago's hand reaches down to grip the rifle and at the same time he revs the engine. To my relief, the noise startles the massive animal. He turns his giant body and bolts into the brush. I let the air escape from my lungs, though I hadn't even been aware that I'd been holding my breath.

"Everybody good?" Junior says, grinning. He isn't really asking.

I'm happy to put distance between us and the elephant as the vehicle coasts forward. Behind me, Phee claps her hands. Arden whistles through his teeth.

"That was something else," Dad says loud enough for Junior to hear. "Wow."

Something else? That's an understatement. What's wrong with him? How was that scare-fest even remotely enjoyable?

"I can't imagine how they'll top that," Dad says to me. "Wish I could have gotten that on video. But it doesn't even matter. I'll never forget that experience. Amazing. Ab-so-lutely amazing."

He's serious, and I've promised to be a model daughter, so I nod and don't say a thing.

CHAPTER TWELVE

The dirt road splits and we veer to the left. There are no signposts. The landscape appears the same to me. Even if Kago is using a particular tree to navigate by, what if an elephant knocks it over? I don't understand how Kago knows where to go and how to get us back to camp. I'd be lost almost before I left.

Up ahead, a giraffe and its young graze on treetops as the sun begins its descent. We stop, but they're pretty far away, and Dad doesn't take photos. Instead, he unclips his water bottle and gulps down some Malarone-spiked water. He offers me some. I shake my head no because I haven't seen a single mosquito.

"Claire, you need to stay hydrated," Dad says yet again.

"We'll be having sundowners soon," I say.

Junior shifts in his seat at the front of the Land Rover. He winks at me. "It is almost time for sundowners."

I'd like to crawl to the front of the Land Rover and reward Junior with a big kiss when Dad caps his water bottle without further fuss.

"Since we are staying within the reserve," Junior continues, "the usual six o'clock curfew doesn't apply. And since we are diverting from the normal route for your surprise, we'll have an opportunity to seek out night animals afterward."

I was hoping we'd be back at camp before dark. Isn't that when lions hunt? But then I think about predator alley next to bush camp and shudder. Nowhere is safe.

"What kind of nocturnal creatures?" Dad pipes up. "Owls?"

"Bush babies?" Phee chimes in. "I wouldn't mind another peek at them."

Poor Junior. Do they think the bush is like a fast food restaurant where you can order up what you want to see?

"Actually—" Junior says.

The radio crackles and Afrikaans words follow. Kago lifts the walkie-talkie and answers. He converses in the undecipherable tongue before saying something to Junior. Kago signs off with the one Afrikaans phrase that I actually understand.

"*Baie dankie.*"

It is pronounced "buy a donkey" and it means thank you very much.

And then it's Ferrari safari time. I have to admit that despite the bumps and jolts, I do enjoy the Mr. Toad's Wild Ride. We round a curve and slow. Up ahead three other Land Rovers are stopped near a termite mound. One Landy holds a full car of eight tourists. The other two vehicles each hold four. All the onlookers have binoculars trained on something hidden from my view on the far side of the mass of gray earth which is as wide as a rhino is long and as tall as a giraffe.

"We'll move forward when one of the other vehicles leaves," Kago says. "The reserve has a rule that no more than three vehicles at a time can be close to the bigger creatures. It benefits both the animals, which don't get harassed, and the tourists, who can take better photos without worrying about cars spoiling their pictures."

"Is there a time limit when a car is waiting?" Phee asks.

"I'm afraid not," Junior says. "Senior guides are the worst. Sometimes they'll pull rank and keep another group from moving in until the animal wanders off. A waiting car might not get to see the sighting at all."

I'm surprised Dad hasn't asked what animal we are hoping to see. His eyebrows are scrunched together, and his skin has morphed into the same light-gray color of Vervet monkey fur.

"Are you feeling alright?" I whisper.

Dad nods, but I don't believe him. Since there isn't anything alive to see at the moment, Junior provides information about the giant pyramid of sandy, gray material. He describes how the termite activities enrich the soil and how on average these structures are taller than most men. I tune him out to fantasize about hushing Junior by kissing him as he further explains about the subterranean tunnels underlying these hills. Dad nudges me as though he's read my mind. I sit up straight, my cheeks flaring heat.

"We often see the above-ground structures more than one hundred feet wide," Junior continues. "The visible part is the small part. There are huge unseen structures beneath the ground for aeration that also help regulate temperature. The termites are farmers too, growing the fungus that comprises their major food source."

My thoughts drift away again and I imagine running my fingers through Junior's blond hair as he goes on to describe how many predators use the added height of the ground to scan the area for prey. But then his words register. Great, Africa has both predator alleys and predator hills. There's truly nowhere to hide.

Dad should be eating this information up, but he seems distracted. My eyes fall on his water bottle. Could the

Malarone be affecting him? It seems unlikely, but maybe the pill didn't dissolve and he swallowed it whole.

"You sure you're okay, Dad?" I ask.

He smiles and pats my hand. "I was a little dizzy for a moment, but it passed."

I'm tempted to tell him to stop drinking, but then I'll have to explain what I've done. One of the Land Rovers finally drives off and Kago moves our vehicle into the spot they vacate. My concern for Dad vanishes at the sight before us.

A leopard and cub sit on top of the far side of the mound. The tiny cat-sized creature is lying down, but Mom is standing as though modeling for a nature magazine.

"Wow," I gasp.

"Aw," Phee says. "Oh, Arden, it's brilliant, isn't it?"

The mother is magnificent with her yellow coat and hodge-podge of black spots. She has a saddle back like an ancient mare that has carried too many heavy loads. Her belly is rounded as if she still hasn't lost her pregnancy fat. I love the way her tail curls up into a U-shape.

Her neck curves in a regal way. She reminds me of a domestic cat, not a wild animal. I'm amazed to find that I'm not frightened. Not at all.

Another safari-inspired fashion idea develops. I envision a leopard blazer with a black leather skirt for a *Project Runway* bombshell challenge. A swallowtail style with the front panels of the jacket dropping down into points like rhino horns. Hah! A perfect date night outfit. I wonder if I could get Dad to go out with Mom if she wore it, but then the image of Jan-Puss wearing my ensemble forms, and I push that thought away.

Dad's camera swings into action, so I whip out my sketchpad. When I complete my drawings, Phee leans forward. "May I see?"

Dad still clicks away, twisting the camera in various angles. Phee does dress well and I suspect she's going to give an honest opinion. If I make it onto *Project Runway*, I'll have to endure harsh critiques. I grip the cover before handing over the notebook.

I'm suddenly nervous and face forward to avoid seeing Phee's reactions. Junior's studying me with his blue, dazzling eyes. Is he curious about my work too? Would I have the courage to let him look if he asked? My breath catches under his steady gaze. Embarrassed, I smile then look away.

I examine the flat, grassy landscape dotted with acacia trees. For the first time, I appreciate how exotic and wonderful the African landscape can be and I understand what draws people to come on safari. This wild land where nature lives as it has for thousands of years.

"These are bloody fantastic," Phee says, handing back the sketchbook. "You are a very talented young lady."

I nod my thanks and put away my sketchpad, grateful that Dad is too preoccupied with the leopards to take notice.

"Look, look," Dad says, nudging me.

I gasp as the mother leopard bends down and licks her cub's face.

"I told you staying on was a cracking good idea, Arden," Phee says.

"I say, you were right," Arden says.

Then the leopard stretches and lies down in a way that hides our view of the cub and shields her face from us. Dad lowers his camera. He glances in the opposite direction to the leopards and his grin fades. I follow his gaze.

"Well that's different," he says. "Both horizons are orange."

I glance at Junior and Kago. Neither seems perturbed. The other guides in the two other cars aren't worried either. Surely, someone must have noticed the glow behind us.

The second Landy backs away and the mother leopard sits up. Kago moves us into prime photography position, close enough to see the details of the cat. The other tourists have stopped taking photos and seem content to lean back and observe the elegant cats. I smile at a gray-haired woman and she waves. Dad's camera clicks in my ear. Everything is back to business as usual, so I relax and turn my attention to the cats.

The cub's eyes are pale green, while its mom's are yellow, almost identical to the man-eating lion's, sending a stream of dread through my core. But then the baby leopard bats at his mother's twitching tail like a little kitten, and I smile.

The radio crackles. When Kago responds, his tone is serious. Junior stares at his fellow guide and chews on his lower lip. I haven't seen this nervous expression before, not even when facing the bushbuck. Something is wrong.

"*Haibo*?" he says with eyebrows raised.

Dad leans close and whispers. "I know that word. Denvin used it last night at the campfire after you left. It means he's either surprised or confused."

The radio in the other Land Rover crackles, and the guide in that vehicle answers. In a matter of minutes, the driver fires up the vehicle's engine and backs away. The man shouts something in Afrikaans at Kago and points toward the eastern horizon where the orange sky mimics a sunset.

Junior turns and flashes a strained smile at us before returning his attention back to Kago. Dread descends. It seems to have affected all of us in the car. Dad hasn't resumed taking photos. Arden and Phee face the front of the car, ignoring the leopard. Something's wrong.

"Dad?" I whisper.

He gives his head a slight shake to shush me. I don't like the urgency in Kago's tone during a series of back and forth conversations. I don't like the way Junior sits stiffly in his seat. When Kago gently replaces the radio receiver, Junior turns to face us once again.

"There is a fire in the brush back at base camp. The tourists are being evacuated, and all staff are digging trenches to create a fire break. We've heard that a second fire has broken out near a camp close to Kruger. There's no storm, no dry lightning, so the fire outbreak is a little suspicious."

Suspicious? Did someone light the fire on purpose? Why would anyone do that? I peer around at the dead trees, victims of the elephant's insatiable appetite. The elephants have created a landscape of firewood.

"Everyone at camp is okay though, right?" Dad asks.

"Ay-a, ay-a," Kago says.

He turns to Junior, and they have a brief discussion. Junior frowns and shakes his head. I may not understand the words, but these two guides are arguing. Kago looks concerned, but eventually nods.

"Okay, then," Junior says, "we're going to proceed with tonight's plans."

I wonder who wanted to abort the trip—Junior or Kago? Both men seem somber, especially Kago who usually seems to find everything funny. I glance at my father, but he is flipping through his bird book. How can he be so calm with two fires blazing? I haven't seen any fire hydrants during our game drives. Ever. Maybe such a thing doesn't even exist in the bush.

"What's really going on here?" I ask.

Junior turns his blue eyes on me. It's as if the flames have crossed the reserve and tunneled inside me. Desire burns deep. I look away, afraid my eyes will reveal my feelings.

"Kago wants to return to base camp to help with the firefighting," Junior says, "but if we do that, we'd have to drive you to safety first. I imagine all the local camps and hotels are full. It is better for us to sit tight and stay at the bush camp, which is far from the fire. There's really no reason to change our evening schedule. Does everyone agree with the plan?"

Around me, I hear murmurs of assent. Stay here? In this remote area? What if the fire shifts direction or it drives that man-eating lion toward our camp? While there's no smoke, no scent of burning vegetation, a crowded hotel sounds like a better plan. Hell, I'd share a room. I'd sleep on the floor.

"Now," Junior says, "we are off to sundowners and your surprise. We will be traveling away from the fire to get there."

The engine chugs to life. I think about how fast the other Land Rover left the area. Were those people leaving the reserve? I want to go too.

"Wait," I say.

"Claire," Dad pats my hand and shakes his head to silence me. "Remember your promise?"

He would throw that in my face. I want to remind him about his vow to love my mother till death do us part. But I hold my tongue and lean back into my seat.

We round a curve in the road. Before us, the sun is a perfect yellow ball set against a vibrant orange sky. A single acacia tree is backlit.

"Wow," Dad says. "I didn't think it was possible, but the sunset tonight is even more spectacular than last night's."

"I say," Arden says, "that view alone was worth sticking around for. This drive is the best one yet."

Junior beams. All our guides have seemed genuinely concerned with pleasing the tourists—even difficult ones like me. I smile at Junior and lock onto his shining eyes.

"The view is amazing," I say.

Junior grins and winks, and I blush at being caught at my double meaning.

"Well, the best is yet to come," Junior says. "We still have one more thing to show you on this drive."

Kago turns the car away from the fantastic fiery ball. I sniff the air and catch a whiff of smoke. Even though the air is warm, a cold chill passes through me. I thought we were far from base camp, too far to detect the brush fire. My resolve to keep my promise wavers.

"Do you smell that?" I ask Dad.

His neck cranes upward as he stares at a circling hawk. I suspect he didn't even hear me.

"Junior," Dad calls. "Is that a *bought-le-er* eagle?" It sounds French and I wonder if Dad has pronounced it wrong. "Those are the ones that don't appear to have tails, right?"

Junior cranes his neck. "*Lekker* spot," he exclaims. "And, a-ya, that is a bateleur. Easy to identify with those legs poking out, eh?"

Dad pulls out his notebook and jots down his sighting.

"Da-ad?" I say, tugging on his arm.

"What is it?" he asks.

"Seriously? I asked if you smell smoke."

"Claire. Really? I swear if someone said there was a stampeding elephant on the African continent, you'd think every gray beast we encountered would be that rogue animal. Junior assured us that we're miles from the fire. Okay?"

"I smell it, too," Phee offers from the back seat.

I sit taller and turn to smile at Phee. She nods, and I see worry in her eyes. Perhaps my fashion sketchbook has changed her opinion of me.

"Nothing to worry about," Junior adds. "We are upwind from the fire at base camp."

The radio crackles. Kago slows the vehicle and picks up the receiver. I can tell by the way his back straightens that the news is not good. He speaks to Junior who shakes his head and turns to face us. He purses his lips and seems to be trying to choose his words with care.

"What is it?" I ask.

"A third fire has been set," Junior says. "This is no coincidence. Denvin says that it is a diversion and that poachers are behind it. He thinks they are trying to flush the rhinos toward them to take their horns."

"Has this ever happened before?" Dad asks Junior.

"Once, but it was a small group and they only set one fire. Their scheme failed because the wildlife fled in different directions. But this time it seems more coordinated." Junior turns backward to face the direction that we came from and chews on his lower lip before adding, "This time it appears that they are flushing them toward a central location."

I don't like the way Junior shifts in his seat or the way Kago stares at the road we came in on.

"Is this new fire close?" I ask.

"We aren't in any danger," Kago says, a little too quickly.

That wasn't what I asked, but before I can push for a direct answer, Dad pipes up.

"Is there anything we can do?"

"I am afraid not," Junior says. "Every man in the area is out fighting the fires. Denvin would never allow tourists to put themselves at risk. And he has gone to great lengths to arrange your surprise. If we don't follow through, there will be hell to pay for us guides. But I think we'll skip sundowners for now. We'll have drinks back at camp."

"We're almost there," Junior says, looking at me. "It would be a shame to lose out on this rare opportunity."

"Agree," Phee says.

"Yes," Dad adds. "Let's continue."

Kago lifts his foot off the brake, and the decision is made. I try to put on a brave face as we traverse the same scrubby brush, the usual felled trees, and more sparse grassland with a few of the ever-present termite mounds.

At last, we descend into a ravine where a dank smell like moldy leaves fills my nose. Another predator alley. I glance to the left and right to make sure there aren't any lions ready to pounce. I let my breath out as we climb upward. The road is steep. I worry that we might not make the ascent, but then the land flattens into a plateau and Kago stops.

To our right in the distance, the orange glow of a fire highlights the horizon. Is this one of the three fires or is it a fourth? How massive is the poacher's plan? All this destruction so they can get money for a rhino horn.

Junior peers over his shoulder and flashes his dimples. He is so gorgeous. But his smile suggests mischief. My attention is drawn to the reflection of the setting sun on a watering hole. At its edge… at its edge are the silhouettes of two rhinos.

At some point, Junior had placed his camera around his neck. Now Kago reaches under the dashboard and brings out one, too. The waterhole reflects the heads of the two rhinos.

The scene is stunning, and I take a selfie with them on my iPhone. This will be my screensaver. I put my phone in my backpack.

"The term "white rhino" is actually a mistranslation from the Dutch. When they first came to South Africa," Junior says, "they described them as *weid mond rhino*, meaning wide-mouth rhino."

Junior laughs then looks at Kago, "You tell them."

"Ha ha," Kago laughs. "These animals aren't white rhinos."

What? Now, I notice the difference in the head shape. Black rhinos. We're looking at the last two black rhinos in the world.

The full magnitude of what Denvin has arranged for us hits. He must have had to pull in major favors. We're seeing the equivalent of Noah's ark for a species whose very survival is hanging on a thread.

"But that's not possible," Phee gasps. "We aren't allowed..."

Junior is grinning. Dad clicks away at a faster rate. He's using his zoom lens.

"Black rhinos are solitary," Junior says. "The only place you see them together is at a watering hole. We are not only seeing the last two remaining black rhinos, but we are viewing them side by side."

"I'm getting great shots," Dad says in wonder. "Amazing. Oh wow. Oh wow. I can't believe this is our surprise. Impossible. How did Denvin... How could he possibly... Tell him," Dad laughs. "Tell him 'buy a donkey'."

"Yes, yes," Phee agrees.

"Oh wow," Dad continues to gush. "This is like a dream come true. Can you believe it, Claire? We are two of the few people on the planet that get to see these magnificent animals in the wild."

Dad shows me one of his shots. The folds of skin near the front leg and wrinkle around the ears remind me of armor. I glance at Junior—my knight in shining armor.

"Nice," I say, grinning.

Dad shakes his head and I blush, realizing Dad knows exactly what I think is nice. I turn my attention back to the rhinos. I must design an outfit based on these special animals. My mind races with the idea of a textured black leather dress with a plunging neckline. Spaghetti straps would hold the bodice in place. I would design it as a single piece, but it would appear to be separates. Irregular geometrical shapes everywhere including "V" shapes pointing seductively toward the pelvis.

The sun has changed to a fiery red as it nears the horizon. It lies behind the two grazing creatures. A termite mound separates the Land Rover from the animals. They are at least a half a football field away, and I suspect that we won't get any closer. But it doesn't matter. The mood in the car has switched from despair to wonder.

"The male is noticeably biggah," Junior says.

I can tell he is excited because his accent has become more pronounced. It makes this moment all the more special to see him so happy. Rhinos are rotund by design, but even I can see that the smaller of these animals is bloated with pregnancy. The only thing that could possibly make this experience more memorable would be if she started giving birth.

"Take photos quick," Kago says. "Five minutes only here."

"I can't really tell in this light," Dad says. "Are they black?"

"No," Junior says, "there's no color difference between white and black rhinos. The black rhino is smaller. Both species have two horns on the snout, though rhinos from different areas may have horns of different shapes and sizes."

"I say," Arden says.

"But that's not all," Junior says. "Another way to tell a black from a white rhino is to observe the mouth. The black rhino has a hooked top lip, as opposed to the flat-based lip of the white rhino, because of their different eating habits."

"Don't forget," Kago adds. "Black rhinos like to charge."

"Where is the anti-poaching team?" Dad asks.

"Don't worry," Kago says. "They are out there, hiding in the bush. It is a very dangerous job. If they made themselves visible, they would be easy targets for the poachers."

"How many men protect these two?" I ask.

"Six full-time stewards work around the clock. You can imagine how valuable those horns are to a poacher." Junior shakes his head. "The rhinos are followed and are pretty much allowed to go as they please, but the anti-poaching unit may guide them out of areas if they feel there is a way that they can be cornered."

I survey the open area with only a few scattered, barren trees. I don't know why the rhinos have sparked a protective, motherly instinct within me, but they have. Maybe it's their resemblance to dinosaurs. *Jurassic Park* is one of my all-time favorite movies.

"When's her baby due?" I ask.

"Well, she's been pregnant for at least fifteen months. The gestation period is reported to be around seventeen months. So soon. We hope."

"How big is a baby rhino?" Phee asks

Kago arches his back, puffs out his stomach and guffaws.

"Her calf will weigh up to forty-five kilograms," Junior says. "That's about one hundred pounds."

We all chuckle, but when the laughter dies down, a watch alarm goes off. Crap. I don't want this experience to end. I say a silent prayer that the female rhino has a successful birth. What if she can't get pregnant again? Then, the very survival of this species may depend on this calf she carries now.

I'm so grateful that Denvin has arranged this viewing. I'm so grateful that Dad forced me to come on this trip. Even if I return to Africa in the future, there will never be another day like today. We're some of the privileged few who will ever have this opportunity.

As the Land Rover backs up, I stare at the orange sky. What if the blaze spreads in our direction? What if these fires were set by the poachers as a diversion so they can take the horns from those two rhinos?

CHAPTER THIRTEEN

K ago navigates the Land Rover toward the ravine to leave the plateau. Dad is silent, but Phee chatters nonstop about the black rhinos. Even Arden responds with more than "I say." It's also adorable how he prefaces each sentence with his wife's name.

"Phee, did you notice the rhino's reflection in the water?"

"Phee, I'm so bloody glad we saw them together."

"Phee, I'm so bloody glad you wanted to stay for one more drive."

I hope that someday I have a husband who loves me as much as Arden cherishes his wife. I doubt Dad ever felt that kind of love for Mom. Does he feel that way toward Jan-Puss?

The yellow flickering light of the fire in the distance is fringed in a soft glow, but I can't tell if it has lost its intensity or if my eyes are playing tricks on me.

"You're so quiet," I say to Dad.

"I'm in awe," Dad says. "Did you see the size of the male's horn? It was as long as a saber."

Dad loops his camera through an arm so that the strap crosses his chest. As the nose of the Land Rover dips down, and we descend into the bottom of a ravine, we both grasp the seatbacks in front of us. The Land Rover bottoms out into a landscape that resembles the predator alley next to our bush camp.

We've started to ascend when a blast of gunfire cracks

through the air, so loud and unmistakable that I jump.

"Blimey," Phee exclaims. "What was that?"

"Dammit," Junior curses. This is the first time I have heard any of the guides swear.

"Was that a gunshot?" Arden says.

"No," I say. "The rhinos…"

Has the female rhino been shot? Are the last of the western black rhino dead? Was that sound of extinction?

Another shot rings out. Closer to us this time. I clutch Dad's arm.

Kago shouts into the radio. "Contact. Rhinos. Contact."

"Claire," Dad says. "No need to be frightened. Probably a ranger firing a warning shot to herd the rhinos away from the fire."

Is he nuts? Do I need to spell it out for him? They're. Shooting. Guns. Goosebumps sprout on my arms and I scoot closer to my father. This is insane.

"Daddy," I whimper. "I want to go home."

Dad puts his arm around me and pulls me under the crook of his arm. The camera grinds into my rib, but I don't care. He plants his chin on my head. His heart beats like a jackhammer and I realize he was lying to keep me calm. Despite his words, he's scared, too.

"Yes," he says. "Tomorrow we'll go home. I'm sorry, honey. This wasn't what I planned. This was supposed to be a fun vacation. This was supposed to bring us closer together. But when we get home, you'll remember the good things. Like seeing the black rhinos and the baby elephant trumpeting at us."

Maybe so. But I won't forget the lion chewing on a human arm either.

Dad kisses the top of my head. "It's okay, honey. It's

going to be okay."

Kago revs the engine, and the vehicle rockets out of the gully onto the opposite plateau. My heart thunders, and I can hardly breathe. As the nose of our Land Rover levels out, the headlights of a vehicle flash on directly in front of us.

"Everyone get down," Junior shouts.

A spray of gunfire explodes in our direction. Dad shoves me all the way to the floor and covers me with his body. The Land Rover careens around in a U-turn, and I grip the footrest near my head as we plunge into the gully again, heading back in the direction of the rhinos.

Through the metal bars that anchor the seats I see Phee cowering in the row behind us. Arden lies on top of her. Fear wafts off Phee in waves. Arden whispers something comforting, but I don't catch what he says.

I can't believe this. It's so surreal. They can't really be shooting at us. It feels more like a scary amusement park ride than reality.

Radio static is followed by Kago's shouts. I hope he's trying to contact the anti-poachers to ask for help. Headlights from another vehicle slice through the night darkness as we rise up onto the plateau. Another volley of gunfire is directed at the front of our Land Rover. This can't be happening. Now we're sandwiched between two gun-toting maniacs who are shooting at us.

Kago slams on the brakes, and the vehicle careens to one side. A silence fills the air when the engine stalls. No. No. No. Kago turns the key but the engine only whines in protest. We're stuck. This can't be happening. I hear a sound like a dry branch split in two. They're coming. I have to get away. I have to get out. I have to get out. They're going to run up to our vehicle and spray the interior with bullets. We can't stay here. We have to run.

I shove my father to get him off of me. He must have thought he was crushing me because he lifts his body enough for me to scramble out from under him. And in my panic, I don't think. I hurl myself over the side of the Land Rover.

"Claire," Dad shouts. I feel his hand graze my foot as I tumble from the car. "Claire, don't run."

His words seem to come from very far away. I scramble to my knees and crab-walk to distance myself from the vehicle. The Land Rover's engine rumbles to life. More gunshots are fired, but I can't go back.

Somehow, I find my feet and flee. Terror snaps at my heels like a herding dog nipping at sheep. My mind shouts its mantra. Get away. Get away. They're shooting at us. Get the hell away.

Acrid air irritates my throat as I sprint across the clearing. A plume of smoke covers the moon. A yellow glow stretches from the horizon in the wrong direction. Another fire? It cannot be a coincidence.

The thud of boots descends behind me. I don't know who is chasing me. A single flashlight beam illuminates the ground. My heart races. My feet pound the earth.

"Clar," Junior shouts over the chugging sound of the Land Rover's engine. "Don't run."

"Claire," Dad adds. "Stop. Right. Now."

I now understand that Dad and Junior are the men chasing me. I want to listen, but I can't. People have been shooting at us. I have to get away.

My father continues to call my name. I see Junior's shadow, the long thin outline of the rifle in his hand.

Somewhere nearby, wood snaps as it is engulfed in the blaze. Are the poachers chasing the three of us?

The moon peeks out from behind the smoke and clouds, illuminating the ground. My eyes dart around for a place to hide. The fires have corralled the rhinos closer to me than I expected. Only then do I remember that black rhinos are prone to charge. I shift direction to avoid getting closer.

I head toward a thin haze of smoke that blankets the air like wispy clouds, hoping this will limit the poacher's view of me. I cover my mouth with my shirt to avoid breathing in the smoke. More gunfire erupts from behind. One of those pyramid-like termite mounds towers in front of me, and I sprint toward the far side. I hear heavy breathing and pounding feet. I've almost reached the protective cover of the mound when the moonlight illuminates the flash of blond hair in my peripheral vision. Junior. He snags my arm and pulls me down. The back of my head thuds to the ground. Air whooshes from my lungs as I land.

"Bloody fool," he chastises me, flipping onto his belly.

I suck in air. The thump, thump, thump of Dad's feet announces his arrival. He collapses next to us. I lift my head, but no one else follows.

Above, smoke creates a thin layer of haze over the moon like a translucent shower curtain. My heart thuds as the sound of more gunshots fill the air. But it isn't too close. The fire may have saved me. I hadn't thought that I would feel afraid of humans on this safari. I only thought the animals would be dangerous.

Silence falls. The three of us gulp air. The quiet is eerie. Then an engine is gunned and a vehicle much smaller than ours appears out of the hazy air about five hundred feet from the rhinos. It coasts in the direction of the giant beasts. This must be the people who ambushed us, but they have somehow skirted around our Land Rover to reach the rhinos. The animals startle and move back toward the watering hole, but they stop when the poacher's vehicle comes to a halt about a dozen car lengths away from them. I want to move behind the termite mound, but I'm too afraid.

Two men get out. One is heavyset and taller than the second man who is lanky with arms like rolling pins. They're probably beyond shooting distance of the two rhinos, so the men creep closer on foot. Junior raises his firearm and points it in their direction. He mutters something in Afrikaans, and from the tone, I suspect that he is cursing. He braces the gun on his shoulder but does not fire. They've moved around five car lengths from their vehicle when the smaller, female rhino, snorts and the two men freeze. Junior takes aim again, then lowers the weapon.

"Agh," Junior says. "They're too far away for me to stop them."

He whispers something in Afrikaans into his radio, and I recognize Kago's voice when he responds. Moments later, Kago appears, his distinctive dreadlocks in silhouette, as he walks towards us from the direction of our Land Rover. The beam of his flashlight swings back and forth. One of the poachers lifts his rifle in Kago's direction.

"Crap," Junior says. Then he speaks into his walkie-talkie. "Kago, turn off the torch. Turn off the torch."

Kago doesn't falter. I can't see a radio on his belt. He must have left it behind. He plows forward so he still must not see the poachers.

"Oh my god." I squeeze my father's arm so hard that I feel him wince. "Daddy. Oh my god. Oh my god. Oh my god. Kago's going to get shot."

Dad pulls my face away. I hear another loud blast followed by an exclamation then a whoop in the distance. I turn my face in time to see Kago's form collapse onto the ground.

I can't catch my breath. Fear steamrolls over me. This can't be really happening.

"It's okay. It's okay," Dad says. "He could still be alive. People survive gunshot wounds all the time."

But then as if in slow motion, the heavyset poacher runs about twenty yards across an expanse of flat land. He lifts his rifle. I turn my head back towards Dad's chest, but I'm not fast enough. I see the big man fire a second bullet into Kago's head.

"No," Junior cries.

He bursts into a stream of Afrikaans. I don't need to understand the words to feel the pain behind them.

The ground shifts under my feet. It feels like an earthquake. The last round of gunfire has spooked the two rhinos. The moonlight is bright enough to see them run across the flat terrain into the path of the lanky poacher who now stands by his vehicle. He jumps into the jeep, but the heavyset poacher who killed Kago takes aim at the charging animals.

The rhinos veer out of the jeep's path, but the big man does not lower his weapon. The female is out front and he's going to kill her. And in doing so, he'll murder her unborn baby. Not after all this. I grip Dad's arm, and he pulls me close.

Beside me, Junior raises his rifle again. This time he cocks it, but then hesitates. He has seemed so competent and self-assured, but now I see how young he is. He isn't much older than me and he's being forced to choose whether to shoot another human being or let a species go extinct. The poacher steadies himself, standing evenly on both legs as he takes aim. A rage as hot as molten lava surges in my chest. Not the rhino. He's killed Kago and now he's going to kill an endangered animal out of greed. Angry tears stream down my cheeks.

"Do it," I say.

Junior swallows hard. His finger trembles before he pulls the trigger. The big man tilts toward the earth clutching his chest. His crumpled form lands next to Kago. The rhinos roar past. Junior shoves his rifle at Dad as if he can't bear to touch it anymore.

The world seems to shift. I hear the buzz of death in my ears. Have I caused this? Would Junior have pulled the trigger without my encouragement?

The lanky poacher jumps out of the vehicle and runs to the side of his fellow poacher. He squats down, shakes the fallen man, and screams something incoherent. He lifts his head, howls—an eerie sound that turns my blood cold—then turns in slow motion to face our hiding place.

"*Ek sal jou neuk!*" he shouts in our direction.

The poacher backs up screaming and cursing as he returns to his vehicle. Moonlight glints off of the barrel of his gun. He's reloading. And then he's coming for us. I can feel it even if I didn't understand his words.

"What did that poacher say?" Dad whispers to Junior.

"He said that I killed his brother," Junior says in a quivering voice. "He said that he'd get me for this."

The threat hangs in the air. None of us move. Then the knowledge sinks in through my shock. The poacher has a car. We can't outrun him. Fresh tears sprout from my eyes. I hate that I'm weak when what I need to be right now is strong. I sniffle and wipe my face.

"You two need to crawl behind the termite mound," Junior says.

I do as I am told. Dad shifts his camera out of the way and follows close at my heels. My father still holds the rifle in one hand. Junior takes up the rear of our retreat.

Junior looks at my father after we are all safely out of the poacher's crosshairs. "You know how to shoot a double-barrel?"

"Been awhile," Dad says, "but I think so."

What? My father knows how to shoot a weapon? He was never in the military, so why would he have handled a rifle? What else don't I know about him?

"Here," Junior says in a strange tone, while reaching into his vest then handing several bullets to Dad. "Reload it."

When he separates the barrel from butt of the gun to open the chamber and remove the empty casing, gray smoke wafts out. I had no idea rifle ammunition was so big, at least as long as my forefinger. Dad adds a bullet to replace the one just discharged, snaps the unhinged barrel back in place like a pro, and pockets three spares that are spectacularly large. I'm floored that my father knows about firearms.

"Pulling the trigger further will discharge the second bullet," Junior says.

Dad nods.

Junior peeks around the termite mound.

"He's run back to his brother. Maybe to find the keys to the vehicle. This is our chance," Junior says.

As I gather my feet underneath me and try to stand, my stomach cramps and my vision blurs. I tilt my head up to clear it. Above, the moon and a rainbow halo forms at the periphery. That can't be normal. Is this another reaction to Malarone? What if I can't see straight enough to run?

"I don't feel too good, Daddy. I'm seeing things and my stomach hurts."

"*Kak,*" Junior's hand trembles as he fumbles for the radio attached to his belt. "The car is not far. But we can't risk having them come get us."

Dad wipes an errant piece of hair from my face. I feel feverish. I must be burning up, but Dad doesn't seem too concerned when he presses a palm to my forehead.

"Phee? Arden?" Junior says into the radio.

What's his plan? Check to see if they are still in the same spot?

The wide expanse of tall grass we must cross is mostly barren of trees to hide behind. The moonlight is bright enough and the smoke thin enough that I can see the crumpled forms of Kago and the poacher. The noise of the engine from the poacher's vehicle grows in volume. We'll never make it.

A second termite mound blocks our view of the poacher's progress. But it doesn't matter. We're running out of time. Even if Arden attempts to drive to us, he has to get past a man with a gun. The radio crackles, but there is no response. The silence on the other end feels like a stone in my gut.

Junior speaks into the radio again. Static is the only answer. I'm thinking about all the gunfire that preceded the poacher's death. Were Arden and Phee shot? Are they dead too?

My stomach cramps even more, and I double over. Junior stands, lifts the radio high and leans around the termite monstrosity. Seconds later a shot rings out, and he dives behind the mound.

"You'll have to be strong, Clar." Junior says. "The poacher is probably reloading again. This could be our last chance to get back to the Landy. Keep your head down. We have to go now."

As Dad stands to help me, the crack of a rifle fills the air.

"*Kak*," Junior says as he thrusts the radio into my hand. "He must have a double loader."

"You dead now," the man shouts in broken English.

"Don't worry," Dad whispers and gathers me close. "I'm not going to let him hurt you."

"Hey," Junior shouts, "you are shooting at tourists. Let them go. They had nothing to do with your brother's death. Come after me." Then he spews angry words in Afrikaans. To us, Junior adds in a whisper, "Run. Now."

Before I have time to react, before I can try to stop him, Junior darts from behind the termite mound, running toward the orange glow of the fire in the opposite direction of the Land Rover. He's trying to lure the poacher away. For a moment, I stare at Dad who clenches the rifle. Good god. Junior has left his weapon behind. Junior has no way to defend himself. I feel the weight of the radio in my hand. He has no way to communicate with us either. A mixture of pride at his bravery, anger at his foolishness, and terror at our predicament fills me. Dad grabs my arm. Somehow my feet cooperate and we flee towards the Land Rover.

CHAPTER FOURTEEN

The earthy smell of dried grass fills my nose as Dad tackles me to the ground amidst a gunshot blast. We've covered less than half the distance to the termite mound that separates us from our Land Rover. The poacher didn't follow Junior for long before shifting his focus and shooting in our general direction. Apparently, he also blames us for killing his brother. How far do voices carry on this plateau? Did the poacher hear me tell Junior, "Do it"? He must have. That's why Junior's heroic plan has failed.

Light beams down from the full moon, cutting through the murky air. There are a few low-lying shrubs, but the rest is knee-high grass. There's a fallen tree, but it's not in a straight path toward the camp vehicle. Its bare limbs wouldn't fully shield us.

I feel exposed in this short grass. Dad belly crawls up next to me. He's breathing hard and has that same shocked expression on his face as when I barged in on him and Jan-Puss. I poke my head up peering through the grass to see if the poacher is coming. The lanky man has returned to stand by his vehicle. He's scanning the area with binoculars. Does that mean he doesn't know our exact position?

"This way," Junior's voice travels from far away. "I'm the one you want."

The poacher doesn't react. And now I know for sure that he has decided he'd rather take his revenge on Dad and me.

"We've got to get help," Dad says.

He takes the radio from my sweaty hand. In my panic, I'd forgotten all about it. He pushes a button.

"Hello?" he whispers into the rectangular box. The walkie-talkie is about the width of my palm and the length of my sewing shears. Impossibly small relative to its importance.

"Phee? Arden? Are you there?" Dad adds.

At first, there is no noise then static. I wince. What if the poacher hears it? Dad fiddles with the dials.

"Err, hello," Dad says. "This is a tourist. We need help."

Dad curses. He twists a different knob. He tries turning it in the opposite direction. He gives the contraption a little shake.

"What is it?" I say.

"The radio battery seems dead."

I try not to panic. How will anyone find us if we can't tell them where we are? The wind shifts and carries smoke from the fire toward us. What if an anti-poacher confuses us with a rhino killer?

"Are you sure?" I say.

"There was a flickering green light. Now it's gone." Dad says frowning. "But don't worry. I'm sure Junior told the anti-poaching team our position the last time he called in."

But he doesn't sound certain. And I heard no such thing.

"Okay, here's what we'll do." Dad runs his hand through his hair. "We're almost to that termite mound up ahead then it's a short jog to the Land Rover. Can you run?"

"I think so," I say, because my stomach really is better.

"Good. Junior said that the poacher had a double-barrel shotgun. He just shot once. Now we have to get him to shoot again. When he reloads, we'll race to the termite mound."

"Okay, but what are we going to do when we get to the Land Rover? We can't leave Junior," I say.

"That's why he ran off," Dad says, "to give us a chance to get away. Junior will probably circle back to the Land Rover. Maybe he's heading there now."

I hope Dad's right.

"Scoot closer, Claire," he says. "It would be a good idea for you to know a thing or two about this rifle given our circumstances."

Dad shifts position so that he faces the direction of the poacher. I track the man's progress creeping toward the termite mound that we had been hiding behind just minutes ago.

"Do *you* even know how to shoot a rifle?" I whisper.

"I went to a shooting range a few times as a kid. My father taught me with a gun similar to this. It had a hell of recoil."

Dad shifts his camera so that it rests against his back, then lifts the weapon. I know he's right. I have to learn so I inch closer to him. He shows me that there are two triggers, one for each chamber. Dad then demonstrates how to slip back the safety lever. He presses the firearm against his shoulder and explains how to aim using the express sights feature, essentially a very wide and shallow V with a white line marking the bottom. He tracks the poacher as the man arrives at our former hiding place. I'm stunned once again. Dad looks and sounds like he's a skilled hunter.

I gasp as my gut suddenly clenches. Sweat sprouts on my forehead. What is going on? As a kid, the pink earache medicine used to give me cramps similar to these. Could I be having a reaction to the Malarone? Or... oh no. No. No. No. Have I caught malaria despite all my precautions?

Dad says to me. "I know you're scared, but this is important."

"I can't focus right now," I say. "My stomach is cramping."

Dad is silent for a moment. The smoky air thickens like a dense fog.

"All right," Dad says at last. "We'll belly crawl. It will take longer, but the termite mound isn't far."

We creep forward. The grass rustles. Other than that, the occasional call of a bird is the only sound. And yet, my mind conjures all kinds of noises that I think are made by the poacher stalking us. My head aches. I fight the urge to throw up.

Dad was correct about the pace. It doesn't seem as if we're making progress. I poke my head up to see what the poacher's doing. He is bent over, examining the ground by the termite mound maybe one hundred feet away. He's tracking us like we're prey.

How long has it been since I panicked and fled the Land Rover? A half hour? An hour? We are about fifteen feet from the termite mound that separates us from where our camp vehicle stalled when I hear a loud sputter from that direction. I pancake myself to the ground because I mistake it for gunfire. But then I realize it's the Land Rover. This is followed by the whine of a reluctant alternator as the vehicle roars to life. Shrubbery crunches under tires and then the noise of the engine recedes. This can't be happening. Arden and Phee must have stayed in the Land Rover this whole time. Now they're going the opposite direction. They're leaving us behind.

"WAIT," Dad screams.

The crack of the rifle from behind us sends a bolt of fear through me. Arden and Phee couldn't have heard Dad's cry.

Not over the roar of the engine, but they must have detected the gunfire.

I close my eyes. Maybe they'd been trying to radio us. Maybe they established communication with the base camp, and were instructed to leave. But whatever the case, if the Land Rover departed without us, we are dead. I'm about to get up from our grassland cover and sprint in the direction of the vehicle when I feel Dad's hand clamp down on my ankle.

"Don't run, Claire," he says. "It's too dangerous."

My eyes come in and out of focus as I try to locate the poacher. When my vision clears, I spot a dark figure squatting on the ground about fifty feet away, as if studying our tracks. This man is a skilled tracker and he's following our trail of trampled grass.

"Daddy," I whisper. "We have to go."

"Hang on," he says so quietly I'm not sure he actually spoke. "Not yet."

The poacher stands still, staring in the direction of the Land Rover. Between the thickening smoke and tall grass, we are still hidden.

The poacher starts to run toward us. But then he veers off course, and I let out my breath as I see that his new route won't intercept us. Dad had been right to make me stay put.

"When he gets behind that fallen tree," Dad whispers, nodding toward an uprooted acacia, "we are going to stand up and run around behind that termite mound straight ahead, okay?"

My throat is so dry I'm not sure I can respond.

"Okay," I manage to whisper.

My stomach twists into knots.

"Ready? He's almost there," Dad says.

I'll have to do something I haven't done in a very long

time. I'll have to ask my father for help.

"I'm not sure that I can make it. I've got really bad cramps and things are blurry."

"Don't worry, honey. I'm not going anywhere without you. Okay. Now."

Dad pulls me to my feet. He flanks me on one side while holding the rifle in his free hand. The two of us scramble toward cover. I'm doubled over, but with Dad's support I make it without vomiting. I lean into the termite mound and pant. It's small, only waist-height, but a tree grows from the base of the mound with a trunk large enough to hide us. I peer around it to see what the poacher is doing. The man switches on his flashlight and appears to be backtracking to his vehicle.

"He probably thinks we were in the Rover and has given up," Dad whispers. "Arden and Phee probably saved our lives."

Or abandoned us to die. We're stranded in the bush with no food and little water. I'm so thirsty. My tongue feels like sandpaper. All we have is the Malarone-spiked water bottle around Dad's belt. Water neither of us should drink.

Dad reaches behind and I hear the click of his carabineer as if he has read my mind. He hands me the stainless-steel bottle. It has a flip top and a straw—an adult sippy cup. Thirst gets the better of me. I reach out and take the bottle. It's heavy and doesn't slosh too much so I know that it's still almost full. I know I shouldn't have any. I'm already seeing double and having cramps.

"Don't drink too much," he says. "We don't know when we'll be rescued. We need to ration."

I intend to only wet my mouth, but thirst takes control and I suck greedily. Dad stops me after two swallows.

The water settles my stomach. I blink a few times and to my relief my vision clears.

"Thanks," I whisper.

A rhino snorts from across the clearing. I thought they were long gone, but the sound is closer than I expect. I raise my head in time to see that the big creatures have not yet descended into the ravine. If I crane my neck to see about fifty feet further beyond these animals, I spot where the Land Rover should have been.

"I was going to say that we should follow the tracks of the Land Rover," Dad whispers. "But with the rhinos so close, we'll have to sit tight for the moment."

The putter of the poacher's car engine grows louder as if it's coming back. Dad lifts the rifle. My heart beats so fast I'm afraid I'll pass out. The poacher is coming after us.

Yellow headlights appear, revealing a small dune-buggy-like vehicle, with a giant windshield. Dad and I duck around the far side of the tree, but the vehicle swerves. I sneak a peek and see the profile of the lanky poacher. The car now heads in the direction of the rhinos. He's decided to complete the job that he and his brother had set out to do. He's coming for the rhinos. Where are the people who are supposed to protect them? Where is Junior?

The jeep coasts slowly toward the animals to get close without scaring them off. Now the vehicle stops and the poacher steps out. He takes out his shotgun and places his elbows on the hood of his jeep to line up his sight.

"We can't let him kill the rhinos," I say.

"I don't know." Dad sounds nervous, not at all like my self-assured father. "If I shoot to scare the rhinos, he'll know we didn't escape in the Land Rover. He's going to realize that we're still here—and he thinks we're his brother's killers. He'll come for us again. I can't risk it. I can't let anything happen to you."

"We have to do something," I say.

"Okay, okay," he says then straightens his back. "Plug your ears," he says. "And stay back. I'm going to try to disable the car."

Dad anchors the butt of the rifle into his shoulder, takes aim. I plug my ears as Dad pulls the trigger. He's propelled backward but keeps his balance. He leans to see around our natural fortress. I look, too. The poacher stares in our direction. It's just as Dad feared. Now, he knows where we are. Worse, the rhinos haven't startled.

The larger male rhino snorts and paws the ground. The barrel of the poacher's weapon comes up, aiming at us, not the rhino. Dad shoves me to the ground behind the mounded soil as two shots are fired in quick succession in our direction. Sand sprays around us. Dad hunkers down to reload.

The ground shakes as the rhinos finally bolt. It feels as though the whole world is shifting. I raise my head and scramble backward. They're headed in our general direction. The moonlight highlights the cloud of chalky dust that forms behind them. I chant Dugger's words in my head. Don't run. Don't run. Dad grips my arm as if he knows I'm thinking about fleeing.

I curl up into a ball wondering if being trampled hurts more than being shot. Dad lies beside me so that the giant beasts will reach him first. I wait, muscles tense, but the shifting earth suddenly tapers to a tremor as the rhinos veer off toward the lip of the plateau. I raise my head and watch the two giant beasts disappear from view into predator alley. If the poacher hadn't been out of bullets from shooting at us, he might have killed one. We've saved them. At least for now.

There's a click as the reloaded barrel of Dad's rifle engages then Dad peers around our earthen fort again.

"Bloody hell," he says. "He's... "

Dad ducks down as two more shots pepper the gray material of our hideout. I cover my head and try to make myself small. I can't believe this is happening.

Dad pops up and shoots then ducks. After a moment, he pokes his head around the tree.

"I got the bastard's front tire," Dad exclaims, "and the engine is billowing steam. My first bullet must have hit the radiator. But now we only have three more bullets. I think we should save them. We might need to fire one into the air to attract the attention of rescuers and we need more for protection."

He doesn't say from what—animal or human. But I agree with his plan. What has become of Junior? He must have heard the gunfire. Has he gotten into some kind of trouble?

"We have to hide," Dad says. "We'll go into the ravine. Can you run?"

"Yes," I say. "The water helped. I'm feeling better."

"See that opening in the shrubs behind us?" Dad says. "If you stay low, the termite mound should block his view. You go first. I'll follow. You ready?"

I nod. My legs wobble then engage as I sprint toward the edge of the plateau. I remember the presence of scrub brush and giant boulders in predator alley. There will be places to hide.

Dad and I skid down the slope. I dive behind a boulder and Dad follows. A branch snaps from above us on the plateau. Dad lifts the rifle and turns around as he pulls back the hammer. My heart thunders in my ears. But then leaves crunch further away. I tremble, imagining the man looping around and confronting us. Dad lowers the rifle then pats his pockets.

"Dammit," he whispers. "I lost the walkie-talkie."

"It wasn't working anyway," I say. "But how are we going to get out of here?"

Dad closes his eyes. At first I don't think he heard me but then he straightens his spine.

"I know exactly what we're going to do," Dad whispers. "We'll follow the rhinos. They're probably tagged with GPS trackers and the anti-poaching unit will make finding them their first priority. It's our best hope. Don't worry. We'll be safe."

Safe? A vengeful poacher wants to kill us. We don't have food or drug-free water. We're lost in the bush surrounded by fire, which could be flushing lions and leopards and hyenas toward us. We are far from safe.

CHAPTER FIFTEEN

Dad walks beside me as we venture further into predator alley to follow the rhinos. I still can't believe that we've been abandoned in the bush. In two short days, I've experienced strange colors, seen a man-eating lion, had a near miss encounter with a bushbuck, developed stomach cramps, and Kago—funny, charming Kago—is dead. My ears buzz from gunfire, and, oh yeah, I've been shot at by a poacher who is probably tracking us. I wish we had never come to Africa.

The ravine is a U shape with slopes ascending up to the plateaus on both sides at about a forty-five-degree angle. If I were to stand on Dad's shoulders, I might be able to view the plateau. The swale at the bottom is patchy, mostly cluttered with gravel, but sometimes coated with a mosaic of dead leaves from the scattered trees that line each embankment.

"I hope the rhinos were scared enough to poop," Dad leans close to say this in a quiet voice, so I know he's worried about the poacher. "The ground before us is too gravelly for tracks."

My eyes comb the earth at our feet for a large pile of gross, brown mulch. Finding these rhinos could mean the difference between being rescued or not.

I cringed when Junior handled the rhino dung. But his detailed explanation had stuck. The difference between rhino and elephant dung was that elephant excrement is orange and rhino poop is dark brown. It doesn't take a seasoned wildlife biologist to tell the difference. I don't see any big, dark brown piles, though a crusty white blob that practically glows in the moonlight lies a few feet ahead. Hyena spoor. Dugger had said that the bright white comes from the crunched bones that these carnivores ingest. The faded, dog-like footprints in the patch of nearby bare soil suggest the hyena activity is probably not recent.

No prints large enough to be rhino are anywhere around here. Did the creatures already lumber out of the ravine?

Dad stumbles. He shakes his head as if to dislodge something that has crawled into his ears.

"What is it?" I ask.

"I think I'm having a reaction to the Malarone. I'm seeing double," he says.

It takes me a moment to digest what he says. He might have to shoot the rifle, but he won't know which of the two objects to aim at. How will he protect us?

"I'm sorry, honey. The side effects of Malarone are supposed to be rare."

Side effects? Malarone causes double vision. What else? Could it also have caused my hallucinations? I've been a fool taking more than the recommended dose.

"I don't usually react to medicine," Dad adds. "Maybe I'm particularly sensitive, or maybe it's the stress."

No, it's the double dose I gave him by spiking his water. I should tell him what I've done. But now is not the time. We need to focus on getting out of this situation.

"Take my arm," I say.

As we walk side by side, the ravine changes from gravel to cobble. I still don't see any poop. I keep my head down, but Dad has the weapon raised. I don't know how he'll hit anything if he can't see straight. Our footfalls are making way too much noise. If the poacher is following us, we won't be hard to find.

"Keep searching for prints," Dad says. "Three toes. Elephant and hippos have four."

It's ironic that our survival may depend on keeping track of an endangered species.

"How will I know it's not white rhino tracks?" I say.

"The rear of the foot pad of the white rhino has an indentation in the middle and looks like a rounded W."

I hadn't paid attention to these details. But of course, Dad, the wannabe safari guide, had soaked up every word. I'm in way over my head.

"O-kay," I say. It comes out snarkier than I had intended.

"Claire, don't. Not now."

He's right.

"We will get through this," he adds. "But we have to work together."

I nod.

"Let's stop when we reach that boulder," he says. "I want to reload the gun anyway."

In the distance, hyenas chortle but not loudly enough to mask the deep "hun, hun, hun" of a lion's roar. According to Junior, lions don't vocalize when they are hunting. The sound sends a chill down my spine anyway. The image of the lion chewing on a human limb forms, and I can't push it away. Please, all I want is to escape this nightmare alive.

When we reach the big rock, Dad opens and empties the used casing from the chamber. I watch for movement in the shrubbery on the slopes of the ravine. Even if the poacher isn't tracking us, snakes or other dangerous animals could be lurking in there. Dad curses. He appears to be trying to insert the bullet slightly to the left.

"Do you want me to do it?" I ask.

I don't even think he heard my question. He must be concentrating too hard.

"Dad," I say, holding my hand out. "Let me help you."

He passes it over. The metal casing is cold, and given how much damage it can cause, way too light. I slip the bullet into the chamber. I hinge the barrel closed and keep possession of the rifle. I'm not sure I could shoot anything, but unlike Dad, I can see straight.

Behind us, the crackle of leaves makes me jump. My heart lurches into my throat, and I can't breathe. Is the poacher or some other animal stalking us?

It's too steep to crawl back up to the plateau. The eerie orange glow above us means the fire is nearby anyway. No choice. We have to keep going straight.

Dad cups my elbow. He's totally dependent on me to guide him. The thought terrifies me. One misstep could mean the difference between life and death. We have probably left tracks and been too loud. We've been fools.

A stretch of soft sand lies ahead, if we continue, we'll leave a clear trail for the man stalking us. A twig snaps behind us. Then light flashes. I turn and watch the beam sweep back and forth. The poacher's flashlight. He's closing in.

I move my father's hand off my elbow then, place his hands on each of my shoulders so his footsteps will fall where mine do. It's the only thing I can think of to keep him from stepping on leaves that will give away our position.

"We have to hurry," I whisper.

I set out at a steady pace. The rhinos' tracks are now clear in the sandy bottom, so I know we're going the right way.

A curve lies ahead. I tell myself it's going to be okay. We

can hide there. When we round the corner, a scream catches in my throat as a long-bodied animal about the size of a ferret runs up the bank and disappears into the brush, flicking its ringed-tail as if dismissing us.

"I think those were genets," Dad whispers. "Don't worry, they won't harm us."

They? How many did he see? I don't tell him there was only one.

Behind us, I hear a sneeze. A very human-sounding sneeze. The poacher is gaining on us. It's a straight shot ahead. No curves to hide us for a long stretch. I search the ravine to the left and right hoping to see a place to take cover, but would that be safe? I remember how Junior and Dugger scoped out the area for scorpions, snakes, and who knows what else, before allowing tourists to go behind a bush to relieve themselves. We shouldn't stop anyway. Staying close to the rhinos is our lifeline out of the bush.

I push forward then falter as the ravine fills with light as if a helicopter spotlight shines on the path ahead. I blink, confused. Above, a white streak extends down to the earth. A spiked halo surrounds the moon and it resembles a glowing magic wand. I blink at the mirage. This must be a Malarone side effect.

I hear a rustle. My head tilts upward in the direction where the noise originated from at the lip of the ravine. I remember Dugger's story about black mambas and spitting cobras. We're surrounded.

"Did that sound like a snake?" I whisper to Dad.

"No, honey," he says, pointing up. "I think it's the shrubs burning."

I crane my neck. The sky glows yellow. I want this to be a Malarone hallucination, but I catch a whiff of smoke. This is real. We are probably walking straight into the heart of the wildfire. We're lucky that the haze hasn't migrated downward into the ravine. But if the wind shifts, we could be in serious trouble. Outrunning the fire would be difficult in the best of circumstances but fleeing the flames to charge straight into the gunfire of a poacher is the last thing I want to do.

"Would the rhinos still go this direction if there's fire up ahead?" I whisper.

"I don't know," he says in a low voice.

Up ahead, the ravine forks into two paths. A large boulder protrudes at the apex of a narrow strip of land bisecting our two options.

"We could hide behind that rock," I whisper. "Maybe he'll walk right by us then we could follow him instead."

"But what if he spots us and shoots?" Dad says in a low voice. "No. We can't risk it. We need to keep to our original plan."

Err. Maybe not. The tracks reveal that the rhinos have gone in separate directions. One set follows the left fork, the other to the right.

"That's just great," I say.

"What's wrong?" Dad asks.

"The rhinos split up. Oh, Dad. We can't protect them both."

"Well then," Dad says, "we'll have to follow the female."

He's right. If the poacher kills the last female, the species will go extinct.

"How do I know which tracks to follow?" I whisper.

I raise my hand to keep my father from responding. Was that the shuffle of leaves? The man could be closer than

I thought. I don't hear anything more but I know we don't have much time to decide.

"What do you think?" I ask in a hushed voice.

"See which tracks sink deeper into the sand," Dad whispers. "She's heavy. That'll be her."

I wouldn't have thought of that. I drop to my knees next to the tracks that head left, grabbing a stick to measure the depth. Then I scramble to the other. The difference is slight, but I'm pretty sure the ones to the right are deeper. I see the glint of a flashlight again.

"Okay," I say with authority, even though I have my doubts, "to the right."

We walk fast. The central thin plateau is free of fire as is the raised land on our right. It's less smoky here.

"How's your vision? Is it better?" I whisper.

"Afraid not," he says. "I think it might be getting worse. Maybe I need some water."

"No," I blurt.

"Just a sip," he says.

I'm not ready to tell him the truth. But how do I deny him a reasonable request? We're both sweaty and need to stay hydrated.

"Not yet," I say, "we need to keep moving."

To my relief, Dad doesn't argue. I'm thirsty, too. I fantasize about filling my mouth and letting the tepid liquid trickle down my throat. It would taste better than chocolate, better than ice cream. Just a sweet mouthful of water.

I stare at the rhino prints as I progress. Are we following the pregnant female? What if I picked the wrong path? This may be one of the most important decisions of my life. The survival of one of the most spectacular animals in South Africa depends on the course that I've now taken.

Wait. Crap. What a fool I am. I stop short and Dad bumps into me. At least we haven't gone far down this path.

"I've made a huge mistake. We have to go back. We have to follow the male," I say. "The poacher is following us, so we've got to lure him *away* from the female."

Dad doesn't say anything for a moment. "You're so right, Claire. The poacher isn't going to care about the sex of the animal. He only wants a horn. But I don't know. What if it's too late? What if he's already following us on this fork and we are backtracking straight to him? He's got a gun and he thinks we killed his brother."

"We can avoid encountering him if we hurry. It's not far. Come on. We don't have time to debate this."

I step behind Dad to face back toward way we came and say, "Turn around and put your hands on my shoulders."

He does. I clamp one of my hands down on top of Dad's and clutch the rifle with the other. I'm trying to align Dad as if we are in a chain dance so that we can move faster. Soon we are almost running. It's an awkward gait, but Dad adjusts. Now, more than ever, I hope that I've read the tracks correctly. We have to beat the poacher to the fork and lead him toward the male rhino. We just have to.

CHAPTER SIXTEEN

We reach the fork without intercepting the poacher and enter the other path. Now, we have the narrow bit of land on our right and the plateau with the raging fire on our left. Our confusing tracks probably haven't fooled the poacher. I can almost feel the man's presence pressing in on me. Dad must sense something too because he keeps urging me forward. We don't even know how far ahead of the male rhino we are, but the female will be safe. We've made a good choice. My heart strums with fear as the fire crackles above.

"I'm okay, I'm okay," I say over and over.

"Shh," Dad whispers.

He's right. I need to calm down. I'm on the verge of hyperventilating. And the smoky air burns my lungs.

Above us, on the plateau, burning trees snap and pop making me jump. Oh, oh god. I can't breathe. I stop. My breath slows to a wheeze.

"Deep inhale," Dad says as he glances up at the crackling fire. "We're going to be okay. The ravine will act as a natural fire break."

Then Dad nudges me forward and I move on, because what else is there to do? As my history teacher had preached back on that horrible day when my life fell apart, there's no going back. If the poacher rushes at us, there's only one direction to run: straight ahead, toward an animal that weighs several tons. Hadn't Dugger said that every time he'd encountered a black rhino, the animal had charged his vehicle? Wasn't the dent on the Land Rover bumper the result of a rhino horn?

Stop it. Stop it. Stop it. Sweat drips down my face, blurring my vision. In my head, I hear my yoga teacher telling me to take in a deep breath, and I do as I stare at the ground. The rhino tracks are there along with cat-like prints large enough to be made by a lion. I'm too frightened to utter even the smallest of whispers to tell Dad.

"Halloo," a male calls from behind.

I stop so fast Dad slams into me. I'm about to shout a response when Dad clamps his hand over my mouth and shoves me forward. What is he doing? The anti-poaching unit has found us.

"Keep moving," he says into my ear, "that could be the poacher trying to trick us."

It hadn't crossed my mind that we'd have to figure out if anyone we encounter is part of the anti-poaching unit, a guide, or the poacher trying to kill us.

"An anti-poacher wouldn't say that," Dad whispers. "He'd ask if we were all right and tell us he wanted to help us."

My heart sputters like a car engine on a cold morning. Dad's right. Of course, it's the poacher. No one else knows where we are. I nod and Dad drops his hand away from my mouth.

"Halloo. You there. Stop. I help you."

Terror hatches in my heart and spreads through my veins. I surge forward. The poacher's voice had come from close behind us. Too close.

"That's right," Dad whispers. "Keep moving and don't say a word. He probably wants to gauge the distance between us."

Up ahead, a large, feathered creature erupts from a tree in soundless flight. It's huge—bigger than a microwave. I duck.

"It's okay. Only one night bird is that big. It's an eagle owl and it won't hurt you," Dad whispers.

The bird passes overhead and back along the ravine in the direction we've just traveled. Seconds later, gunfire shatters the air. Dad pushes me forward though I don't need the encouragement. The poacher must have shot at the owl, which means he's jumpy. But he'll have at least one more bullet before he needs to reload. I shudder. He's closing in.

"We need a plan," I say in a hushed voice. "We're stuck in a ravine between a poacher and a hostile rhino."

"Keep going," Dad says.

I don't argue, but I still can't think of a scenario where we don't end up dead. I'd been clinging to the idea that the anti-poaching unit would magically appear and save the day. But can they get to us in a vehicle with the fire raging up on the plateau, assuming they are even tracking the rhino? And we don't know how far behind we are. The animal could be a mile away by now.

Arden and Phee, if they're still alive and can find their way out of this park, probably wouldn't be able to direct anyone to the last place we were seen. And there's the chance that the English couple could presume we're dead anyway.

"I think... I think we have to go to Plan B," Dad says.

I wish he'd said that with conviction.

"Ooo-kay," I say.

"We'll use a bullet to shoot the poacher in the leg," he says. "It's our best chance."

Except you can't see straight enough to shoot. I've never fired a rifle and we have three bullets. Three chances and then he figures out we've run out of ammunition. Great plan.

"We'll have to do it soon," Dad adds. "He's not far behind, and if he catches us…"

Dad doesn't need to say more.

"The next curve in the ravine or the next big boulder," Dad says.

I want to protest. I want to tell him that we have to wait until he can see well. I can't shoot a person. Hell, I can't even shoot.

"I'm sorry," Dad says as if reading my thoughts. "It's going to have to be you. All you need to do is hit a leg so he won't be able to follow us."

"Hallo," he calls again. He's almost upon us now. "I hear you. Stop now."

I move faster because I can't shoot him. I just can't. I survey the area for an escape route. We're surrounded by steep banks, too much loose soil, and only sparse vegetation. It would be impossible to exit this gully. Up ahead, the path curves. If we don't make a stand here, he's so near that we'll surely be shot. I start to shake. This is where Dad and I will have to stop and I'll have to shoot him. What if I miss?

"Is that one boulder on the hill?" Dad says. "Or two?"

"Just one," I say.

"Then this is the place. You can do this," he says. "Remember how good you were at archery in Girl Scout camp?"

Really? That was six years ago. I was shooting arrows, not bullets. Girls giggled beside me. My life didn't depend on whether I hit a moving target. And I wasn't trying to hurt a fellow human being.

We catch a bit of luck. There is an animal trail skirting around behind the boulder. Probably during winter months when water fills this ravine, wildlife has made a path down into the gulch to grab a quick drink. We head up the slope. The worn track prevents us from crunching leaf litter. The air smells of sage intermixed with burning wood. The moonlight is strong, but the shadow of the boulder hides us.

My hands clench the rifle as we squat behind the big rock. I don't want to hurt this man and I can't stop quivering. How will I hold steady long enough to take aim?

I visualize the classroom floor of my yoga class. I seek only stillness and after a moment of focusing on my breath, I calm down. I position myself at angle that gives me a clear view of the gully.

"That's my girl," Dad says. "Stay centered. You can do this."

Pressure forms behind my eyes. It's as if the world has been emptied of air. Breathe, I tell myself. Find your core. Be present in the moment. Think about aiming. It's a target. Just a target. Just his leg. That's all.

The boulder will shield us from any return fire that the poacher might deliver. This is the best situation we could hope for. If I miss, the man might retreat, but he'll be back for us. I can't think about missing. We need spare ammunition. What if we encounter a lion or leopard before we're rescued? I have to pretend that I have one bullet. I get one shot. Please, let me hit his leg, maybe a knee or an ankle. That's all I need to do.

I lean against the rock, and as I place the rifle butt on my shoulder, I glimpse the scissor tattoo on my fingers. I'd been strong when I'd had that done. I hadn't cried out once. I must find that same inner strength now. I peer through the scope. Four crosshairs meet in the center. I close one eye then wonder if that is the right thing to do.

"Release the safety," Dad says.

"Where is it?" I ask.

"There's a lever on the barrel," he whispers. "Toggle it so that the arrow doesn't point at the word safe."

The orange light of the fire along with the moon above provides enough light to see the lever, but not enough to read any engraved words. I follow his instructions, hoping that I've moved it to the correct position.

"You'll want to brace the butt into your shoulder to steady your aim," he continues.

Leaves crackle. A dark form appears lit by the orange glow of the fire. As he rounds the corner, I notice his rifle points at the ground. He doesn't seem concerned about an ambush at all. Perhaps he thinks all tourists are fools.

"It will have a kick," Dad says. "Hold tight after you shoot and don't let go of the barrel. Don't forget to aim low."

You can do this, I tell myself. The man is slender. The only thing remarkable about him is that his left arm clutches the barrel of a shotgun. He is in dark clothing. If it weren't for the firelight, I wouldn't have been able to make out his form at all.

"Now," Dad says.

No time to think. No time to chicken out. I sight the barrel at the man's left foot and feel cold steel curl around my index finger. I squeeze the trigger.

The force of the blast pushes me backwards and the noise in my ears creates a loud ringing. Right before my finger curled around the trigger I had closed my eyes.

When I open them, there is no body lying on the ground. He's not standing clutching his leg. There's nothing at all. I've missed. The man must have retreated around the curve in the path. And now he knows we are at war.

CHAPTER SEVENTEEN

My knees vibrate so much that they won't hold me. I collapse against the boulder. The gun feels as heavy as my overloaded school backpack, but I clutch it tight. I have failed. I expected the poacher to taunt us with another "halloo" or deliver a nasty curse. If he has, I can't hear him because my ears still hear the thunder of the gunshot.

"I missed," I lean close to Dad's ear and say "Oh Daddy, I missed. He's going to come back."

I glance up to my right at the central finger of land then to my left up at the edge of the plateau that lies about ten feet above us. Has the man climbed atop of either of these land features? Is he looking down at us? From there we could now be in the crosshairs of his rifle. We'd be most vulnerable if he chose the plateau.

"We have to go," I say. "Now."

Dad doesn't budge. He eases the weapon from my grasp. He reloads with our final spare bullet, engages the safety and hands it back. A fully loaded gun, but with only two shots. Two chances.

"Let's wait a minute," he speaks into my ear.

His words sound muffled as if he is talking to me from inside a metal box. I blow air through my nose, and my ears clear although an unpleasant buzzing persists.

Dad takes a drink of water. He hands me the bottle, but I don't take it.

"I'm okay," I say, though every fiber of my body screams for water.

Dad frowns and opens his mouth to protest, but a loud noise silences him. I duck as if it were gunfire, but it neither sounded like a rifle blast, nor did it come from the direction of the poacher. Dad's eyes widen as the roar amplifies and the earth shifts under our feet. It has to be something big. Perhaps the gunfire spooked the rhino, or maybe the fire has spread into predator alley. Whatever the cause, a very large animal is coming toward us. Dad and I press against the boulder on the bank. I think we'll be out of harm's way as long as the panicked beast doesn't shift direction and turn up the slope.

And then it's upon us. Without the elevation and protection of the Land Rover, the rhino seems even larger out here. It's the male and he's not encumbered by the weight of pregnancy. This creature moves like a Humvee or a small tank and is fast despite its short, trunk-like legs. Didn't Junior say rhinos could reach speeds of thirty-five miles per hour?

This enormous tank of gray flesh is armed with a sharp weapon. His horn protrudes from its skull as if the animal is tailor-made for a jousting match. The big animal is close now, but given his awkward bulk, he won't be able to navigate up the hill where we are. The animal races by our boulder, snorting his displeasure and leaving an earthen scent in his wake.

The rhino rounds the bend that we passed a few minutes ago. I hold my breath, afraid the poacher will shoot, but there's no gunfire blast. When I finally exhale, I'm relieved that my ears have mostly cleared and my hearing is restored.

"Do you think the poacher got out of the way?" I say.

Dad shrugs.

He must have though. There was no scream of pain. What will he do now? Will he follow the rhino or continue to hunt us? Surely, his thirst for money will prevail.

The ground beneath me shudders again, and a herd of about six zebras appear, whistling in terror. Two things register: One, we're on a game trail that leads out of the gulch. Two, the panicked animals might try to cut out of this chasm to reach the plateau above us. We'd be standing in their way if they turn.

"Move," I yell at Dad, as I scramble up the side of the boulder.

Dad follows my lead. But the zebras don't turn. They keep to the bottom of the dry channel, leaving behind a cloud of gritty dust.

"The fire," I whisper, "it must..."

The roar of hooves drowns out my words as a small herd of wildebeest stampede through the gully. But these animals also continue straight ahead like the zebras did. After they are gone, I stare down at the compacted trail, at the morass of cloven footprints in the center of the ravine—evidence that we would have been trampled if we'd been down there. Even if the poacher managed to dodge the charging rhino, maybe the zebras and wildebeest have accomplished what I had not.

My muscles tense up in anticipation of another wave of animals, but nothing happens. If we continue ahead, will we encounter raging fire or fleeing hyenas or lions? Going forward seems like a bad option. The only way out is to turn around and backtrack toward the poacher. But is he standing in the center of the gulch anticipating our retreat? Should we wait? If a wildfire is on the heels of these stampeding animals, we don't have time to second guess. The smell of burnt wood registers. Then, tendrils of smoke appear up ahead.

"What should we do?" I say. "I think the male rhino is long gone."

"We have to backtrack and find the female," Dad says. "We need to stay close to one of the rhinos if we're going to be rescued."

Go back toward the poacher who wants to kill us? All I want to do now is get out of this death trap and away from this madman. I bite my upper lip. I'm too afraid. I'm no hero. I've just shot at a man who's already angry at us. Hell, I don't even know how far off I was.

As I've been frozen with indecision, the smoke has thickened. There's no time. The fire is coming. We have no choice but to turn around.

"We have to get out of here," I say.

I turn and Dad reattaches his hands to my shoulders as if we're doing a line dance.

If the poacher avoided the stampeding animals and lurks around the corner, we'll be marching toward death. I swallow and raise the rifle, squinting at the darkness up ahead. Nothing happens. We creep forward around the curve.

The smoky air irritates my throat, but I suppress my cough. I pick up my pace, and somehow Dad matches my gait without stumbling. I can only hope that the poacher is equally afraid of the fire and has decided to abandon his mission.

Despite my careful steps, smooth, light-colored pebbles crunch underfoot. Then our movements are silenced as the ground morphs to a sandy texture. It seems as if it's taking too long to retrace our steps to where the ravine forked. Then I recognize a tilted boulder and know that we're close to where the poacher could be lurking.

I brace myself as if tightening my abs will somehow

prevent a bullet from penetrating my stomach. The moonlight illuminates dark splatters discoloring the sand. Could that be blood? Could I have hit the poacher after all? But it's just as likely that one of the fleeing animals was bleeding. As I trot on, the splotchy trail continues. If the splatters were from the zebras or the wildebeest, wouldn't we have seen drops back near the boulder? If the poacher is wounded, not only will the blood trail offer clues to his whereabouts, but also he'll be weakened. And if the red dots turn at the fork in the direction of the female rhino, then I'll have more confidence that I hit him, and I'll know his whereabouts.

A tree at the lip of the small, dry gorge crashes into the gully behind us about one hundred feet away. The canopy of the downed tree is shrouded in flames and the dry shrubs on the banks catch fire. I sprint forward and Dad tightens his grip. The area is awash in orange and red.

I pull my shirt up to my nose to avoid breathing in the smoke, clutching the rifle in my free hand. Dad coughs and stumbles but regains his footing. I'm jogging so fast that I almost miss the split.

We turn into the other fork. There aren't any new rhino tracks, so the male must have kept running straight. If the fire spreads into this path too, we could end up surrounded by it. My eyes zero in on blood splatters and human footprints. I stop short, and Dad plows into me. I almost do a face plant before I regain my balance.

"What is it?" Dad says between coughing fits.

"Blood," I say.

"What?" Dad says.

"I must have nicked the poacher," I say. "He's bleeding. And I see the soles of his shoes, too. He's chosen to track the female instead of us and he's up ahead somewhere."

"We have to save her," Dad says. "And she's still our best hope for rescue. I doubt we'll be able to track down the male."

He's right.

A knot of anxiety seizes my chest. Instinct tells me to run in the opposite direction. But there is no choice. We must follow the poacher.

"Claire?" Dad says.

"This way," I say.

And with that I move on. Dad gently squeezes my shoulder muscles as if to urge me forward like a cowboy applying pressure to his horse. The rifle seems heavier now.

As we move further up this path, the smoke clears, and the light from the full moon makes tracking easier. For now, the fire hasn't spread into this area of predator alley. The dark splotches of blood seem to be larger. Maybe I already managed to injure the man enough. I slow down because the drops are closer together. I suspect that means the man has dropped his pace. Will the smoke mask the scent of blood or are predators already honing in on this wounded man?

"What is it?" Dad asks.

Sweat drips from my forehead and my khaki shirt sticks to me like a second skin. My breath comes in ragged gasps and my throat feels like brittle leaves. I don't care if Dad's water is tainted. I have to take a drink.

"Water," I say. "Can I have some water?"

Dad hands me the bottle. The container sloshes, but it's lighter than I expect. What if we run out? That scares me as much as the thought of catching up with the poacher, as much as encountering the fire that still rages on the plateau above our heads. I take the tiniest swallow that I dare. Every pore of my body screams for more, but I return the bottle. He only takes one sip, too, even though rivulets of sweat cascade down his temples. He must be conserving the water for me. My heart opens with gratitude. This small gesture makes a bigger statement that a million declarations of love. If only I could change what I've done. I put Malarone in his water and now he sees double. I bolted out of the Land Rover and put us both in danger. I have acted like a horrible brat this entire trip. No, even longer than that. And yet he still loves me.

"I'm sorry, Dad," I say. "For all of it."

He pulls me into a hug and kisses the top of my head.

"No, Claire," he says, "I'm the one who made a mess of things."

Something thuds. I listen for sounds above the crackle and roar of the fire but hear nothing else. The only good thing about this background noise is that it masks our approach. I hope that the poacher has assumed that we would continue our retreat out of the ravine and not track the female rhino.

We navigate slowly through a snake-like twist in the path. When I spot the lanky form of the poacher, I step back out of sight. I put my finger to my lips to indicate to Dad to be quiet then guide him toward a cluster of shrubs growing along the bank. My heart is in jack-hammer mode. The tip of an axe bulges from the man's backpack. He is studying the ground as he walks. In one hand, he grips a shotgun. His other hand glistens red where he clutches his right side. Now I know without a doubt that I hit him.

I can't believe that he still pursues the rhino. Junior said that a rhino horn weighs about five pounds, so this man probably reasoned that he would have the stamina to carry one out. But removing the horn will require a fair amount of strength. This injured man must be desperate.

The idea of shooting him from behind occurs to me, but how could I?

"Any idea how close the poacher is to the rhino?" Dad whispers.

"No."

Maybe the female will charge at first sight of this man. A pregnant mother surrounded by fire isn't likely to be indecisive. She might spare me from an impossible decision.

The poacher would have to shoot her quickly. He must know the exact spot to target. Is that between the eyes? Is it behind the front legs? Is that where a rhino's heart is?

I peer around the shrub. The poacher has shuffled forward. Although he's still within sight, he's too far away for me to take aim if I somehow find the courage to try again to shoot him in the leg. Another patch of shrubbery that we can use as cover lies about half the distance between us.

"Let's move to where I can get a better view of the poacher and maybe even see if the rhino is up ahead."

Dad takes the rifle and releases the safety before handing it back.

"If he lifts his rifle," Dad says, "shoot him. Don't let him kill her and the baby." After a moment, he adds, "Or us."

"Shh," I say.

If I miss his leg again, a second bullet to his torso could kill him. Can I risk it? But then I think about the unborn baby black rhino. I think about the extinction of an entire species. How can I stand by and let this happen?

We inch forward mimicking the way the two lionesses we had seen move in unison as they hunted. The bushes still seem an impossible distance away. Dad smells like my sweaty gym clothes, or maybe it's a whiff of my own fear. I try to think of an outcome where some animal—human or rhino—doesn't end up dead. I don't want that to be the rhino or us. But I don't want to kill the poacher either.

The man has stopped short like an impala about to take a drink at a watering hole and senses danger. I freeze too. Did he hear us?

We're too far from the next clump of bushes to dive forward without making a lot of noise. If he turns and sees us, he will lift his rifle and shoot. We are less than thirty yards away. I'm in front with Dad behind. I will be his first target.

This killer with his double barrel won't miss. I start to tremble. I take a deep breath before slowly lifting the weapon to plant it on my shoulder.

The poacher turns his head. He raises his rifle in my direction, but he doesn't take aim. He probably never expected he'd be shooting a young, blonde American teen.

My heart hammers so hard I can feel its beat at the base of my throat. My fear is so palpable I can taste its metallic venom in my mouth. This is surreal. A man and a girl standing in the midst of fire, pointing double-barrel rifles at each other. I should pull the trigger now as he hesitates, but I can't. Tears blur my vision.

"You? It was you?" he says.

Dad's hands clench my shoulders. I know what he wants me to do. My finger curls against the trigger; the metal cold against my skin. I can't do this. I can't shoot him. My eyes dart from the brush, to the cover, and back to him. Why couldn't Junior have stayed with us? He'd said he'd protect me. Now I'm going to die.

The lavender scent of my mother's perfume fills my nostrils. I think about the pink ballet shoes I've kept in my closet, the silky, golden fur of my dog. Sketches I've made for clothes ripple through my mind. I see my mother's face crumple when she hears of my death. I see her collapse to the ground at the news. And Dad. If he makes it out alive. All the guilt he will endure. He will be forever sad. I don't want to die. I don't want to hurt the people I love. A solid mass of resolve clunks to the pit of my stomach. I have to shoot this man, before he kills me. I grip the rifle tighter.

"For. My. Brother," he says as he takes aim.

I can't do this. My hand starts to shake. I focus on his left knee, but now I'm quaking all over. The voice in my heads screams: *PULL THE TRIGGER*. My finger obeys and squeezes hard. Too hard. I discharge both bullets in rapid succession.

CHAPTER EIGHTEEN

My collar bone aches from the recoil as if it has been whacked by a baseball bat. A high-pitched buzz floods my ears. I had failed to brace myself for the recoil and the second bullet missed. But it doesn't matter.

The impact of the first bullet hitting his belly pushes the man backward. What have I done? I've missed in the worst possible way. I had only wanted to hit his leg.

The poacher's descent to the ground seems to happen in slow motion, even as he yells out in Afrikaans what must either be a slew of curses or a prayer for mercy or forgiveness. He loses his grip on the gun as he falls. It bounces out of his reach.

My body feels as though it will burst from all the fear and horror coursing through my veins. A scream fills my throat, taking up too much space, demanding release.

"Claire," Dad shouts in a panicked voice, "are you all right?"

The urge to run swells in my chest. Don't run, I tell myself. You can't run. I close my eyes and count.

"Claire?" Dad repeats in a rising crescendo.

"Yeah," I squeak. My eyes flutter open then I swallow hard. "I'm okay. Stay here."

I rush forward in the dim light. I'm going to take away the poacher's weapon. I've watched too many cop shows where the villain comes back to life and shoots the heroine even though the bad guy appears dead.

When I reach the poacher's crumpled form, I kick the weapon even further away. Blood seeps through his thin shirt at the center of his belly. His chest doesn't rise and fall. I can't bring myself to touch his neck to feel for a pulse. But it doesn't matter. His eyes are open and unblinking. He's dead.

Oh god. Oh god. This can't be really happening. My head rings and I lose my grip on the gun. My arms clutch my belly as if I'm the one who has just been shot then my hands come up to cover my mouth. I can't hold still. My legs feel like jelly, but they're moving me around on a random course. My stomach roils as though a rhino horn has gored my stomach.

Then the ground slips out from under me. I land about an arm's length from the dead man and start to cry.

"I'm sorry," I blubber. "I didn't mean it."

I hear the snarl of a big cat. A leopard perches on one of the many boulders that line the dry streambed. I squint not believing it. Several things dawn on me all at once. My gun is empty and even though the poacher's rifle might still have ammunition, I have foolishly kicked it too far away. I can't lunge for it because the guides have warned us to never, ever, make sudden movements near big cats. It could trigger an attack.

Dugger's words at our initial safety briefing tumble through my brain.

"What do you do if you see a leopard?"

"Don't run."

"Even if it's coming at you and you see the yellow of its eyes?"

"Don't run."

Now I know why the guides had been so emphatic. I'm sitting before a leopard, and every ounce of strength I have is focused on not getting up to run.

"Claire?" Dad calls. "Is everything all right?"

The leopard's ears flatten. It crouches as if to launch an attack, so I stay quiet, even though Dad is probably freaking out right now.

"Claire?" Dad says.

The direction of his voice suggests that he is standing in the center of the gulch. The leopard hisses. I want to tell him to shut up, but I don't want to blink much less speak. Then Junior's added advice hits.

Bigger. I'm supposed to make myself look larger.

I stand slowly, raising both arms over my head. The leopard curls a lip. Hadn't Junior told me that a leopard will warn you by vocalizing? And Dugger had said it was a good idea to retreat slowly from a big cat, not straight backwards, but sideways and away. I start to move.

The leopard roars so loud that it sounds like a foghorn blasted in my ear. I freeze. My muscles gather to run. It is only my mind counter-screaming the words "don't run" that prevents me from bolting.

"Claire," Dad shouts. "Don't run."

I silently urge him to shut up. The sound of Dad's voice has startled the animal. It turns its head in the opposite direction. I immediately realize the problem. We are both blocking the leopard's retreat from the fire.

"I'm o-ookay." My voice shakes and betrays that I'm on the verge of losing it. "I'm coming that way. Back away sideways toward the right bank of the ravine."

"Don't run," he says. "Even if it charges. Remember the chant Kago taught us."

If I weren't so scared, I would roll my eyes. But I start to recite the words in my head. *I will not run, I will not bolt, for if I do, the leopard will too.* The rhythm gives me confidence.

And as the distance expands and I edge closer to my father, I think I might make it.

But then a tree on the rim of the plateau catches fire. I turn in time to see the leopard leap from the rock and barrel toward me. It charges with its belly low to the ground, its ears plastered to its head. The lower fangs exposed by its open mouth seemed to glow in the orange light of the fire. Four giant, sharp teeth. It delivers a horrible roar as it descends. My legs turn wooden and I can't move, even though my brain screams at me to run. Huge yellow orbs outlined by black bore into my eyes.

I will not run, I will not bolt. Fear clogs my brain and I can't remember the rest.

Time stands still and everything slows as the leopard closes in. My legs quiver, and I'm afraid I'll fall, but then the big cat streaks past my frozen form—passing close enough that I could have reached out and touched its sleek, spotted fur. It reeks of rotten meat and something vile. If "sinister" has a smell, it would be this stench.

My head swivels to check if it will attack Dad. He has moved out of the leopard's direct path, but it veers and leaps at him. Its tackles my father the way a domestic cat pounces on a toy.

"Nooooo," I scream, rushing toward my father.

As Dad falls to the ground, a blood curdling screech erupts from my throat, as wild and as feral as the beast that has attacked my father.

Dad has done exactly what he was supposed to do. He has tucked his chin and curled into a ball, using his hands to cover his neck. The big cat is in a state of frenzy. I feel the heft of the rifle in my hands, but it has no bullets. I fling the useless weapon at the big animal and nail it in the head. It whips around to face me.

I freeze even though every muscle in my body screams at me to RUN. The leopard's tail twitches. Dad remains curled in a ball, not moving a muscle so he doesn't know that the leopard's focus is on me now. Its lip curls back and the animal makes a horrible, deep rumble. I tried to remember the chant but my thoughts dart around before I can grasp them.

Above on the plateau, a tree explodes in flames. The leopard startles and flees back toward the fork.

I collapse next to my father. He's face down on the path, unmoving.

"Dad," I scream. "Daddy."

My heart thunders like a herd of stampeding elephants. Is he dead? Blood oozes from under his fingers where he still clutches his neck and a giant tear in the back of his vest and through his shirt reveals a gash that travels from his shoulder to the bottom of his shoulder blade. Through a rip in his pants, I see a second cut that appears to have sliced open his right thigh. The attack lasted less than a few seconds, but the leopard has caused major wounds.

"Daaaaadee," I screech.

His head turns and he rolls all the way over. Is his glazed expression severe pain or shock? Blood stains the ground beneath him.

My father slowly releases his hand from his neck and I see that his artery isn't slashed. The blood has come from scratches on the backs of his hands. He reaches out his arms like a child wanting to be picked up.

"Oh, Claire," he says in a voice hoarse with emotion. "You're okay."

But I'm not okay. A dead man's body lies ahead.

I'm going to have to tell Dad what I've done.

"I... I killed the poacher, Daddy," I say. "I didn't mean to. He was going to shoot me and I—"

"Oh, baby," Dad says. "Oh no, no, no."

Dad's horrified expression makes my stomach lurch as the full weight of what I have done hits me. I fall into his arms moaning and weeping.

"Not your fault. Not your fault. Oh, Claire. I should have never put you in that position. I should have been the one. Oh, baby."

I shake uncontrollably. I think I might throw up, so I gulp air.

"He didn't give you a choice," Dad continues, petting my head as if I were a dog. "I heard what he said. It was self-defense."

His words help me calm down. I wipe my eyes and see the blood stains on the ground have spread. I reach deep to pull myself together. I sit up.

This is my fault too. If I hadn't shot the poacher, I could have killed the leopard. Or maybe the big cat would have attacked the poacher instead. Or if I hadn't run from the Land Rover in the first place or spiked Dad's water with Malarone, things could have turned out differently. Will there ever be an end to the consequences of my foolish actions?

A voice in my head—the nasty one that usually tells me what a loser I am—snarls at me to *STOP. Just STOP wallowing in self-pity. You need to help your dad and find the rhino. Nothing else matters.*

My inner voice propels me into action. I roll back onto my heels.

I examine his injuries. I remove the camera, which appears undamaged, from his neck and loop the strap around my own then ease off his vest. There's blood. A lot of blood oozing through his shirt at the shoulder and more blood is seeping through his safari pants. My stomach churns and I swallow the bile that rises in my throat.

I have to be strong. I can't let him die. If he dies, I die. He needs to be airlifted. But there is no radio to call for help. A helicopter wouldn't even be able to find us in all this smoke, nor would it be able to land in this ravine.

Dad's first aid kit that he packed and religiously carried in his backpack during the game drives would come in handy now. I had thought it was a ridiculous thing to do since Dugger had said every vehicle had an extensive supply of emergency bandages and other paraphernalia. But what I wouldn't give if Dad had his backpack now with that kit inside. But Dad left it behind in the Land Rover, and it disappeared when Phee and Arden drove away.

I push aside Dad's shirt and examine the wounds on his back. None of them appear too deep. Already, the blood is starting to thicken. I manage to tear a few strips from his ripped shirt and wrap a cut on his thigh. Dad still seems dazed. I leave his vest off.

"Can I have some water?" he asks.

Water. My dry throat aches for it, too. But we have to keep moving. What if the leopard comes back? Or what if hyenas smell the blood?

"Soon," I say. "Can you stand?"

Dad manages to shift to hands and knees then slowly rises to his feet. He winces as he tries to put weight on his right leg. But now that he is up, I have no idea where to go.

If we go forward toward the rhino, the fire might spread into this gully, or we might encounter another stampede. Dad wouldn't be able to scramble up the banks and get out of the way. And yet I can't bring myself to turn around and retreat toward the leopard either. If we find the rhino, surely the anti-poachers will eventually track her down. This is still our best option.

"Lean on me," I say. "I think the rhino is just ahead."

I know no such thing, but if he's aware that I'm lying, he lets it slide. He takes a faltering step forward and then another.

The nasty voice informs me not to look at the dead man as approach. *DON'T YOU DARE LOOK*, it commands. And so I turn my face away from the poacher's body as we pass his fallen form. The scornful creature in my head tells me not to be so stupid. *Go get his gun.*

I have Dad rest against a boulder, while I return to collect the dead man's rifle. And this time I peek at what I've done despite the protesting voice screaming in my head. When I pick up his weapon, the enormity of it all threatens to flatten me. The pooled blood around his body, the vacant eyes seem to hold an accusation. I know this image will haunt me. I will never be able to return to the innocent girl I used to be. The voice in my head agrees. *Stupid girl. I told you not to look. There's no going back from this.*

CHAPTER NINETEEN

Dad insists on taking the camera from me so that I'm free to move unhindered if I need to shoot at a charging animal. We don't get far from the dead man's body before Dad stumbles on a rock in the streambed. His weight drags me forward and I teeter off balance. My breath catches as the earth tilts upward. My hand—the one with the rifle—reaches out to catch my fall. The weapon feels hot in my grip as I realize my mistake. I hadn't checked to see if the safety on the poacher's shotgun was engaged.

I twist to the side, but the gun butt hits anyway. I feel the smooth base slip in my grasp, the jarring thrust of impact. I close my eyes expecting a bullet to discharge straight into my body. But only gravel and dirt spray around me as I hit the ground. Dad makes an *umpf* sound as he lands beside me. He's rolled to one side, too, to protect his camera.

I sit up, brushing dirt from my face. My shaking fingers fumble to engage the safety on the rifle. I check to see if it's loaded. It is. There's one bullet left in the chamber. I hadn't thought about rummaging through his pockets for more ammunition, but I'm not sure I could have stomached touching a dead man anyway.

"You okay?" I ask Dad.

"Yeah."

There's less of a smoky haze this close to the ground. Dad lies on his side breathing hard, clutching his leg.

"Dad?"

What if he can't get up again? Then what? Should I leave him behind and continue to track the rhino? What if hyenas come? If I leave the rifle with him, what will I do if I encounter another leopard or the man-eating lion?

My inner voice chimes in with her opinion. *Are you kidding me? You can't leave him behind.*

This wiser, stronger version of myself is right. The orange glow in the sky suggests that the fire has grown bigger. Dad has to get up. He has to.

"Rise and shine," I say, though it's still nighttime.

I see Dad's resolve dying in his eyes. He's going to tell me to leave him. But I can't let him think that way.

"Claire——" he says.

"Have some water," I interrupt, handing him the bottle that I carry now to ease his burden, even though it weighs next to nothing. I try to take his camera again, but he refuses to give it up.

"Two sips," I say.

He drinks then hands the bottle back.

"Your turn," he says.

My throat feels like it has been scraped with a dull razor blade. I want to guzzle the water we still have, but I have to care for my dad, so I take only enough to coat my parched throat. So far, the Malarone in the water hasn't affected me. I have to keep it that way.

"Okay then," I say. "Up you go."

For a moment I think he isn't even going to try, but he struggles onto his hands and knees then lumbers to his feet.

"Okay then," I say, and although I have no idea where the rhino is, I add. "It's not much further."

I'm worried. I haven't seen any rhino tracks since we left the poacher's body. We've traveled a long stretch of cobbled ground so it's possible we're still on its trail, but I've been so focused on my father I may have missed the rhino's exit trail out of the gully. What if every excruciating step I coerce out of my father takes us away from our rescuers?

I brace myself against Dad's weight as best I can. I don't know how much more either of us can take. How long has it been since we first left the Land Rover? I wish I hadn't left my cell phone behind. There's no reception, but I'd know what time it is. It's still dark, but it could be nine p.m., midnight or four a.m.

When I look over my shoulder to see if we're being followed, I notice splatters of Dad's blood dot the path behind us like a trail of bread crumbs. The gash on his back from the leopard still hasn't closed. Will a hyena pick up the scent? I push the thought away.

Dad doesn't groan or moan, but every once in a while he squeezes my shoulder a little too hard, and I know that a wave of pain has hit. As tired and as thirsty as I am, I know he is in far worse shape.

The patch of rubble under our feet makes walking slow. Dad lurches then yelps. Down we go again. I land hard on my hip. Dad slams his fist into the ground, cursing. He clutches the ankle on his good leg. His face is contorted in pain as he lifts his head skyward.

"No more," he shouts at the sky. "No more."

My heart thunders in my chest. I don't want to ask, but the words come out anyway.

"Is it broken?"

"Claire, I can't go on."

Tell him he can, the demanding voice says.

"Yes, you can," I parrot.

I sprained my ankle on the soccer field once. The pain of

placing any weight on that foot had been unbearable. How can I ask him to keep going? His body is a battered mess.

"I need you to know something," Dad says. "This trip was never really about the birds or the animals. It was about fixing what's broken between us. I hope that someday you'll understand that."

He's talking like he's giving a deathbed confession. *Don't just sit there, do something.* I jump to my feet and offer my hand.

"Get up," I command.

Dad ignores the gesture. A sense of defeat starts to drag me down. His breath comes in ragged gasps. Even in the orange light, his face is pale. His forehead is dry when it should have beads of sweat. He has reached his breaking point.

I imagine steel rods reinforcing my spine and I stand tall. I refuse to give up. *That's the spirit*, the voice in my head says, cheering me on. *You know what you have to do.* I want to tell her to shut up because I know what I need to say and I don't want to. I say it anyway.

"Do it for Janice," I say. "Do it for her."

Dad meets my gaze. So many different emotions pass through his eyes: shock, embarrassment, and then regret. He shakes his head.

"Oh, baby girl." His voice is husky with emotion. "Is that what you think? That she's more important to me. Never doubt that I love you more than anyone else in this world."

My knees buckle as a wave of emotion overwhelms me. I collapse beside him. He gathers me into his arms and smells my hair like he used to do when I was little.

"Oh Daddy," I say. "I—I want you to be happy. I don't want to lose you. Don't you see? We have to keep going."

Dad pushes me away and forces me to look at him. Our eyes stay glued to each other's for a moment longer. Above us, a tree branch cracks and sparks ignite the air.

Enough, Miss Cranky says in my head. *While you're blubbering like an infant, the fire is coming and the rhino is getting away. Get on your feet. NOW.*

My father takes a deep breath. He reaches down and massages his foot. Then he flexes it back and forth. He winces, but he doesn't cry out. I struggle to my feet.

"Okay then," he says, staring up at me with a forced smile. "Let's take her for a spin."

This time when I offer my hand, he takes it. He finds his balance, and with my father using the rifle as a walking stick, we move on as one.

Our progress is painfully slow. The fall has reopened the wound on his back and he's losing more blood. A curve lies up ahead, and I'm praying that the rhino is visible and we can stop. I bend forward at the waist to support Dad's weight. He's so reliant on me I might as well carry him on my back. Even if he can continue to walk on his ankle—which seems doubtful—I will not be able to support him for much longer.

"Claire," he mutters as if talking to himself. "Mistake. Big mistake. Should've stayed at waterhole. Could've hid from poacher."

"Don't," I say.

But he's right. He wouldn't have been mauled by a leopard and... and I wouldn't have killed a man. I've managed to push that thought away more than once, but it keeps coming back and with it the image of his open eyes. The thing that I cannot unsee.

I keep telling myself that it was self-defense. But did I do the right thing? Can I find a way to live with myself even if everyone else, including my father, says I had no choice? This time the voice in my head doesn't offer an opinion. The silence is deafening.

A short snort makes me freeze mid step. The moan that follows lingers in the air. I try to remember if I've heard that sound before. Rhinos are mostly silent. When our vehicle was close to the white rhinos, I could hear them chewing, but that was it.

Heavy panting follows a louder, groan-like noise. Elephants? No. They breathe through their trunks. Could it be the female rhino?

"Do you hear that?" I whisper.

Dad doesn't respond. I'm not sure he's heard me. His eyes are closed and his face is contorted into a grimace. I'm not sure he's even going to make it to the bend ahead in the ravine. I'm hoping that the bank slopes are a little more forgiving. If so, we can rest on the side of the ravine where it will be easier for Dad to stand up again. I'm worried he'll collapse here in the middle of the dry streambed where he could be trampled if another stampede of animals comes through.

"Just a few more steps," I say.

The moaning continues. What the hell is that? Even though whatever creature is making that noise sounds pretty far away, I don't know how sound carries in this gully.

On the plateau above us, the crackling of the fire intensifies. The vegetation is greener in this part of the fork. There's a chance it won't spread downward. The right bank forms a gentle angle in this segment of the gully. The perfect resting place for Dad.

We stagger forward a few more feet and the dry streambed comes fully into view. About seventy-five feet ahead, a giant blob of an animal lies in the center of the ravine. I'm pretty sure it's the rhino, though it could be a fallen young elephant.

I guide Dad partway up the left bank. We both collapse onto the ground, panting. The moans increase in frequency, and I sit up. The camera gouges into my side and I pull it over Dad's head and hand it to him.

All I care about now is water. I roll onto my opposite hip, unclip the bottle, and hand it to Dad.

I'm drenched in sweat. My legs are numb. Will they support me when I try to stand? If that truly is the rhino up ahead, maybe neither of us will have to move until help arrives.

Dad takes a sip and gives it back. The container is so light now that I wonder if he left anything for me, but I shake it and hear a feeble slosh.

A terrible groan fills the air. The sound came from the direction of the big animal. I struggle to my feet. In the darkness, I see a lighter shape has appeared next to it. What the hell is that? I ask Dad to hand me the rifle and when he does, I undo the safety on the firearm.

"I'm gonna go see," I whisper to Dad.

He doesn't reply, doesn't even lift his head. His eyes are closed. I lean over, suddenly afraid. I don't know if he has passed out or has fallen into an exhausted sleep. Finally, his chest moves. He's alive.

I creep forward grateful that the moon illuminates the ground and that I can see well enough to avoid leaf litter. A pitiful grunt of distress makes me cringe. The white shape appears larger as I get closer. Has a predator slashed the animal's belly open and left it to die?

When I have halved the distance, the animal's profile

comes into focus. I'm facing the belly—I think. I'm guessing it's a side view and the white, round, bulbous mass is its innards. The large animal's leg length is too short to be anything other than a rhino's. The pregnant rhino has been attacked? After all this? This beautiful creature cannot survive if it has been disemboweled. It's going to die.

I stagger forward still unwilling to accept that it's too late. Kago's death, the poacher's death, and everything that Dad and I have endured during this horrible night cannot have been for nothing.

The rhino pants and moans, and I freeze. But when it doesn't stop making that awful sound, I press forward, determined to put this poor animal out of its misery. But as I get closer, I stare in disbelief. The white mass is full of fluid and appears to have doubled in size in a few short minutes. Oh. Oh. I almost laugh with relief. This white blob is coming out of the hind end, not the belly. Within the translucent membrane, I see the shape of two small rhino feet. I feel stupid and full of wonder and relief all at once. No wonder the rhinos were slow to startle up on the plateau. She must have already been in labor.

The mama rhino isn't injured, she's birthing her calf and it's coming out front feet first. I wonder if that is normal? Should I try to help? I inch closer.

I'm only about ten feet away. I should back up. If this baby arrives unexpectedly, the mother rhino is going to be fiercely protective. Mama lets out another shuddering groan, and the whitish membrane morphs to a blue color. I'm too mesmerized to move.

Through the thin membrane sack, I spot the nub of the nose on the small head where a horn will grow someday. The one feature that will be the undoing of the animal. But for now, I'm witnessing a miracle.

I lean closer. The head has emerged now, too. The newborn's eye peers back at me through the translucent membrane. Can it really see me? An adult rhino's eyesight is bad, but how about a baby's? Mama strains. She is using one leg to brace the ground to help her push. The front feet are out and I can see the full head now. Doesn't the rest of a human baby slip out after the head is cleared?

Move, Claire.

I back away faster. Another push by the mother, and the shoulders are out. In moments, the torso and the hind end slip through like a greased piston. Gravity does the rest as mama heaves to her feet. The protective membrane stays attached to the mother and the tissue pulls away as she stands, peeling it back to reveal a miniature rhino. Now is the time to turn and run, but I can't.

Mama wheels around to check on her baby. If she is aware of me, she isn't upset by my presence. The newborn's sides expand as it takes its first breath. A glimpse between the legs reveals that it's a girl! When Mama touches her muzzle to the calf's back and inhales, it takes my breath away.

I love that I now I can add an "s". Now two female western black rhinos share our planet, not one. The baby flips onto her belly and her head comes up, but its back legs are stretched behind. She twitches her ears and is so adorable that I want to take her home as a pet.

The mother licks her young's back, reminding me of a cat cleaning her newborn kittens. The little gal's head tips up like a dog's does when you scratch its butt. I smile. The newborn is enjoying her first bath. After a moment, mama shoves her giant horn under its belly. I suck in my breath thinking that she's going to impale her baby with an appendage so sharp it looks as if it has been chiseled to a point. But then I see she only is trying to encourage her calf to stand.

I turn around to see if Dad has witnessed any of this. I don't want him to miss out. But his head is still resting on the ground.

When I face the rhinos again, the baby attempts to put weight on its front forelegs. Mom nudges her young, but its hind end won't support it. The newborn tilts over and falls. The tiny creature tries out her forelegs again and this time they hold. But when she lifts her bum, she falls down hard onto her side. The animal immediately rolls back to her belly. She's a tough little cookie and keeps trying. On a third attempt, she's successful and stands wobbly-legged, shaking with the effort.

I can see why the young need to be able to move so quickly. Surely, that awful stench of this whole messy process of birth will soon attract hyenas and wild dogs.

I'd been rooting for a girl for the sake of the species, so I decide to call her Hope for now. It seems fitting. But she'll need an Afrikaans name.

Hope takes a tentative step. Mom is right beside her, still unaware of my presence. Dad has to see this. I move backwards until I reach him, then squat down.

"Dad," I whisper, shaking his shoulder. "Dad, wake up."

He startles, groans, then struggles into a sitting position.

"What?" he says a little too loud.

"Shh. Look," I say.

Dad squints in the direction where I point. From this vantage point, the fire-lit sky paints their gray skin a strange hue. Mom walks beside her baby, her ears pricked forward.

Dad's mouth drops open. Knowing how temperamental black rhinos are even during the best of circumstances, I freeze, keeping my breath shallow. It's so hard not to exclaim at the little baby's cuteness. I have to keep reminding myself that my father is a sitting duck if the mother rhino charges.

Dad reaches for his camera. I put my hand on his.

"I only want to get a closer view," he whispers.

I let my hand fall away, and he lifts the camera. I imagine what he sees with the viewfinder. A snub-nosed creature with her little hooked lip. Or maybe his lens is focused on the tiny, awkward head bisected by a pointy nub of a horn more valuable than gold. As I visualize his viewpoint, Dad shifts his injured ankle. A subtle movement, not even an inch, but a leaf crunches underfoot, and Mama's head swivels in our direction.

Dad and I freeze. From my perspective here on the ground, I'd swear she was as big as a school bus. Her tail lifts straight up similar to what a warthog's does when it runs. The newborn rhino mewls—such an unlikely noise for this dinosaur-like animal. Mama relaxes, lowers her head, and nudges Hope. Her poor eyesight and Baby Hope's test of her vocal chords must have saved us.

Dad hasn't taken the camera away from his eye. The animals are fully bathed in orange light now. Despite how thirsty and miserable and desperate I feel, I'm grateful to have witnessed this miracle. This experience is all ours. My father's and mine.

The baby rhino turns its head toward us. A *National Geographic* moment if there ever was one. And before I can stop him, Dad depresses the button to take a photo. The shutter click is soft, but Mama's head jerks in our direction. Her enormous horn whips around. It must measure three feet. It glistens orange in the firelight like a glowing sword. She paws the ground and lowers her head. Oh god. What have you done, Dad?

CHAPTER TWENTY

Dirt splays as Mama digs at the ground. Why hasn't the mother rhino charged? Could it be her limited eyesight? That we're up on an incline?

The fire crackles above us. Perhaps this background noise has distracted her, and that's why she can't locate us. It would be better to move even higher where the land is near vertical, but we can't risk making any more noise.

Baby Hope mewls. I hold my breath as Mama continues to paw the cobbled earth and shake her head. Black rhinos are supposed to be smaller than white rhinos, but it doesn't seem like it from where I sit.

Mama snorts, and her head whips toward us again. I inch the rifle up to head height. This double barrel gun is similar to Junior's firearm.

Dad's hand covers the butt and I let him pull the firearm from my grasp. He's right. I can't shoot this animal. I can't take Hope's mother from her.

My eyes meet Dad's. They're full of apology. I don't think Dad could shoot the rhino either. But who knows what we are capable of if two tons of charging flesh with a chiseled weapon attached to its head plows toward us?

Dad nods toward a fist-sized rock. I remember how the white rhino reacted when a flock of babblers flushed from a nearby tree. It had turned its head in that direction. I see his plan. Throw the rock and distract her. But it's a risky move and could only serve to agitate her.

I shake my head, no. But Dad throws the rock anyway. It clatters to the ground behind the two rhinos.

Mama turns, and the world slows as her horn shifts back toward us. As I feared, she's smart. She snorts again then Mama's front legs hop forward and back like a rabbit. I'm fascinated and horrified at the same time. It's hard to believe that such a giant beast is so agile.

Dad launches another rock at her. What is wrong with him? An animal that's built like a bulldozer charges, and Dad can't scramble out of the way.

Fix this, the voice says. *Draw her away*. I don't question Miss Cranky's judgment. I plunge down into the ravine to lure her away from my father.

"Claire," Dad shouts.

But it's too late. I've already violated the number one safari rule. Don't run. Worse, my plan isn't working. I've sprinted a good thirty feet parallel to the bottom of the gully, and she hasn't shifted her attention away from my father who bombards her with a fistful of pebbles. What the hell is he doing?

"Here," I shout at the rhino as I descend to level ground.

I wave my arms, hoping her eyesight is strong enough to see me in the dim light.

Mama finally takes the bait. Her snort rattles the air and the ground rumbles as I turn to scramble up the slope. But the hill is steeper here and I'm not quick enough. She is upon me in the blink of an eye. How can such a heavy creature run so fast? Her breath huffs like a horse's at full gallop. I can smell her rage and the metallic scent of blood from the birth. Hot air hits the back of my arms. It reeks of moldy hay. A boulder fills my vision. It's my only hope. I scramble up the rock face.

But again, I'm too slow. Mama's horn hooks under my thigh and she flings me upward. My arms flail like a bird flapping its wings. I notice green moss on the boulder, the hazy orange of the night sky, the sound of a tree sizzling as the fire consumes its trunk. The slope yawns away from me as the bottom of the ravine reaches up to catch my fall. I hit the ground hard, pebbles scattering under the force of the impact. I hear a pop as my shoulder lands at an awkward angle. The air in my lungs releases with a whoosh as I roll onto my belly. Mama whirls around and lowers her head for another charge. I'm in such agony that I almost wish she would finish the job.

"Claire," my father shouts.

The mother rhino has lost track of me and she runs back up the ravine then stops and whirls around as she senses her mistake. I try to get my legs underneath me, but there's no time. Of all the ways that I imagined I could die, being trampled by a rhino hadn't been one of them.

Up the slope, I spot my father standing with the rifle braced on his shoulder. He's unsteady and wavering. What is he thinking? He can't see straight. He's just as likely to kill me as hit the rhino.

"No," I gasp, though I doubt my father can hear me.

I close my eyes. I feel the thunder of the massive animal's charge. My muscles clench, waiting for the impact. I don't really want to die. Not like this.

A blast of gunfire shatters the air. I open my eyes in time to see Mama falter. Her front left leg crumbles. The impact of her nearly two-thousand-pound torso collapsing in the bottom of the gully makes the ground underneath me shake like a low-intensity trembler.

I don't know whether to be grateful that my life has been spared or cry. Dad has shot the last female black rhino.

Hope runs to her mother who has landed on her side. Mama struggles to get up but can't. A whimper escapes from my dry, scratchy throat. Despite the horrific pain coursing through my body, all I can think is my father... god... my father shot this baby's mother.

CHAPTER TWENTY-ONE

I must have passed out for a moment. But a blast of pain brings me fully awake. The rhino attack comes back as if I'm waking from a nightmare.

I inch my head up. Mama has found her feet but she's still at least a car length away from me. Her barrel-shaped body is tilted because she isn't putting all of her weight on both front limbs. Her sides bulge and contract as she browses on the leaves of shrubs.

I lift my head a bit higher and a searing pain courses through me. Oh crap, crap, crap. I glance at my shoulder and I can see an unnatural bulge. Tears prick my eyes, and my vision blurs. I ease my head back down. This is bad, really bad. I'm in a dangerous situation and I can't think straight.

"Claire," my father calls to me.

His voice seems to come from far away. I want to tell my father to be quiet, but nothing comes out. My tongue feels too thick. I try to swallow but I'm so dehydrated there's not enough moisture in my mouth.

I catch a whiff of the fetid breath as the rhino blows out air. Somehow, I have to get up that slope before she decides to charge again. I slowly pull my knees under my body and ease onto my heels. Mama is still busy chowing down, so I gather my courage, clutch my shoulder, and brace myself for another wave of pain as I stagger to my feet. I bite my tongue to keep from gasping, but it doesn't matter. Mama's head and that lethal horn attached to it have turned toward me.

Idiot, the voice in my head screams.

Her anger slices the air then a cloud of malevolence settles around me. She dips her head and charges.

"Claire," Dad screams.

A rush of wind wafts hair into my face then there is the weightlessness of being airborne. Oh god. Oh god.

Air rushes from my lungs during my descent. When I land, my shoulder shifts back into the socket. The relief is immediate. The excruciating pain has disappeared, leaving a dull ache in its wake.

Less than ten feet away, Mama tosses her head like a haughty mare, but she's lost her balance and has fallen. This is my chance to get away.

"Run, Claire," Dad shouts.

Run? Isn't that what I'm not supposed to do? But I launch myself onto my feet anyway. I choose a steep path up the slope and away from my father. I don't know if a baby rhino would charge or not. But Hope stays beside her mother anyway. Mama struggles to straighten her injured leg to scramble up the incline after me, but she must be in pain because she collapses. When I'm almost at the edge of the plateau, I shift direction and head toward my father.

Dad's sitting on the ground next to a boulder. He seems miles away, though the distance is less than fifty feet. Each jarring footfall sends shooting pains into my shoulder. I glance behind me and see that Mama has stopped trying to get up. She lies on her side. Baby Hope is nuzzling a nipple. That should distract Mama for a bit.

I stop to catch my breath. The sky appears more pink than yellow as the first rays of the morning light appear. It's hard to believe that so much has happened in less than twenty-four hours. I lick my parched lips that have cracked and feel swollen. How long can a person go without water?

I listen, but I don't hear the crackle and snap of fire anymore. Perhaps that's one less threat to worry about. Except what if the wildfire has isolated us? The wildfire could still be burning strong along the roads.

My body sways. My head feels fuzzy and the distance seems impossibly far.

I take one step then another. Birds call. Babblers. They are in a tizzy over something. A snake? When I look down, the world tilts, but I manage to stay upright.

Focus, the voice says. *Think about your safari collection.*

I take a step. A Hope collection. All fabrics made of gray and black leather. Another step. Textured textiles. Another step. A fierce collection. Fashion forward. A crazy headpiece made in the shape of rhino horns. Tim Gunn telling me to "make it work" when I have put in too many spikes and I've been too literal. Two more steps. Oh god. I need water. Focus. Below, Mama's ears flick forward, but she doesn't try to get up.

I'll design graduation caps with unique tassels resembling a rhino's tail. I know I've gone over the top, but I cling to the images. Wrinkles. Maybe I could make 3-D fabric. Curls to mimic the bags under the eyes.

My vision clears. Somehow, miraculously. I'm with Dad. I lean against the boulder.

"Claire," Dad says. "Thank god."

"Water?" I rasp.

My head lolls to the side and I don't have the energy to even look in his direction. Then I feel him nudging me with the water bottle. I reach out and take it. There isn't enough to sip it through the straw. My hand shakes as I twist open the lid. I tip my head back with the bottle against my lips.

Droplets trickles down my throat. And I'm almost crazed with my want for more.

The moment the water is gone, I'm sorry that I drank it. There's a finality in its absence. It is as if by not saving this last little drip, by drinking what meager portion was left, that I have given up on rescue.

I peer downslope to check on the rhinos. Baby Hope is finished nursing. She lies on her belly next to her mother with her front forelegs folded under her. Her eyes are closed. So are Mama's. At least Dad and I don't need to worry about the rhinos charging us.

I stare at the gun next to my father, at the camera by his side, and at his rumpled and bloodied safari clothes. My dad who loves birds and nature above all else, chose me over the rhino.

"You shot her," I say aloud.

"I had to," Dad says. "I had to save you."

"I don't think Mama's wound is too serious," I say.

But I'm worried. If Mama dies will Dad go to jail? I'm pretty sure he will. But he used the poacher's rifle. Is there any way to concoct a plausible story that the poacher shot Mama? But I know there isn't. Forensics will be able to establish the time of death of the man. And then there's the blood pooled under his body. He died too far from here.

I lean into the rock. It feels so good to have support for my body that I rest my head on its hard surface and close my eyes. I want to sleep. I want to escape this place.

"Claire." Dad's voice is a croak. "Don't ever run off again. We're staying right here. Okay?"

I open one eye. I take in a breath and release it slowly like I've been taught in yoga. It helps clear my head.

"What if the rhinos move on?" I say. "I don't think either

of us has the strength to follow them."

I don't speak of the fear that has tunneled inside me. It could be days before anyone comes our way. Safari guides aren't going to bring tourists through a burned-out area.

"They won't," he says in a voice that sounds as creaky as an old man's. "We can't give up hope."

"I named the baby Hope," I whisper.

I peer down the slope. The little rhino's eyes are closed. For now, she has a full belly. She's so young that she has no idea how precarious her situation is. I envy her innocence. And suddenly I want my mother. I want to tell her that everything is okay. Except is it? I've killed one poacher and encouraged Junior to kill another.

"Hope," Dad says.

Dad's dry lips form a half-smile and I know he likes it. I listen for the sound of helicopters or a Land Rover engine, but all I hear is the sound of blood pumping through my ears.

"I shouldn't have brought you to Africa," "Dad says.

"Shush," I say, even though I agree with him.

There's no point in poking his wounds, and he needs to stop talking. We both need to conserve energy.

He reaches out and touches my hand. This small movement is like opening a faucet. I remember when I was a little girl and he'd pretend to take off my nose. Or when he'd ruffle my hair, and I'd feel so loved that I thought my chest would swell until it exploded.

His affair with Jan-Puss ruined everything. Feelings of betrayal bubble up, but then I look at the crumpled shell of my dad. I think of how he saved my life. He shot Mama to protect me. He risked wiping a species off this planet for me. And suddenly all my anger shatters into a million pieces.

"No matter what happens..." His voice trails off.

The depth of his remorse is so palpable that I can breathe in his pain. But there's another emotion hidden under his anguish. The raw feeling of love pours through his eyes that glisten with tears. My throat constricts. It feels like I've swallowed foxtails. The enormity of my love for him scares me.

"I love you," he says. "I'll always love you."

Dad gathers me into his arms and I yelp as he bumps my shoulder.

"Sorry, sorry, sorry," he says, releasing me.

"It's okay," I manage to gasp.

I take deep breaths until the pain subsides. And now another childhood memory surfaces. I'm seeing myself as a little girl rushing to the front door when Dad got home from work. I loved the way he would pick me up and nuzzle my neck and say, "You are so cute, I could eat you for dinner." Then I would laugh and tell him that Mom made meatloaf or chicken. That was how he would know what was for dinner. And then he would set me down and I would turn to see my mother standing in the hall with her arms crossed over her chest, and how he would peck her cheek with a kiss. If it was a good day, she would smile, but most of the time she would say, "Go wash up" then turn on her heels.

My parents had been struggling to repair their damaged marriage for a long time. I could see how Janice might have filled a void in Dad's life, but he should have tried harder. They should have tried harder. And now it's too late. I doubt there's anything I could do or say to change my father's desire to divorce. I may never choose to like Janice, but what I understand now is that my parent's divorce won't change one simple truth.

"I love you too, Dad," I say.

CHAPTER TWENTY-TWO

The sun blazes down. The fire on the plateau above us has fizzled, having burned itself out overnight. Dad and I huddle in the meager shade provided by the boulder. A smoky haze hovers above on the plateau, and it reminds me of a summer day in Los Angeles. I'm no longer worried about fire. I'm no longer even focused on my throbbing shoulder. All my thoughts are fantasies of water. A clear glass full of ice floating in cool, crystal water. Even Baby Hope and Mama rhino can't distract me from my thirst.

"Hey," Dad croaks, jarring me. "Do you remember during our first game drive that Dugger said that the sap of the date palm is drinkable?"

I don't remember that at all. I don't want to expend any energy replying. I don't even bother to open an eye.

"He said that the sap can be collected from a cut flower."

Why is Dad wasting his breath? We're stranded in a swale with shrubs and boulders.

"Isn't… isn't that tree a date palm?" he persists.

I open my eyes and follow his shaking finger to a tree overhanging the lip of a ravine. All I see is a tangled bunch of sticks. He's hallucinating. It could be the Malarone or it could be dehydration or maybe both.

Even though we wouldn't be able to see him from our perch half-way up the slope of the ravine, I avert my eyes from the direction where we left the body of the poacher.

I close my eyes and try to recall where we were when

Dugger was talking about plants. Wasn't it near a watering hole? Yes, that was it. And then I do remember his words.

"No," I say. "The date palm only lives where there's a permanent water source, remember?"

"Right," Dad says.

His face has been rinsed a scary shade of gray. I lift my head and peer down the slope to see if the rhinos have moved on. They're still there. Mama and her young lie about twenty-five yards away from us down in the streambed. Baby Hope is nursing again. I hope she's getting the milk she needs. I hope that means that Mama is going to be fine. I squint. I'm pretty sure her chest is moving, but the light is so bright and my eyes feel so dry that I don't trust them.

I lower my head and lean against the boulder, favoring my good side so that there's no pressure on my injured shoulder. My face and ears are hot where a sunburn has blossomed. My lips feel like they're huge and I don't care. All I want is water.

I hear a knocking sound. At first, I think I'm dreaming, but then I recognize the noise. Land Rovers have a distinct engine noise. A clatter with pings interspersed when the engine idles.

I sit up straight searching for the source of the sound. It seems to come from the bottom of the ravine in the direction of the poacher's body. Then silence. Has the vehicle stopped to examine the dead man? I'm so desperate for water that I don't care whether it's another poacher or a good guy.

"Help," I say.

It was meant to be a shout, but I only emit a squeak. There's no way the driver or occupants of a Land Rover could hear me.

"Claire?" Dad rasps.

"Do you hear that?" I say.

He tilts his head. I strain, and I can still hear it. It's coming from the direction where we started.

"No," he says.

"Well, I do. Yell," I say. "It's a Land Rover."

He tries, but his voice isn't any louder than mine.

"Help," I try again.

I bang a rock against the boulder. It makes a paltry sound and when I stop, the air falls silent. My hope for rescue deflates like a skydiver plummeting to the earth.

DON'T YOU DARE GIVE UP, the voice in my head shouts.

I stagger to my feet. My father doesn't seem to notice. I chew on my lower lip. What if there's a relative of the dead poacher in this vehicle? The soil underneath Dad is a dark maroon. He needs medical attention. I have no choice. I have to get help.

Down below, baby Hope is on her feet and Mama has rolled onto her stomach. Did they hear the engine noise too? Or did they hear us?

Baby Hope mewls like a kitten. Mama struggles and manages to raise her hind end. She straightens one of her front legs, but her other foot can't seem to support any weight. She's already proven that an angry rhino can charge on three legs. More shouting could attract her and trigger an attack, though it's a steep climb.

I'm so frustrated and scared. Assuming these are the good guys, if they choose to collect the poacher's body and don't bother to investigate further up the ravine, my father and I could die. But if I run, the rhino could charge before I even have a chance to get help. Wasn't an injured animal more dangerous than a healthy one, particularly one with a newborn? Hadn't Dugger emphasized that there was no chance that a tourist could outrun any of the Big Five? And then I remember the rifle. All I have to do is shoot it into the air. It is such an obvious solution that I can't believe I hadn't thought of it immediately.

I pick up the firearm and undo the safety before I remember. No bullets. We don't have any stupid bullets. I throw down the weapon in disgust. My head scans the area for anything I could use to make noise. There's nothing. Not one stupid thing.

I sway a bit, even standing is difficult now. I peer down into the streambed again. Both rhinos are on their feet. But Mama wobbles and her bum hits the earth like an obedient dog sitting on command. She snorts, nudges Hope, and lies back down onto her side. Hope squeaks, latches onto an exposed teat, and resumes nursing.

Up ahead, the Land Rover's engine shudders back to life. The volume grows louder and louder. It sounds as though they're coming our way. I pick up the empty water bottle hoping the stainless steel will reflect in the sunlight and attract their attention.

The hood of the car rounds the bend in the gully. I blink. It seems too good to be true.

"Hey," I shout, waving my arms.

"Dad," I gasp. "Get up. They're coming."

But when I look down I see that he's passed out and doesn't respond. The Land Rover hasn't slowed. I should probably wait to see if it could be another poacher. It's not too late to hide, but I don't. Dad could die if we don't get help. We can't stay here. We need water.

The face of the driver comes into view. I don't recognize the dark-skinned man. But then I look at the person sitting next to him. My knees buckle as I recognize his blond, disheveled hair and those broad shoulders. I brace myself against the rock and manage to stay on my feet. Junior is sitting in the passenger seat. His eyes are on the rhino and he doesn't see me. He's on the radio. Twigs poke out of his beautiful golden locks and his face is smudged with dirt. His left arm is in a sling. But what does it matter? On this hot afternoon after a night of horrors, Junior is alive—injured—but alive and he's come looking for us. The car stops about twenty-five yards away. They're probably afraid of angering Mama.

"Hey," I say, my voice breaking apart before the word forms so that it's almost a whisper.

I'm not surprised that neither the driver nor Junior hears me. The driver whips out his camera. I wave my good arm again, but neither of them glances up the slope in my direction. Junior and the man fist bump. They don't yet know that Mama is hurt. They only see the baby nursing. They only see hope for this endangered species.

Oh god. What if they discover Mama is injured? Will they rush to get help? I can't let them leave. The men are so excited that they haven't turned off the Land Rover motor either. I try to scream, but nothing comes out. My ears roar as panic sets in. I wave the stainless-steel water bottle in big sweeping arcs. Please look up. Please, please, please. But they're too excited about Baby Hope. They've both raised cameras to their eyes and are clicking photos now. They can't see me through their camera viewfinders. They could leave once they get the photos. I can't let them. Not with Dad in such bad shape. Not when we are out of water.

"Help," I try again. My throat is so dry that I don't have a chance of being heard over the chuck, chuck of the idling Land Rover.

My eyes zero in on a white Styrofoam cooler on the floor in the row of seats behind them. There's probably bottled water inside. The thought makes me wild and reckless. I drop Dad's water bottle and rush down the slope, holding my injured shoulder.

I'm running so fast, and the hill is so steep that I lose my balance. In my peripheral vision, I see Mama rising to her feet. What a foolish thing I've done. I tumble and cry out as my shoulder slams into the ground. The pain sears through me as if I have been shocked by a cattle prod.

Mama is up, whirling around, clawing the ground with her lame foot, and preparing to charge. Her instinct to protect her young so intense that she ignores her injury. What if I die? I have to tell them about Dad. They don't know he's up there. Oh god. I can't find my voice.

Junior's eyes connect with mine. His gaze communicates many emotions, anger, fear, and disbelief. Mama snorts and swings her head back and forth. Junior jumps out of the Land Rover and sprints toward Mama, flapping his uninjured arm to divert the rhino's charge.

Her inclined head showcases the object of so much greed—her long lethal horn. It's now pointed at Junior. She lunges forward and before he can side-step out of her path, she flips him into the air. The screams gurgle somewhere deep in my throat. I close my eyes, but it is too late. I've been too late so many times. I couldn't stop my father from shooting Mama. It's too late to bring the poacher back to life, too late to fix my parents' relationship, too late to leave Africa when we had the chance. Most of all, it's too late to avoid the horror of reliving Junior's death over and over again. Now, I'll have to live with yet another image that I will never be able to unsee.

CHAPTER TWENTY-THREE

My eyes flutter open. My head feels foggy. I blink, and the room comes into focus. Gray concrete walls surround me on four sides. A fan swivels toward me and blasts warm air onto my face. The room smells of bleach or maybe antiseptic and makes my nose wrinkle. Medical equipment is positioned to the right. I'm in a hospital.

My tongue feels thick and dry as though I've been sleeping with my mouth open. I want water, but there's no pitcher on the small bedside table next to my bed. The thin cot mattress underneath me is a bit lumpy, but not uncomfortable. No metal railings protect me from falling out of bed. I shift position and realize my arm is immobilized in a sling. What happened to me?

No computerized equipment surrounds my bed. It's like a medical set up I'd seen on that old TV show *M*A*S*H*. I try to sit up but stop when I see a clear tube connected to my hand. What happened to me? I remember putting Malarone in Dad's water bottle right before we were leaving on a game drive. And then what?

The single wooden door to the room is shut. The floor is the same gray concrete as the walls. The same color as a rhino.

Wait. We saw the black rhinos. At sunset and... I reach for the memory and find it. There was a fire. In the distance. And then what?

I lift my head and turn to peer beyond the bedside table. My vision blurs, but not before I see that there aren't any other beds. Where is Dad? And suddenly, more than anything, I want my father. Why isn't he here?

"Dad?" It comes out as a hoarse whisper.

The hum of the fan drowns out my voice. No way Dad could hear me. Why is the door shut?

"Dad?" I try again.

My breath hitches. There was a trail of blood. I remember Dad leaning on me. He was hurt and couldn't see or something. Suddenly, I don't want to know what happened, but more memories flood back. He had double vision because of Malarone. My head spins like it's caught in a tornado. The room spins faster and faster. My heart feels as if it might beat out of my chest. The poacher. The poacher. He's aiming his gun at me. I can't catch my breath. I cover my face with my good arm. No, no, no. I shot him. I killed that man. And I can't. I can't. I can't fix it. I want to get out of here. I want to run, but I've got this needle in my hand.

"Help," I rasp. "Help."

But no one comes. My body turns cold as another memory hits. A rhino threw me in the air. Searing pain in my shoulder. And then… and then I was running to tell Junior that my father was by the boulder. That he needed help. And then blackness.

"Dad," I say a little louder this time.

My throat feels like gravel. I stick my tongue on the roof of my mouth and push it side to side, trying to create moisture. It helps.

"Daddy," I try again.

Panic hits. Oh god. Is Dad still out in the bush?

The door opens. A black man with glasses perched on the

tip of his nose walks in.

"Where's my Dad? Is he okay?"

"Yes, yes."

A stethoscope is draped around his neck. He has gray hair and a gray beard. A chipped tooth appears as he smiles.

"You finally woke up," he says. "You've had us all worried."

"Where's my dad?"

"He's in the next room," the doctor says. "He's going to be fine. Just a bad case of dehydration and he needed some stitches."

He comes closer. A flashlight appears from his pocket. He clicks it on and shines the beam at my eyes one at a time. When he gently pinches the skin of my arms, my cinched skin melts down into its original shape. The man nods his approval.

"I'm Doctor Botha," he says. "But everyone calls me Doc."

"Can I have some water?"

Doc nods then turns his head and calls over his shoulder.

"Nurse Anele," he shouts. "Can you bring in a glass of water, please?"

Doc is dark-skinned. He has creases under his cheeks that I suspect come from smiling too much. I like him immediately. My doctor back home is a stiff, snooty woman who makes me feel stupid whenever I ask a question.

"You were severely dehydrated," he says. "Your father has been quite concerned."

A buxom woman waddles in, carrying a clipboard. She hands me a tepid, plastic cup full of clear water with a pink straw. I suck down the liquid and close my eyes.

"Thank you," I say.

As the nurse turns to leave, she drops the clipboard. It clatters to the ground and the noise bounces off the walls making a racket like the crack of gunfire.

I scream and drop my empty cup. I try to make myself small. I'm about to rip out the IV needle when Doc seizes my hands.

"Claire," Doc says. "Claire, it's okay. Nurse Anele dropped a clipboard. That's all. You're safe."

I nod. Doc studies me for a moment, then releases his grasp.

My hands tremble, so I pull the sheet up to my chin. Doc takes the chart and whispers something to Nurse Anele. I don't know if I'll ever feel safe. I hear the gunshot, see the poacher fall as if it's happening all over again. I killed a man. I'm probably going to jail.

"Am I in trouble?" I ask.

Doc shakes his head no, but he is busy writing and doesn't say anything more. My heart starts to race. He doesn't want to tell me. I'm going to prison. And what about Dad? He shot an endangered rhino. Maybe this is the medical ward of a prison. I try to think straight. My chest tightens and my breath quickens.

"Claire?" Doc says. "Are you all right?"

I have a horrible thought. What if they think my father shot the poacher?

"I did it," I say.

"Yes, everyone knows," he says. "They've named you Queen of the Rhino."

I'm not sure I heard him right. Everybody knows I'm a killer? The thoughts in my head swirl. I feel like I'm tumbling down a hill. Did he call me a queen?

"The what?" I finally ask.

"News headline today. I don't know how the newspapers got it, but your photo is on the front page in the *Citizen* and *The Daily Sun*. *The Daily Sun* is the most widely-distributed newspaper in South Africa. I wouldn't be surprised if you made the front pages in the States, too."

They must not know that I killed the poacher. My eyes fill.

"But I—"

"Are you in pain?" he interrupts.

I shake my head no.

"You have been through a great deal." He puckers his lips as if he is about to say something else but pats my hand instead. Doc unwinds the stethoscope from around his neck, puts the ear pieces into his ears, and places the disc on my chest. I take in a long slow breath and let it out without being asked. He steps back and peers into my eyes.

"But I didn't mean to do it," I say. "It was an accident."

"Maybe not," he says. "But you did a good thing. A very good thing."

How is it possibly a good thing when a man is dead? I close my eyes and more memories flood back. Running down the slope, Mama charging, Junior intercepting the rhino, the big horn hooking him. Oh, god. My eyes fly open and I sit up straight.

"Is Junior... is he alive?"

Doc nods. "Is that what's upsetting you? He's going to pull through, too."

I ease back onto my pillow and let out my breath. I wonder if Junior will have permanent scars. I know I will, even if there isn't any visible evidence. No one walked away unscathed from that horrible night. Not even the rhinos.

"And the rhinos?" I ask. "Is the mother rhino still alive? Is the baby an orphan?"

"Because of you," he says, "the rhinos are safe. The female rhino's leg injury won't cause any permanent damage. Her baby is thriving. Everything's going to be fine. So now let's talk about your health. How is the shoulder?"

I lift my arm. No shooting pains, only a dull ache.

"Not too bad," I say.

I spot several red bites, which immediately start to itch. I hear a buzz in my ears. Is it a mosquito or my imagination? I start to cry, frustrated at my foolishness, but unable to stop.

"Claire?" he says.

I sniffle and wipe my face.

"How long have I been here?" I say.

"About a day and a half."

A hundred electrodes seem to fire across my brain. I've gone a day and a half without protection against malaria. I fold my arms across my chest.

"Am I...am going to get malaria?"

Doc frowns. "That's not likely. The mosquitoes in this part of South Africa aren't prone to carry it. I haven't heard of a single case from this area."

I'm reassured, but I probably won't be able to take the pills when I'm in prison. I hug my arms closer to my chest. *Idiot*, my inner voice says. *Malaria is going to be the least of your problems.* I close my eyes and start to cry again.

"What troubles you, child?" Doc asks.

Doc hands me a tissue and I blow my nose. Then I take a few deep breaths. I don't know where to start. *Yes you do, says the pesky voice.*

"I killed a man. Am I going to jail?" I ask.

Doc takes my hand. "No, Claire. From what your Dad has

said, it was self-defense."

There have to be consequences. I can't just walk away from what I've done.

"Will there be a trial?" I ask.

"Probably just an investigation," he says, "but as I said, you're being called a hero."

How can I be celebrated when a man is dead because of me?

"All you need to worry about is getting better," Doc adds. "Speaking of your father, are you up for a visit? He's been asking about you."

I start to nod. But all of a sudden I'm afraid to see Dad. He almost died because of me. Doc seems to understand something's bothering me. He cups my chin in his hand. His gaze plows straight through me and somehow it grounds me and gives me courage.

"Yes," I say.

Less than a minute after Doc leaves, Dad pops his head through the door. His face is the color of watermelon and his lips are speckled with white flakes, like coconut shavings. My face is warm, but I don't think my sunburn is nearly as bad.

When Dad opens the door wide enough to enter, he's pulling a mobile IV. His blue hospital gown distends at an odd angle at the shoulder. And the memory hits me like a rogue wave—how the leopard attacked the curled form of my father. I hear the snarl of the leopard. I see the cat pounce, its giant teeth ripping into my father. The image is so real it's as if I'm living the horror of it all over.

"Are you…"

I can't finish. I start to cry again.

"Oh, Cara-Cara," he says.

He hasn't called me that name in years. I was twelve when I discovered that his pet name for me was an eagle-like bird that fed on dead things. I got angry and wouldn't respond until he stopped using it. But now I remember how he used to say it with such affection, tousling my hair. Now the nickname somehow reassures me. As he crosses the room, the wheels of his IV clatter. His hand covers mine and I remember how safe I used to feel as a child when he picked me up.

"I need to tell you something and I'm so, so sorry," I say.

"Claire—"

"No, Dad. Listen. I put a Malarone pill in your water bottle at the bush camp right before the game drive. I should have told you. That's why you had double vision. I was so stupid."

He chews on his lower lip, then sighs.

"Honey," he says. "There's enough blame to go around for both of us. In fact, I want us to go to joint counseling together after we get home. But I promise you that I'll help you work through what happened. And when you're ready, we'll figure out how to mend our relationship, okay?"

I nod. He's right. It's one thing to profess love and forgiveness like we did when we were about to die in the bush, but we'll have to go back to our old life where he's divorcing my mother, and where I'll have to make peace with Jan-Pu... Janice.

And then there's dealing with all the bad decisions I made while on safari. My recklessness put others and myself in danger. I finger my sling, thinking about the rhino attack and how Junior put himself in harm's way to save me.

"Dad," I say. My lower lip quivers. "I broke the most important safari rule. I ran. And Junior... he paid the price."

I burst into sobs.

"Hey," he says. "Take it easy. Junior's fellow guide shot the rhino with a dart gun, so the attack didn't last long and Junior's wound wasn't deep. He's in the room two doors down. He's expected to fully recover."

I sniffle and wipe my eyes. Doc had said that too, but I'm still having a hard time accepting it.

"Junior's really okay?" I manage to say between shuddering gasps.

"Yes," Dad says. "He'll sport a battle scar, but now he has a great story to tell."

I can see Junior milking that. I hiccup a few times. Then I take a deep breath. I imagine he'll love seeing the wide-eyed expressions of future safari guests.

"Listen," Dad says, "you might as well know that the media are going crazy, but in a good way. They're saying you're a hero for saving the rhinos."

"Doc said that, too," I say, wiping my runny nose with the back of my hand.

"And… your mother's on a plane. She's… err… not too happy with me."

I bet that's an understatement. But I'm not going to throw my father under the bus. Most of it was my fault. If only I hadn't run from the Land Rover.

"Is Janice flying out, too?" I say.

"No, I asked her not to come."

I'm glad Dad's kept her away, but there's a wistful expression on his face, and the corners of his mouth are turned down. He misses her. And as much as I wish he would feel that way about Mom, that's not going to happen. And because he's put my needs before his for a change, I swallow my resentment and straighten my spine.

"Is she into birds?"

Dad's eyes light up, but I can see him trying to not show too much enthusiasm.

"Even more than me. Bet you didn't think that was possible."

"And hiking?" I ask.

He nods. A smile slips out, but he quickly puckers his lips, as if he's afraid that he'll blow it if I see how much my questions please him.

"That's good," I say.

I can't quite read his expression, but I think I see gratitude. I've never asked about Janice before. I may never like her, but maybe I can find a way to appreciate that she makes him happy.

"We'll be transferred to a hospital in Joburg soon," Dad says and squeezes my hand. "We were taken to this local hospital. It's a little rustic here, but I assure you, the care is more than adequate."

I don't really want to go to a big, impersonal hospital. I scan the sparse, sterile room. I like Doc and I want to stay close to Junior. I think about his battle scars and the pain he must be enduring because of me. I need to go apologize to him, but I can't do that until the Doc says I can get out of bed.

"Have you visited Junior?" I say.

"Yes," he says. "He isn't allowed to walk around yet. Otherwise, I'm sure he'd come by to see you."

Suddenly I'm so tired that I can hardly keep my eyes open. Dad has bags under his eyes, too.

"I need some rest and so do you," I say.

He doesn't argue. He shuffles across the floor, dragging his IV. Outside my window, a bird trills, mimicking a muffled alarm clock. Moments later, a dove lands on the ground and calls, "work hard-er, work hard-er." Amidst these exotic sounds, I lean back into my bed and close my eyes.

CHAPTER TWENTY-FOUR

In this dream, I hold a gun against the base of the poacher's neck. My hands shake. I say aloud to myself, "Do it." The man's head turns to glare back at me. But it isn't the poacher who looks over his shoulder, it is my father.

I sit up in the hospital bed. My ribs seem to have compressed, making it hard to breathe. Moisture drips down my temples. My gown clings to my sweaty body.

The words "do it" echo in my head. But even if I could change the past, I'd still encourage Junior to shoot that first poacher. If I hadn't, Mama would have been killed. Baby Hope wouldn't have been born.

Doc walks into the room. Wrinkles form on his forehead before he rushes to me.

"Claire?" he says.

He sits on the edge of my bed. His hairy eyebrows and gray speckled beard remind me of a schnauzer.

"You are drenched," Doc says. "Did you have another nightmare?"

So, he knows this isn't the first one. Nurse Anele must have told him about how I woke up screaming last night. That nightmare had been worse. I had been aiming the gun at myself in a mirror.

I don't want to talk about my bad dreams. I don't want to think about guns or shooting people, but how can I hide the truth when my hair is plastered to my head?

"Yeah," I say.

He nods and smiles at me in a grandfatherly way.

"It's to be expected after what happened in the bush," he says. "You shot a poacher, watched a leopard attack your father, had a rhino attack you and, earlier in the day, Junior told me that you observed a lion eating a human arm. Any one of these events could result in trauma, and you experienced all of them in a very short period of time."

The image forms of the poacher falling to the ground. Tremors flow from my fingertips to my toes. My throat thickens so I can't breathe. I want to get out of this bed and bolt. But how do you run from yourself? I start to cry.

"Okay," he says, covering my hand with his. "It's okay. You're safe. What you are feeling is normal."

He sits beside me as I sob. When I've exhausted myself, I wipe my eyes. I focus on my yoga breathing. After a moment, my heart slows and I feel better.

"That's good, Claire," Doc says and pats my hand. "Do you want to talk about it?"

My chest cinches as the panic returns. I pull my hand away and shake my head. I focus on my breath again. It takes longer this time, but soon I'm steady.

"Claire, I think you are experiencing PTSD."

I blink. Have I heard him right? PTSD? Like war veterans? Are they going to lock me up in a mental hospital? Will I end up on a street corner? No, I can't have that.

"I'm fine," I say, but my voice trembles.

"You will be." Doc says. "But it may take a little time. You're going to get through this. I've already called a colleague. It's important that we address your condition. PTSD, if left untreated, can cause all kinds of problems. Depression, substance abuse, anxiety, panic disorders, difficulty in school—any of those would be a normal reaction."

I think about the homeless veteran who hangs out by the grocery store and yells out that people are out to get him. Is that what I'll become if I don't get help?

"You really think I need a therapist?" My voice comes out as a squeak.

"Yes," he says. "The sooner you start the better. My colleague is an expert in behavioral therapy. He'll do an assessment and help you find someone back in the States. It's going to take some work, but you're young and strong."

I collapse back onto my pillow.

"Will my nightmares go away?" I ask.

"Probably," Doc says, "But it would be better to ask a trained therapist. I'll see if Dr. Tatowa is available this afternoon. I have to go make my rounds now. Do you want something to help you sleep?"

I'm not tired and the last thing I want is to risk another nightmare. Judging from the amount of light streaming through the window, it's mid-morning. But I need a distraction. There's no television or Wi-Fi here. Not even a magazine.

"No. But how about something to read?" I say.

"I will ask Nurse Anele to bring you something," he says. "I know just the thing."

His wide grin reveals straight white teeth. He seems a little too enthusiastic.

Doc leaves and moments later returns with Nurse Anele. She carries a newspaper folded under her arm. She's a big woman with biceps bulging like the fat end of a bowling pin. She reminds me of Mammy from the movie, *Gone with the Wind*.

"Doc here said you wanted something to read," she says.

Her smile widens as she snaps open the paper, and hands it to me. There's a photo of me on the front page with the words "Queen of the Rhino."

I'm taken aback. I hadn't quite believed that Doc was telling the truth when he first called me that. I glance up and Nurse Anele smiles at me.

"Wow," I say.

"Ay-ya," she says.

Doc nods, grinning before exiting the room.

I scan through the article. It says that the fires are now out, and that this was the most coordinated plan by wildlife traffickers ever implemented. It says that two poachers were killed but not who shot them. It says that the gunshot wound to the mother rhino's leg was minor. It does not say that my father was the one who shot her. It says that Junior thwarted the rhino's charge at me. It says that my brave actions spared the lives of both the mother and newborn rhino. That the whole of Africa was indebted to the "Queen of the Rhino."

I blush. I suddenly feel like a celebrity. But then the guilt descends. Two men are dead.

I look through the article again. There's no mention of Phee or Arden. Did they survive the night? I can't believe this is the first time I've thought to ask about them. They could have been boxed in by fire or ambushed by poachers. They could still be lost in the bush.

"Do you know what happened to Arden and Phee?" I ask Nurse Anele.

She shrugs. "No patients here by that name."

"Can you ask my father or Junior if they know?"

"How would you like to ask Junior yourself?" she says. "He's been asking about you. And Doc told me it's time for you to get up and move around."

My heart flutters at the idea of seeing Junior. But I need to rinse off the sweat and freshen up.

"Can I shower first?" I say.

She purses her lips.

"Yes," she says. "Doc says your IV can come out, but I'll have to help you support your arm while it's out of the sling."

I nod, pull the covers back, and swing my legs over the side of the bed. I offer my hand to Nurse Anele so she can extract the needle. This Queen of the Rhino is ready.

*   *   *

The shower restores me, and now that my arm is back in the sling, my shoulder pain has subsided. The blue hospital gown has a slit through it for my arm and lots of ties down the back so I don't feel exposed as I walk down the narrow hallway.

When I poke my head into Junior's room, he is lying on his back and appears to be asleep. Stubble dots his upper lip and chin. His five o'clock shadow makes him appear older.

His room is almost identical to mine, but his window to the outside is smaller. A barren tree with an enormous trunk blocks the sun. The small fan next to his bed makes a rattling noise as it swivels so I can't tell if he's snoring.

I stand in the doorway wondering if I should back out of the room and let him rest. But then a slow smile forms on Junior's face. That crooked grin melts my heart. I grip the door. Even in a funky hospital gown, he's so handsome that I want to sneak up on him and plant a kiss on his lips.

He opens one eye and then the other. When our eyes

connect, I clutch the front of my hospital gown, suddenly self-conscious.

"So," he says, "Howzit?"

"I'm okay," I say.

"I hoped you'd come today," he says. "Nurse Anele said you were better. Your face is all the *muti* I need today."

I have no idea what *muti* is, but I assume it is something good.

"Come here," he says. "Sit with me."

The bed squeaks as I settle on it. He has an IV attached to his hand. He scratches at the collar of his hospital gown then lifts a flap on the garment so that I can see the yellowed, bruised skin below his ribcage. I cringe inside but force a smile.

"You look great," I say. "I think hospital food agrees with you."

"Yes, and I am almost ready to wrestle lions again," he says laughing. "They took out my chest tube for the collapsed lung today. My broken ribs are healing. I should be able to go home in a few days."

His injuries are way worse than I thought.

"I'm so sorry," I gasp. "It's my fault you got hurt."

"I promised to protect you," he says. "And I meant it."

I slip my hand over his. I want to bend over and kiss him, but my cheeks flame at the thought.

"But—"

His hand covers mine.

"No, buts," he says. "Don't worry about it."

"Um, okay," I say. I'm having a hard time focusing under the heat of his touch. "Err, how are the rhinos?"

"Dugger says that all three are doing fine. They were helicoptered to a remote area of Kruger. The female is hobbling a bit, but the bullet exited her leg and didn't do any permanent damage. She's receiving veterinary care and expected to fully recover. Her baby is thriving. All three are under twenty-four-hour surveillance."

I breathe a sigh of relief. Dad won't be in any serious trouble. Then I remember my original purpose for the visit. I need to find out what happened to the English couple.

"Did Phee and Arden make it back to camp?" I ask.

"Yes," he says. "They asked Dugger for your contact information so that they can apologize for abandoning you and your dad. They were ordered to leave when the ranger heard the gunfire on their end of the radio. They resisted but were assured that an anti-poacher was coming to pick up the three of us."

The tension in my shoulders eases. They're okay. That's the most important thing.

"Our rescuer," Junior continued, "encountered the brush fire before he could reach us and had to turn around. By the time the man finally found a route around the fire to where the Land Rover had been, it was morning. He found me stranded in a treetop. After I left you and your dad, my plan fell apart. First, I encountered a leopard so I had to make a wide arc around the poacher. Then a wild boar charged me, and I had to scramble up the tree. The boar eventually settled down, but it wouldn't leave so I was stuck. I'm so sorry, Clar. It was my job to protect you and Jackson but I failed. Anyway, the anti-poacher chased the boar away, and the two of us went looking for you and your dad. We found your tracks in the gully and followed them. When I saw your Dad's vest I thought... but, well, you know the rest."

"You did your job," I whisper. "You saved us."

I imagine what might have happened if he hadn't found

us. Dying a slow death from dehydration. A herd of stampeding elephants mowing us down. Becoming the man-eating lion's next meal. My heart races and my chest tightens as another panic attack threatens to overwhelm me.

"Clar?" Junior squeezes my hand, "Hey, Clar."

His accent, the sweetness of his voice, and the gentleness of his touch pulls me back from the abyss. My eyes connect with his and I draw in a breath.

"That's better," he says as if addressing a skittish horse.

My shoulder muscles relax.

"I'm okay now," I say, offering a small smile.

Junior nods and we sit quietly for a moment.

"Hey, I almost forgot," he says. "Your backpack and luggage will arrive later. Your Dad's stuff, too. But Uncle Denvin left this when he and Dugger visited. I said I'd give it to you when you woke up."

Junior reaches under his pillow and pulls out my safari sketchbook. For a moment, I'm mortified. What if he thinks my sketches are horrible? Worse, what if he thinks I'm planning on using the hides of these wild animals as part of these designs? But then he smiles.

"I peeked inside," he says. "I hope you don't mind. But you are truly amazing, Clar."

Heat flushes my cheeks and I study my hands. I finger the sketchpad. I'm proud of my safari line. It occurs to me that the news that I stopped the poacher from killing the rhinos may have reached back home. Even if it did help me to be selected as a contestant on *Project Runway*, my appearance on the show doesn't seem as important as it once did.

Junior moves his hand so that it covers my arm. He rhythmically strokes my skin with his thumb. I close my eyes to enjoy the sensation. I know I have to tell him what I've done. And I'm afraid of how he'll feel about me once he knows what I'm capable of. I blurt out the ugly truth anyway.

"I killed the second poacher," I say. "The brother."

"I know. Your dad told me. It's a strange thing to have in common," he says. "I'm having nightmares about the man I shot."

My eyes widen in alarm. It hadn't occurred to me that Junior might have been as affected over killing another human being as I have been.

"Me, too," I whisper.

"We're both going to be okay though," he says with confidence. "We did what we had to do."

Something shifts inside me. I know he's right. I am going to be okay. I close my eyes, tilt my head, and press my cheek into his hand.

Desire swells into hunger. I've had crushes before, but not like this. But then my feelings threaten to overwhelm me, so I pull away.

Junior clears his throat. I can't read the expression in his eyes, but I sense that he's not ready for romance either.

"I'm supposed to fly to Joburg in a few days," I say.

Junior chews on a knuckle and looks away. He shakes his head and won't meet my eyes.

"But we haven't even had a real date," he whispers. "You know, I've been staring at your photo in the newspaper and thinking, 'she is from America, you have to let her go,' but, Clar…"

For a moment, I'm stuck on the fact that he's been looking at my picture, but then the reality that we live on different continents descends.

"I know," I say, my voice husky with emotion.

"What if…" he says, "okay, this is crazy. I know this is a

crazy, but Dugger suggested it and the more I think about it, the more it makes sense."

His cerulean blue eyes latch onto mine. There's such intensity in his gaze that it sears through my chest and into my heart. He takes a deep breath, then seems to lose his nerve to say more. He stares out the window at the giant tree with its spreading branches that look like roots.

"That's a baobab tree," he says. "It's very special to our culture. There's a tradition in Africa to sit under the baobab tree and work out differences peacefully. And some people believe that if you soak baobab seeds in water then drink it, you will be safe from attack."

"That's pretty cool," I say. "Do you believe that? About keeping you safe, I mean."

He rubs the stubble on his chin.

"When I was stuck in that tree that night watching the fire spread and wondering if I'd make it out of the fire alive, I thought about what I want my life to be about. In Africa we have a saying, "If you don't stand for something, you will fall for something.""

He turns to face me. A kind of fever glints in his eyes and I feel myself melting to the floor.

"Dugger and I want to start a foundation to help the rhino. We're going to call it The Rhino in the Room to honor... Kago."

Junior's voice cracks at his friend's name. A glossy film forms on his eyes and he looks away. I squeeze his hand and a flash of warmth tingles through me. He shakes his head as if flicking away his pain, then takes a deep breath.

"Kago loved twisting that American 'elephant in the room' phrase around to make tourists laugh."

Rhino in the Room. The idea that Kago will never crack a

joke again brings on a wave of anger. He died so some greedy men could try to become wealthy. I chew on my lower lip. A foundation honoring him, while a wonderful gesture, won't change the fact that Kago won't ever again be able to make people laugh with him.

"I'm sorry," Junior continues. "I've upset you."

"No, I'm okay." I swallow hard and focus on my breath to calm down.

"The foundation is a way to make his death meaningful," Junior continues, and now there's a sense of urgency in his voice, "and we plan to ask America for financial help and..." Junior looks me in the eye. "And... Duggar and I agree. We want you to be involved. People are going crazy on social media talking about the brave American girl. The Queen of the Rhino. You'd make a great spokesperson."

Me? Wait. What? I'm both flattered and stunned. I haven't even graduated from high school. There must be more experienced people.

And yet I want to pay tribute to Kago's death too. The Rhino in the Room. I love the name they've chosen. I think of Mama and Hope and how close the planet had come to losing a subspecies of black rhino. I stopped that. I rose up and did what had to be done and prevented the extinction of a species.

The confidence beneath his words fills me with hope. He wants to keep me around and for there to be an "us" and so do I. And that means we'll find a way to stay in touch whether or not I agree to do this.

"Are you sure I'm qualified?" I ask.

"Yes," he says. "You're perfect."

Being involved with the foundation could help the rhino and keep me in contact with Junior. But this is a life-changing decision.

"I'll need to know more," I say, then add thinking about my panic attacks. "I like the idea, but I'm kind of messed up."

Would Dad support me? After what I've been through during this trip, he'd probably let me do about anything, except maybe sacrifice my education.

"And I need to finish school," I say.

"We can work around these things," Junior says. "We can start slow—like taking your photo with the baby rhino and writing a blog post or two for a social media campaign. We'll wait until you're ready to take on more. Dugger and I could work locally and you can gather support in the U.S."

"But the rhino needs help now," I say.

"Agreed," he says. "We're going to partner with an anti-poaching foundation to help fund more rangers and equipment like night goggles and better guns. And Dugger thinks the long-term solution for both the black and white rhinos is to relocate them into areas with better protection."

"Why can't you cut off their horns?" I say. "Take away what they're being killed for."

"It's been tried. And it's failed for three reasons: One, the poachers kill the hornless rhinos so they won't waste time tracking the animal again. Two, if done humanely, there is still enough horn left at today's prices, to make it worthwhile to harvest the stump. Three, the horns regrow and constantly cutting them off is too costly. It doesn't work."

I nod. The magnitude of the problem is overwhelming.

"And," Junior adds. "We cannot focus on only one solution. What we are doing now is not working."

I chew on my lower lip. I stare into his eyes. There's such passion there that I blush and turn away.

Nurse Anele walks in carrying a basin and a teal washcloth. I stand up as though I've been caught doing something wrong.

Junior grins. "I think it's time for my sponge bath," then to the nurse he adds, "Give Clar that *lappie*."

"Agh, shame," Nurse Anele says, as she herds me out of the room.

CHAPTER TWENTY-FIVE

I shuffle down the hall in my disposable paper slippers as I head back to my hospital bed. My emotions are all over the map. I have to pass Dad's room to return to my hospital bed. His door is open. I have my sketchbook and I'm afraid he'll insist on seeing it. I've been able to keep it hidden this whole trip by only pulling it from my backpack when he was busy taking photos or watching birds and using my body to shield what I was sketching. Now I tuck my drawing pad under my bad arm. The sling covers most of it.

I move close to the opposite wall, hoping he's asleep. The swish, swish of my oversized footwear echoes down the empty corridor.

"Claire," Dad calls as I pass. "You're up!"

Crap. I'm not ready to talk with him about Junior's proposal. I can already hear his objections to my involvement in Kago's namesake rhino foundation: What about the rest of your senior year of high school? What about college? Being a spokesperson could be dangerous. Rhino poachers are usually linked to organized crime. I turn to enter his room.

"Hi, Dad," I say, walking to where he's propped up in bed. "How are you feeling?"

There's a spark in his eyes now, but he's still pale.

"About the same. It's good to see you up. Been to see Junior?"

I nod. "He told me that Dugger is bringing our luggage here."

"I heard."

An awkward silence settles around us. Perhaps we said too much to each other when our lives were in jeopardy out in the bush. Or maybe he has nothing left to say. Neither do I, so I fiddle with the edge of his blanket.

"I need some rest," I say at last then turn to go.

"Claire," he says. "Wait."

I hesitate.

"Come," he says. "Sit next to me. I…"

His voice cracks. Naked emotion is laid bare in his eyes—sorrow, fear and something else I can't quite discern. I stand beside the bed. He reaches out his hand and I take it with my good arm, but I don't sit. His touch is warm and comforting and I cling to his grip like I used to hold tight when I was little as we crossed a busy street.

"Doc tells me you might have PTSD," Dad says. "I'm… I never meant for any of this to happen."

"I know you didn't. I made mistakes, too. I shouldn't have fled the Land Rover."

I'm not about to tell him about my nightmares.

"Doc's scheduling an appointment with a shrink later today. His name's Dr. Tatowa, and I'll see a therapist back home, too. Doc says I might have a mild case. I've already been using some coping skills based on my yoga practice."

I hate the tortured look on his face.

"It's okay, Dad," I say. "I'm going to be fine."

"No, Claire. It's not okay. I've been self-centered and selfish for far too long," Dad says, shaking his head. "It's not okay that I was careless, and you saw Janice and me together. It's not okay that I forced you to go on this safari when you didn't want to. But most of all, it's not okay that I put your life in danger." His voice turns husky as he adds, "Oh, Claire, this is all my fault. Even before this trip, I was a poor excuse for a father."

Before this trip, I would have agreed with him, but now I say nothing. I stare at my chipped fingernail polish and the crust of dirt under my thumbnail. Before this trip, I would have been mortified at my messy manicure, but now having perfect nails seems trivial.

When Dad squeezes my good arm, a corner of the sketchpad under my sling slips into view.

"What's that?" Dad asks, nodding at it.

Like so many other things that used to feel important, hiding my designs from him now seems less so. I take a deep breath. My safari line idea flows from my lips. I expect him to start yelling about how I need to attend a traditional college. Instead, he extends his hand.

"May I see?" he asks.

There's a calmness to his request. I sense genuine interest, so I pass it to him. There was a time when his praise would have meant everything, and his criticism would have devastated me. But after what we've been through, clothes and fashion don't seem to matter so much. Dad turns each page, studying each sketch as if he were examining exquisite art in a coffee table book.

"These are good, Claire. Really good!" Dad nods as if making a decision. "I've been thinking about a lot of things. And, well, if designing clothes will make you happy and you want to attend a fashion design school next year, I'll support your decision."

"Really?"

I imagine myself walking with my models adorned in my safari-inspired clothing at New York Fashion Week. With

Dad's help, I can focus on learning to sew, something I'm not all that good at yet and, if I'm honest with myself, would keep me from getting on *Project Runway*. My talent lies in designs, not executing them. But I could learn at college and in time I could hone my skills.

But does that matter anymore?

I shift the magazine he was reading out of the way and sit beside him. I glance at the front cover and freeze. It's a photo of a dead rhino. The headline reads "Custodians of Giants Fail Again" In small print below it says, "Rhino Deaths from Poaching at a 15-Year High."

Junior's words come to mind. "If you don't stand for something, you'll fall for something." Ever since I first watched these animals graze, I had a sense that something had shifted for me. But now... now these creatures could change the direction of my life. My breath hitches. The enormity of what Junior has asked of me hits. I'm standing on the cusp of something big.

The photo shows a rhino on its side, a bloody gash where its horn used to be. A warden, with his head inclined as if in prayer, stands beside the fallen creature with his hand on the animal's elongated head. I think of how close to extinction a subspecies of black rhino came. Maybe everything that happened on this trip was fate. I wouldn't have cared about these dinosaur-like animals if I hadn't come to Africa. I wouldn't have glimpsed any other future than fashion for myself. But I have a chance to keep a species alive—something way more important than clothing design. I stare at my sketchpad and make up my mind. For now, I have to set aside my ideas for my safari collection. I have to help Junior and Dugger start up their rhino foundation.

I decide to tell Dad what I want to do. I describe the

Rhino in the Room Rescue Foundation and Dugger and Junior's ideas. I tell him that I'll still finish high school and go to college. That I can do it all.

Dad frowns. "It's certainly honorable. But I think it's too much, Claire. You have to address your PTSD."

I'm not surprised by his reaction. Before this trip I would have lashed out in anger and run from the room. I'm surprised at how calm and rational I feel. My newfound maturity gives me confidence that I'm making the right choice.

"I know, Dad. I'll go to a therapist for as long as it takes. I can do school, and therapy, and foundation work at the same time. I promise I'll make it work. And—"

"Claire..."

Worry is scrawled across his brow. He grabs my good hand in a way that reveals my scissor tattoo. I wonder if there's a way to modify it into the shape of a rhino. Dad stares at my inked finger, but he doesn't react. He's not the same person, and neither am I.

"If I wait until it's convenient to try to help rhinos," I add, "it might be too late. The rhino needs their queen."

"Oh Cara-Cara," he sighs.

Dad offers a crooked smile. I've almost won him over. I see pride in that grin.

"Were you there when Junior said one bird can affect the path of a whole flock?" I say. "If someone doesn't do something soon, poachers will push rhinos off the edge of the earth. What if I can change that?"

Moisture glistens across the surface of Dad's eyes. He pinches the bridge of his nose and clears his throat. He stares down at the rhino photo.

"You don't know how proud of you I am right now, but I don't know," Dad says. "You've been through so much."

"But it's because of these experiences that I want to help rhinos," I say, surprised by how emphatic my voice sounds. "I know there's a lot to learn about... about everything."

The irony of it all hits me. Dad was right. Nature changes you in ways you can't possibly imagine. He's been pushing me to study the sciences, and if I'm going to help African wildlife, I'll have to do just that.

"Let's talk about this after your session with the therapist. I'll want his or her opinion."

I nod, satisfied for now. Even if I need a little more time to recover, I'll find a way.

Dad reaches out and pulls me close. The magazine slides toward me with the dead rhino photo revealing the brutal reality of poaching right under my nose. It's far too late for me to stand by and do nothing. Not when the rhinos still have a chance. I have to do everything I can to save this species from extinction. For me, there's no going back.

AFTERWORD

Let me first say that as Dugger states in the novel, you are far more likely to be involved in a serious car accident than to be harmed by a wild animal on a guided safari. I sincerely hope this novel doesn't discourage anyone from going on safari and visiting Africa's amazing natural wonders. And as Jackson states, a few precautions such as taking an antimalarial appropriately and using bug spray will minimize the risk of catching malaria. Viewing the jaw-dropping wildlife in their native environment really will change you in ways you'll never imagine.

The first white rhino I encountered during my South African safari in September 2015 seemed too large and too odd-looking to be real. I felt like I had traveled back in time and witnessed the resurrection of an ancient dinosaur. During zoo visits, the rhinos had been far away and behind moats. But on safari, this giant creature had grazed its way toward our vehicle until it was only a car length away—so close that I could see the almond-shape of its tiny eye. The bags and wrinkles surrounding that dysfunctional organ (rhinos have very poor eyesight) gave the creature a weary appearance, like a wise old grandmother whose value has been forgotten.

Our safari guide had explained that three rhinos each day are killed in South Africa for their horns, which can be worth half a million dollars on the Asian black market. As I listened, a call to action rose in me. What if I could bring awareness by writing a novel that illuminated the complex causes of rhino poaching and through this book support solutions to prevent their extinction?

This novel focuses on African rhinos, but population declines for Asian rhinos are just as grim. The statistics are appalling. Levels of rhino horn poaching have increased by 5,000 percent since 2007[1] and time is running short to save this species. Historically, there were eight subspecies of black rhinos, three of which have become extinct. Within their natural range, four of the remaining five rhino species have declined so severely that they have been given threatened status. Three are critically endangered.

In the early 19th century, the rhino population was estimated to be one million. In 1970, their numbers fell to around 70,000 or seven percent of their peak population. Today, there are only around 28,000 rhinos surviving in the wild.[2] And the situation is worse for some subspecies. Only two northern female white rhinos remain. The chances of saving this subspecies are slim.[3] All subspecies of white rhinos in the wild could vanish in the next twenty years. If this happens, rhinos will be the largest land mammals to become extinct since the woolly mammoth.

The loss of rhinos could affect the survival of other species as well as impact local economies. Rhinos, in addition to being a draw for tourists, serve a critical function in maintaining a healthy ecosystem.[4] A 5,000-pound white rhino can consume 50 or more pounds of food in one day. But it isn't only the sheer bulk of vegetation consumed that makes them so important. Unlike elephants that browse on trees, rhinos act as giant weed whackers, selectively grazing on certain plants and grasses, creating biodiversity in the landscape. These dietary preferences also form a mosaic of habitat that is more attractive for other grazers such as zebras and antelope, who, in turn, are food for lions, leopards, and hyenas. Therfore, extinction of this animal can adversely impact the survival of many more species.

In 2011, the International Union for Conservation of Nature and Natural Resources, the world's most comprehensive information source on the global population status of vulnerable species, declared the Western black rhino extinct. The south-central black rhino is native to northeastern South Africa. While it has gone extinct in portions of its range, it has been reintroduced successfully into Botswana, Malawi, and Zambia.

Although only two surviving black rhinos exist in my novel, in reality, about 5,055 black rhinos were estimated to be alive in 2016. Still, this species remains critically endangered. According to the World Wildlife Fund, about 96% of African black rhinos were lost to large-scale poaching between 1970 and 1992.

Demand continues to grow in Asian cultures for the keratinous material that makes up rhino horn. The misguided belief that horn powder cures everything from hangovers to impotence to cancer has created a frenetic seller's market, driven largely by China and Vietnam.[5] Top dollar is spent on purchasing essentially the same material as fingernails. In 2014, the Vietnamese Ministry of Health confirmed that rhino horn had no medicinal value, but this has had little impact on demand. The hope is that a Vietnamese campaign starring celebrities will have better success.[6]

England's Prince William, who serves as president of United for Wildlife, a consortium of wildlife charities, is a strong advocate for rhinos. In March 2016, he unveiled a global agreement to crack down on wildlife trafficking routes.[7] Forty transportation authorities, representing airline, shipping and custom agency leaders signed the declaration to stop the movement of poached animal products into the black market.

Many solutions have been proposed to address poaching, including horn removal. However, dehorning, once touted as an ideal solution, has not been as effective as once hoped. Most poachers will shoot the dehorned animal either to harvest the stub of remaining horn or to avoid tracking a rhino without a horn. According to the Save the Rhino website, in the early 1990s in Zimbabwe, the majority of dehorned rhinos were killed by poachers within a year and a half after being dehorned. However, a new dehorning technique that removes all the horn except for a couple of hundred grams covering the actual growth plate shows promise as a poaching deterrent.

The dehorning operation is also risky because the animal may die while under anesthesia. Yet, dehorning may still have merit and may not be as harmful as once thought. While it has been suggested that rhinos need their horns to protect themselves and their young, a study of dehorned black rhinos found no significant difference in survival in the young of dehorned black rhinos when compared to the offspring of horned rhinos.[8]

Other options to combat rhino extinction from poaching include poisoning the rhino horn, development of synthetic horn material, legalization of trade, captive breeding farms, improvement of anti-poaching techniques, and relocation of rhinos out of high poaching areas.

Poisoning the horn seemed like a fail-proof solution that would make rhino horns worthless. A colored toxic dye that didn't hurt the rhino was injected into the horn, and the outer skin of the rhino's horn was painted a bright color. But poachers soon discovered that the poison didn't penetrate far inside the dense fiber.[9]

The International Rhino Foundation opposes the sale of synthetic horns. Critics believe that creating a fake version will drive up the cost of and demand for poached rhino horn. The consequences could mean an even bigger market for a natural product seen as more potent and, therefore, more desirable.

Sale of rhino horns became legal in South Africa in 2017. Proponents of sustainable harvesting of rhino horns argue that the horn can be removed humanely and painlessly[10], although they admit the procedure does involve anesthetizing the animal, which is not without risk.[11]

Opponents of legalization suggest it will only worsen the problem. Poaching would be cheaper and faster than farming due to the low reproductive rate of rhinos. With permits, private rhino owners could sell horns illegally obtained from poached rhinos to circumvent the system for their personal enrichment.[12] Corruption is rampant. Legalization may even increase demand by legitimizing its use for consumers who would not buy an illegal substance but will after it becomes lawful. The World Wildlife Fund reports that the connoisseurs of rhino horn are mainly financially successful Asian men over the age of forty who buy entire horns as a symbol of their wealth. Thus, there are potentially millions of customers waiting for the price to drop. Time will tell whether legalization in South Africa will harm or help the rhino.

Anti-poaching efforts have largely failed in most areas of Africa, although exceptions have occurred in some countries such as Botswana, which has reduced its poaching rates. Areas where rhinos roam are large, usually in terrain with limited sight distance. Poachers are often outfitted with the latest technology in tracking tools by black market dollars whereas anti-poaching units are typically underfunded. When game wardens are provisioned with anti-poaching equipment such as cameras, drones, trained dogs, and night-vision binoculars, they have a better chance of preventing rhino poaching.[13] After donations of equipment provided by the Rhino Protection Programme, a game reserve in Limpopo, a province of South Africa, reported success using military thermal cameras to track the movements of poachers[14].

Overall, 121 fewer rhinos were poached between 2015 and 2016 and 26 fewer were killed between 2016 and 2017 in South Africa. But considering that only thirteen rhinos were killed in 2007 compared to 1,028 in 2017, South African anti-poaching units may occasionally win a battle, but it appears they are still losing the war.

The Rhinos Without Borders campaign based in South Africa seeks to relocate rhinos away from high-poaching areas. This effort comes with a price tag of $45,000 per rhino. Other efforts to establish a breeding rhino population outside Africa involve the relocation of 80 rhinos from Africa to Australia. With up to a sixteen-month gestation, replenishing wild rhino populations will not happen quickly. Still, these transplants may have a better chance of success than if they were sent to zoos.

Rhinos born in captivity rarely produce young. An exception occurred in California at the San Diego Zoo Safari Park. In April 2016, a southern white rhino was born to a captive female after ten years of breeding efforts.[15] The success was attributed to a change in the mother's diet. Artificial insemination has failed to produce young in the critically endangered northern white rhino.[16] As of May

2018, using artificial insemination in a common southern white rhino female has resulted in pregnancy.[17] Time will tell if the pregnancy will produce a viable calf. Thus, it is possible that some rhinos living in captivity may be able to save northern white rhinos from extinction, if the two remaining northern rhinos can be impregnated with frozen sperm from the last male of its kind that died on March 21, 2018.

A multi-layered approach is needed to combat the current rhino-poaching crisis, and the time to act is now. Progress is being made. The number of rhinos killed in South Africa dropped from 1,175 in 2015 to 1,054 in 2016 to 1,028 in 2017. But these minor decreases in poaching rates are not large enough to maintain a sustainable population. We must do more to protect rhinos, these living dinosaurs of the African savannah.

How You Can Help Rhinos

In addition to contributing to organizations dedicated to saving rhinos, such as World Wildlife Fund, Save the Rhino, or the International Rhino Foundation, individuals can adopt a specific rhino through the International Rhino Foundation or purchase a Rhino Keepers Association Calendar: http://www.rhinokeeperassociation.org/. Join the Rhino Resource Center forum and learn more about rhinos (www.rhinoresourcecenter.com/forums/) or donate to this organization and help them keep their rhino literature database up to date. Follow me or any of the save-the-rhino organizations on Facebook to learn more about the current status of rhinos, and actively share posts with friends and family. The more people become familiar with these amazing animals, the more likely they'll get involved. As Junior says in this book, a single bird can change the direction of a flock. If you stand against rhino poaching, maybe you can be that bird.

SOURCE MATERIAL
AND FURTHER READING

1 Starzak, K. (2014, May 30). New study: Infusing rhino horns with poison doesn't work, *Earthtouchnews Network*, Retrieved from http://www.earthtouchnews.com/environmental-crime/poaching/new-study-infusing-rhino-horns-with-poison-doesnt-work

2 Audubon Nature Institute. (2016, September 21). *Audubon Zoo Raises Awareness About Rhino Crisis*, Retrieved from http://newsroom.audubonnatureinstitute.org/audubon-zoo-raises-awareness-aboutrhino-crisis

3 Martin, S. (2015, September 22). World Rhino Day 2015: Rhinoceroses in Numbers, *International Business Times*, Retrieved from http://www.ibtimes.co.uk/world-rhino-day-2015-rhinoceroses-numbers-1520744

4 Nuwer, R. (2014, February 27). Here's What Might Happen to Local Ecosystems If All the Rhinos Disappear, *Smithsonian.com*, Retrieved from http://www.smithsonianmag.com/articles/heres-what-might-happen-local-ecosystems-if-all-rhinos-disappear

5 Larson, R. (2010, July). Rhino horn: All myth, no medicine, *National Geographic Society*, Retrieved from http://voices.nationalgeographic.com/2010/07/07/rhino_horn_and_traditional_chinese_medicine_facts/

6 Aldred, J. (2016, January 13). Richard Branson fronts nail-biting campaign against rhino poaching, *The Guardian*, Retrieved from https://www.theguardian.com/environment/2016/jan/13/ richard-branson-fronts-nail-biting-campaign-against-rhino-poaching

7 Leithead, A. (2016, March 15). Prince William in plan to tackle wildlife trafficking, *BBC News*, Retrieved from http://www.bbc.com/news/uk-35814135

8 Du Toit, R. and N. Anderson, 2013. Dehorning rhinos. *Wildlife Ranching,* Autumn: 82-85. Retrieved from http://www.rhinoresourcecenter.com/index.php

9 Ferreira, S., Hofmeyr, M., Pienaar, D., and D. Cooper. 2014. Chemical horn infusions: a poaching deterrent or an unnecessary deception? *Pachyderm 55:*54-61.

10 Nuwer, R., (2016, December 2). A tipping point for slaughter. *Newsweek 167(20):* 50-53.

11 Hart, A. 2016. Could legalising the trade in rhino horn save the species? *The Biologist 63(6):*7.

12 Swartz, M. (2016, April). Will Keeping the Rhino Horn Trade Illegal Kill More Rhinos? *National Geographic*, Retrieved from http://voices.nationalgeographic.com/2016/04/23/opinion-will-keeping-the-rhino-horn-trade-illegal-kill-more-rhinos/

13 Starr, M. (2016, November 27). Can tech save the rhino? *Cnet Magazine* Winter. Retrieved from https://www.cnet.com/news/rhinos-endangered-poaching-synthetic-horn-tech/

14 Peace Parks Foundation News. (2015, July 10). Night Vision Equipment for Kruger National Park Rangers. Available from http://www.peaceparks.org/news

15 Chiusano, S. (2016, April 6). Southern white rhino gives birth to calf at San Diego Zoo, *New York Daily News*, Retrieved from nydailynews.com

16 Hubbard, A. and T. Perry. (2014, December). Only 5 northern white rhinos are left; artificial insemination difficult, *Los Angeles Times.com* Retrieved from http://www.latimes.com/local/lanow/la-me-ln-white-rhino-dies-safari-park-20141214-story.html

17 Watson, J. (2018, May 17). Rhino in San Diego pregnant, could help save subspecies, *The Associated Press*, Retrieved from https://www.telegraph.co.uk/news/2018/05/17/pregnant-rhino-san-diego-zoo-could-help-save-endangered-subspecies/

BOOK CLUB QUESTIONS
AND DISCUSSION GUIDE

1. Do you agree or disagree with Mr. Garcia's statement: There's no going back? How does this statement affect Claire throughout the book? Are there instances in your own life where there was no going back?

2. Whenever Claire is uncomfortable, she runs. How did this aspect of her personality shape the action in this book?

3. Do you agree with the concept that nature can change you? Describe an incident from your life where the natural world affected you.

4. Did this book inspire you to learn more about South African animals? If you could see one safari animal in the wild, what would it be?

5. Did Claire do the right thing by killing the poacher?

6. How were Claire's actions motivated by Sylvia's illness? How will Claire's choices affect her for the rest of her life?

7. Before reading this book, were you aware that poaching threatens the long-term survival of rhinos?

8. How did you experience the book? Discuss if you were immediately drawn into the story—and, if not, at what point were you hooked?

9. Is Dad a likeable character? Do your feelings toward him change over the course of the book? If so, when?

10. Did you find the end satisfying? If so, why? If not, how would you end the novel?

ACKNOWLEDGEMENTS

First and foremost, I must thank my family. My husband, Eric, has never once complained about the many hours I've spent with my head tucked into the computer. My two daughters, Kelly, and Lindsay also endured leftovers and crumpled clothing that had been left far too long in the dryer while I learned craft, sent out query letters, and despaired over rejections. This book wouldn't have been possible without your loving support.

Special thanks go to my critique family, Writers on the Journey (WOTJ), especially Elisabeth Tuck whose editorial eye is unmatched and who first proposed my inclusion into this talented group after a writing setback that had me questioning whether to continue writing. Each and every member of WOTJ improved this novel with their own special point of view. This book would not have the depth and accuracy I strive to give my readers without IPPY Award winner Melanie Denman's command of character development, Cheryl Spanos' knack for finding flaws in plot, Fran Cain's eye for faulty logic, Susan Berman's insights from her experiences in Africa and her refinement of the Southern drawl for my Texas characters, and David George's skill in painting setting and nature into the landscape of words.

I must also express my gratitude to the members of Avid Readers Book Club. Through book discussions, you all have taught me so much about writing and what constitutes a good read. Thank you Mary Anderson, Miriam Belsa, Carla

Bergez, Susan Bruno, Ann Gray, Cheryl Monroe, Amy Pennington, Joy Pinsky, Linda Summers Pirkle, Terry Pixton, Catherine Stafford, Laura Walsh, and Tamara Wickland. And Tammy Jacobson who is no longer with us. Thanks must go to my die-hard Shush and Write cohorts B. Lynn Goodwin, Aline Soules, and especially Ann Steiner who not only opens her home, but also sets aside an evening each week for quiet writing time. Cameo thanks are owed to Debbie Stiffel for her editorial prowess, Linda Scotting for reviewing Arden and Phee's dialogue for proper English dialect, and Wendy Blakely for her expertise on Africa. My gratitude also extends to Chessa Mehlman and Ian Sumner of Chasing Light Studios (http://chasinglight.pro/) for creating an awesome book trailer. Kudos to Andrew Benzie and Anne Pentland for the amazing book cover design and artwork, respectively.

These acknowledgements wouldn't be complete without thanking Grant Faulkner for starting National Novel Writing Month. The majority of the first draft of this novel was written in November 2015 as part of this wonderful program.

Lastly, hats off to you, dear readers, for making it all the way to the last page. If you've enjoyed this book, join the mailing list on my website (www.jillhedgecock.com) for announcements about my four other novels that are in the works.

ABOUT THE AUTHOR

Award-winning and internationally-published author Jill Hedgecock is dedicated to taking readers on high-stakes adventures in exotic settings. Her short stories, personal essays and nonfiction pieces have appeared in multiple anthologies, newspapers, and magazines. *Rhino in the Room* is her debut novel. She lives in California with her husband and three adorable dogs. Visit www.jillhedgecock.com to learn more.

Made in the USA
Lexington, KY
16 November 2019